BARLOW GOES FORTH

by

John McAllister

BY THE SAME AUTHOR

THE BARLOW SERIES

The Station Sergeant

Barlow by the Book

Barlow Laid Bare

JIMMY & DOC SERIES

Fight or Flight

Pursuit

Line of Flight

SHORT STORY COLLECTION

The Fly Pool

For Trish
And
Daniel who acts as unpaid researcher
And
Lucie, my publicist

My Guru, Kevin Hart

Published by Glenlish Publications

ISBN: 978 0 9956338 7 2

Blank Page

MONDAY

Blank Page

Chapter 1

The body of a man lay in the river, caught up in the rocks at the weir. It lay neatly wrapped up in a salmon poacher's net. A salmon net in a trout stream seemed all wrong to Station Sergeant Barlow.

Barlow looked at the police doctor who stood beside. The police doctor was ageing and splashing through river water would ignite his rheumatism.

Barlow gave him a nudge. 'Doc, I could do with quiet week. Now if you made it suicide…?'

The doctor gave a shiver at the coming trudge through cold water. 'I'll make it an "Accidental Death" if you bring the body to me.'

'Gillespie,' Barlow yelled.

'What now?' said Constable Gillespie.

Gillespie stood in the river beside the body, and he at least had the sense to bring his waders with him. All the same, cold water on a cold day with no off-duty line to cast ran counter to Gillespie's chits for: bad feet, bad back and a weak chest – which was why Barlow had sent him wading through thigh-deep water to have a closer look at the body.

'Bring the "Accidental Death" to the bank,' said Barlow

'Some "Accidental Death".' Gillespie held up a tangle of fishing line attached to the body. 'Hogtied and….' he shook the length of line, 'held down by a stone, but it broke free.'

'We'll go with suicide,' said the doctor.

'Done,' said Barlow and jerked a finger at the young constable standing beside him. 'Right, Wilson, get in there and give the man a hand.'

Two steps in the river and water poured into Wilson's Wellington boots. Wilson splashed on. No hesitation, no complaints, Barlow noted, though he expected no less of the boy.

'What about me?' asked WPC Susan Day.

''Hop in there and give the boys a hand.'

She flickered her eyelashes at him. 'Papa Bear, who brings you all those lovely cups of tea?'

‘Or you could call the station and tell DS Leary to get his murder bag up here.’

Susan nodded and walked away. That was one thing he liked about her, she didn’t always find it necessary to talk. It gave a man peace to think.

Barlow hadn’t gone near the body himself – no need to when there was someone like Gillespie to bully into the water – but he had a horrible suspicion he knew who it was. Tommy Weir: water bailiff, small farmer and self-important pain in the ass.

The late Tommy Weir had traded height for weight. He was a heavy lift and an awkward carry in fast-flowing water but Gillespie didn’t oblige by falling in. Barlow helped with the final heave onto the bank.

Hogtied was a good way of describing the body. The fishing line stretched from head to foot, with loops of fishing line wrapped around the body at elbow, hip, knees and ankles.

‘Poor ignorant old git,’ said Gillespie, still breathless from the heavy lift.

‘Just because he nearly caught you poaching a couple of times,’ said Barlow.

Wilson sat pouring water out of his boots, with Susan fussing over his wet socks. The doctor hunkered down over the body, and checked the carotid artery for a pulse. ‘Dead,’ he said.

What people were doing, what they were saying helped distract Barlow from the picture he was getting of Weir’s death: Tommy Weir’s eyes and mouth were open, his fingernails broken in those last moments of clawing for life. Both eyes were puffy, the nose pushed sideways. The man had been beaten to pulp, then wrapped in a net and, still conscious, weighted down in the water and left to drown.

Barlow shivered as if someone had walked on his grave.

Chapter 2

With Wilson's feet encased in a spare pair of socks carried by Gillespie – The spare socks didn't surprise Barlow, sometimes Gillespie displayed a spark of intelligence – he told the two constables to go break the news of Tommy's death to his wife. While there, they were to have a good look around the Weir farm.

Barlow ached to go to Weir's farm himself and get involved in the physical search, but the police station and month-end reports called. Anyway, heading there himself would be sheer indulgence. Gillespie and Wilson between them would spot anything of interest.

As an afterthought, he sent Susan Day as well.

'Good practice for when you make sergeant,' he said. 'But don't expect any tears from that old witch.'

Susan was studying for her sergeant's exams, but he thought it more to do with snuggling up to Wilson than anything else. Gillespie objected to being the gooseberry in the group but if he skipped a study session, he found himself on foot patrol.

'You can't make me sit the exams,' he said.

'No I can't,' said Barlow, and added another foot patrol for luck.

Back in the station, he ignored the month-end reports stacked on his desk. Instead, he leaned on the counter in the Enquiry Office and stared into the flickering flames of the coal fire.

Tommy's death had got to him. Whatever had been going on in Weir's life had to be nasty, and it had nothing to do with local poachers. A poacher knocking Weir into the river during a struggle was one thing, but a person or persons unknown had tied up the man the way butchers parcelled up meat for the weekend.

A constable came running up from the Radio Room. 'Sergeant, Gillespie's been hurt.'

Barlow was already reaching for his cap. 'Fell in the midden? Tripped over his feet?'

'He stepped on a gin trap. It's bad.'

Barlow paused, sick to the stomach with fear for Gillespie. 'How bad?'

'Just below the knee. They say the leg's broken.'

He knew he should have listened to that feeling of unease and gone himself. 'Son, that's not a gin trap. That's a mantrap.'

Barlow scooped his hat and gun-belt out of the cupboard and ran for the car. Instinct for trouble had made him leave the squad car handy at the front door instead of running it into the yard.

He detoured by the Larne Road – always referred to locally as the Larne Line – then the Moat Road, rather than risk being caught up in town traffic. In short minutes, he was driving along the ridge looking down on the town.

Way past the Catholic Chapel, he managed to stay ahead of the ambulance coming up the Woodside Road. Past Blacks' Estate and then a turn, taking him deeper into the hills. The ambulance stayed tight on his tail as he swung down a rutted track and bounced the last stretch into the farmyard.

Barlow parked beside Gillespie's car, got out and put on his cap. He had already spotted Susan waiting for him at a boundary hedge. She waved at him to follow her into a copse of trees that weren't even on Weir's land. They were part of Blacks' Estate, the grand house long abandoned and fallen into decay. From memory the only inhabitant left was the headless horseman, whom everyone feared but no one had seen.

Barlow hurried down the field, the ambulance bobbing along, hard on his heels. Nearing the gap in the hedge, he saw Gillespie lying on the ground. Knowing that Gillespie could now see him, Barlow slowed his pace and took his time pushing through the gap.

Gillespie was white-faced, his teeth gritted against the pain. Wilson and Susan between them had bandaged the broken leg and then extended the bandaging to the other leg, immobilizing both. Blood stained the bandage just below Gillespie's knee. Two inches higher and the teeth of the mantrap would have shattered the knee joint, crippling Gillespie for life.

Someone, Wilson presumably, had cut away the waders.

Barlow stood over Gillespie. 'I suppose you're going to indent for those waders?'

'I was thinking of buying a new pair anyway.'

Gillespie's face went blank as he fought down a spasm of pain. 'You'll tell the wife?'

'Aye, we'll send her a letter.'

Barlow pointed to Susan, then away across the field to the police car. Susan nodded and hurried off. Mrs. Gillespie would be at the hospital almost before Gillespie himself.

Barlow helped load Gillespie onto the stretcher and from there into the ambulance. The ambulance crawled out of the field and down the rough track.

When it finally disappeared behind the hedgerows, Barlow squared the cap on his head and turned to Wilson. 'Show me,' and let Wilson lead the way back through the hedge onto Blacks' land.

Barlow asked, 'Any chance of that trap being here since the Blacks put their pheasants before the peasants' empty stomachs?'

'Someone's kept it oiled.'

'Frigging hell.'

So far, Barlow had focused solely on Gillespie, assessing the severity of the injury and having him rushed to hospital. Now he had time to look around him and to think. Had to think, because the mantrap implied other hidden dangers for his men.

They were on Black's land. The feet of Wilson and Day had churned up the immediate area around Gillespie. The mantrap itself lay on top of the churned earth, but a thick layer of autumn leaves covered the undisturbed ground under the trees. That would need checked and declared safe before he dared send men in.

Stepping carefully on ground already trodden on, Barlow retreated through the hedge, taking Wilson with him. Once through, he looked the length of the field between them and Tommy Weir's house and outbuildings.

'Okay, son, tell me. What brought you down this way?'

Wilson said, 'Gillespie thought someone might have escaped, a woman.'

Chapter 3

Of all the answers Barlow had been expecting, Wilson's "someone might have escaped" wasn't even a possibility. A loose animal, it happened. Gillespie slipping through the gap to assess the chances of a rough shoot? That happened too.

'Say that again, son.'

Wilson pointed back to the farmyard. 'There's a byre up there with a bucket for personal waste and a plate with spilled food at the door.' His hand drew an imaginary line from the farm buildings to where they stood. 'We could see a track through the grass of two or three people heading this way and….' He stepped back to the gap in the hedge and seemed to search the ground. 'Damn! It's gone.'

'What has?'

'A footprint, no shoes, no socks.'

Barlow looked carefully as well. Any footprint had disappeared under the solid boots of Gillespie's rescuers.

If Wilson hadn't been there, he'd have taken off his cap and scratched his head while he made sense of an escaped prisoner and a mantrap. He knew the late Tommy Weir got up to a bit of petty larceny and was not above guiding poachers to the right pool, for a share of the catch. But involved in a kidnapping, and who? There was no reports of anyone missing this side of Liverpool.

'A footprint you say?' he asked.

Wilson's head vibrated up and down as if a series of nods would convince despite the lack of physical evidence. 'Size five, Susan….' He didn't even wait for Barlow's glare before correcting himself. '….WPC Day thought.'

Size five, which made it a youth or a woman. Bare footed and maybe not much else. Barlow looked back across the field with the dew still weighing down the grass. And out in this weather.

Priorities, he had so many priorities he hardly knew where to begin, but one stood out. It was vital that they found the youth or woman before they died of exposure. He tried not to think what would happen if the men who killed Weir caught up with them first.

He led the way back to the farmyard. 'Right, son.' He pointed to the crumbling farmhouse. A curtain flick closed as they looked that way. 'Don't let the family go anywhere until I talk to them.'

He settled himself sideways in car, with his feet on the ground and called into the station. Like himself, Inspector Foxwood was incredulous of an escaped prisoner, but he was glad to get away from the paperwork that Barlow always kept piled in his "In Tray".

Foxwood would be out straight away with DS Leary and his murder bag, and the dog handler and his dog. Barlow imitated a spit at the mention of the dog. He liked dogs in a neutral sort of way but never patted them. He had enough trouble with a Jack Russell that had taken over his house and his favorite chair. The brute snarled every time it saw him.

Barlow signed off on the radio call, stretched out of the car and had a good look at the farmyard. He hadn't been there in years – a question of sheep straying onto Weir's land and not returned to their rightful owners. Weir hadn't spent any money on the property in the meantime. From the front of the house, two rows of outhouses stretched out on either side to form the yard. The outhouses, like the house, had thick lava-stone walls that still stood solid. However, the wood had rotted: the roofs concave, the doors hanging off their hinges.

Except one outhouse where someone had bricked up a window and sheeted the raw wood of a new door in tin.

Barlow nodded in that direction. 'In there, you think?'

Wilson led the way over but didn't go in, didn't even touch the door. DS Leary's snarled contempt of the uniformed branch did more to keep a crime scene uncontaminated than all the lectures at Headquarters. 'In there.' His head seemed to stretch a foot ahead of his body as he looked in to double-check. 'It's gone!'

Barlow looked in as well. No plate, no spilled food, no bucket for personal waste, but the floor around the internal door had recently been brushed. He spotted something Wilson hadn't mentioned: dark drips on the dirt on the floor. If he was a betting man he'd put a fiver on it being blood. He looked again at the house and again a curtain flickered over.

There wasn't a hope of finding the missing plate and checking it for fingerprints. It had to be in the house, washed and put away with the rest. As for the food? He glared at hens clucking around a feed trough.

Wilson had gone red-faced, a mixture of anger and embarrassment. 'When we heard Gillespie scream, Susan and I just ran. We … I never thought ...'

Barlow let the "Susan" go. 'Son, when you're up against a bunch of bad ones, it's like wartime. You deploy your forces, you don't go charging blindly in.'

'Yes, Sergeant.' Wilson looked annoyed with himself. 'I take full responsibility.'

'This is a major cockup, leaving a potential crime scene unguarded,' said Barlow, determined to drive the lesson home. 'You'll both be on the mat with the DI, but WPC Day, as the senior constable, will bear most of the responsibility.'

'That's not fair,' said Wilson.

'Who said life was.'

Chapter 4

Inspector Foxwood arrived, driving his own car. Behind him, bumping up the rutted track came the dog handler in his van.

One good thing about a dog handler, in Barlow's opinion, was that the animal needed a lot of exercise. Foot patrols, especially on a Saturday night when a snarling Alsatian knocked the fight out of an aggressive drunk quicker than a couple of thumps.

The dog handler, Constable McGinn, could go out anytime he wanted on a full pension but he stayed on rather than lose the dog to another handler. Rumor had it that having taught the dog to do everything else he was now training it to eat with a knife and fork.

McGinn approached Barlow, the dog's nose never more than an inch from his leg, and nodded equal to equal. 'I need something to give the dog the scent.'

'There's enough of a smell in the air,' said Barlow and McGinn smiled.

Inspector Foxwood hadn't been in Northern Ireland long enough to know the smells of the countryside, and roasted sugar wasn't one of the ones he'd learned. Somewhere in one of those outbuildings they'd find Tommy Weir's moneymaking sideline, a still for making poteen.

Barlow pointed to the outhouse. 'Try in there.'

Foxwood had already briefed McGinn, who was quick on the uptake. 'Leary will moan.'

'Leary's always moaning.'

McGinn disappeared into the outhouse, the dog still a nose-length from his leg. Barlow used the waiting time to suggest to Foxwood that he might have a word with the grieving – Barlow added a question mark to that word – widow.

'What have you got against the woman?' asked Foxwood whose musical background, tuned him into subtle changes in tone. That made him a good interrogator and a hard man to bluff.

'Ah now, Sir, I'd rather you made up your own mind.'

'Have it your way.'

Foxwood went off to speak Mrs. Weir.

Barlow liked that about the man that he tended to play things Barlow's way because he trusted him to achieve the right result. However, Foxwood also agreed with anything District Inspector Harvey said, when their superior needed a subordinate who'd tell him he was a bollocks.

Barlow hunted out a wooden hay-rake. By that time McGinn had reappeared.

'Well?' asked Barlow.

McGinn shrugged. 'There's a mattress and an old blanket. Half the countryside could have slept in there, but we'll see. We'll see.'

The dog was standing, its head moving in quick jerks as it sniffed the air. More and more it's head turned in the direction of the house where Inspector Foxwood stood thumping the door and getting no response. Barlow trusted the dog's instinct. It was tracing the mixture of scents found in the outhouse to their source. It confirmed in his mind, not that he needed it, that one or more of the inhabitants of the house had been involved in guarding the escapee. However, that wasn't his concern right then.

He said to McGinn, 'Why don't we start at the gap in the hedge?'

First he took time to explain to the increasingly frustrated Foxwood what they intended to do. He was also tempted to open the door for the man, but decided not to. It kept the inspector busy. Anyway, Foxwood had spent the formative part of his career in a nice part of London. Kensington if he remembered right, where people didn't kick doors in.

Foxwood looked wistfully after them as they set off. The rumble of his increasingly rapid thumps on the door followed then down the field.

Barlow stopped at the gap and pointed to the mantrap. 'It was set to catch anyone coming or going through the hedge. The unknown barefoot person must have kept hard against the hedge to avoid it.'

McGinn eyed the mantrap. 'Master or Miss Unknown were luckier than they'll ever know.'

'Maybe, but if you look around, all Weir's fields are well fenced and this is a definite gap.'

'For Weir to do a bit of poaching on Blacks' Estate?'

'And I'm guessing the trap was set to keep people off his land.'

‘So what had he to hide?’ asked McGinn.

‘When you find out, you can tell me.’ Barlow ignored the bared teeth aimed in his direction and waved the dog on. ‘Fetch, Towser.’

McGinn sniffed in disapproval. ‘Designated Constable Rex Number 421, please. Rex for brevity sake is acceptable.’ He kept Rex on a tight lead. ‘I’m not sending the dog in there. There could be another trap hidden under those leaves.’

‘Then you go first,’ said Barlow, but he went himself, using the flat head of the rake to prod hard at the bed of leaves. He angled the search along the hedge away from the house, assuming that any fugitive would head in that direction.

He found himself sweating. Every prod, every rustle of leaves brought back buried memories of his time with the Bomb Disposal Unit during the war. In those days, he prodded gently to see where the ordnance was, because he didn’t want it going off in his face.

After ten yards of an increasingly wide sweep, McGinn said, ‘We can risk it now.’

He let the dog go to the end of a long lead. It ran the hedge for a few yards, angled in through the trees and came back again. The men followed at a distance. To Barlow the dog looked like it was doing the human equivalent of scratching its head. Every so often it glanced McGinn’s way as if to say, ‘Give me a bit of guidance here.’

‘Atta boy,’ said McGinn.

‘That’ll really help the brute,’ said Barlow.

He couldn’t blame the dog, it was doing its best. What he really needed was a squad of men sweeping the estate, with every farmer in the area asked to check their outbuildings for a fugitive. There was no knowing whom they were up against so it was a question of “Do not approach. May be armed and dangerous”.

All the same, it was a nice day even if frosted leaves crackled under-foot. His feet were dry and he wore a pullover under his uniform to keep himself warm. And wasn’t the government paying him to take a walk in the woods.

Suddenly the dog stopped and sniffed the air. Its head turned to the left and the right as if trying to get its bearings. Then it sprang forward to the end of its lead. McGinn stumbled with the suddenness of the pull. Barlow grabbed him by the gun-belt to stop him from falling.

'He's onto something,' said McGinn, recovering his balance.

'Probably a rabbit,' said Barlow, rather than hope that they could avoid hours of trekking across fields after a Will o' the Wisp character who might not even exist.

The dog pulled hard on the lead. They had to pick up their pace to keep up with it as it hauled McGinn through a stand of fir trees. Dust from rotted pine needles stuck to their boots. Then the dog sat down. He looked pleased with himself.

McGinn had stopped as suddenly as the dog. Barlow looked back. 'What now?'

McGinn licked dry lips. 'Sarge…' He wiped at his forehead though he wasn't sweating. 'I've been training Rex to find meat. Hidden meat.'

Barlow looked to where the dog sat. The ground in front of it was a different tone of color from the rest and there was a dip in the earth. A clearly defined dip, the shape and size of a grave.

Chapter 5

Barlow resettled the cap on his head and hitched up a belt that didn't need hitched. Tommy Weir running up against a ruthless gang of poachers, was one thing. A fugitive who for some reason didn't dare go to the police. That happened as well. But a grave, and one that had been there for some time?

Barlow turned and looked through the trees in the direction of Weir's house. Whatever the late Tommy Weir had got himself involved in couldn't be good.

'Call the dog back,' he said.

McGinn gave a short whistle. The dog came to him, though it kept glancing back at the grave as if to say, 'Are you not going to look at what I found?'

McGinn made a fuss of the dog and gave it a treat.

He looked apologetically at Barlow. 'It's only a game to him.'

'Aye.'

Barlow went over to the nearest bush. He used his penknife to cut off two sticks and stuck them in the ground, about six foot apart, lining them up, they pointed straight at the grave. He pulled out a good linen handkerchief. 'Vera's going to kill me,' he said as he cut it in half and tied the halves to the two sticks. Now, even in the dark, the useless detectives who made his station untidy and used most of their investigating skills to fetch buns out of Matthews' home bakery, could find the grave.

He looked at the sky rather than his watch. Still barely lunchtime but darkness came early these days.

'Onwards,' he told McGinn.

McGinn pointed at the dip in the ground as if Barlow couldn't see it, didn't know what it was. 'But, Sarge…'

'If it's a body, it's going nowhere.'

He realized he'd spoken sharply and eased his tone down. 'First house we come to with a phone, we ring it in. But if there is a fugitive out there, it's important we get to them before other people do.'

McGinn lengthened the dog's lead and sent it ahead of them.

Barlow reckoned that at least he and McGinn had an idea of what they were looking for. The dog spent more time sticking its nose under brambles, searching for rabbits, than anything else.

'I'll dock his pay if he doesn't sharpen up,' said Barlow.

'Trust him, Sarge. He's still on the job.'

'He and Gillespie would make a great team.'

Which brought Barlow's worries for Gillespie back into his mind. Things were shaping up to get nasty and this time he hadn't Gillespie to watch his back.

They went on. He couldn't make up his mind if they were following the dog or if it was leading in the direction it thought they were heading. Eventually they forced their way through a hedge, out of Blacks' Estate onto a county road. The dog picked up its pace as it headed across the road and into the next field, which gave Barlow hope.

All the same, the day was moving on rightly and the woman/youth could be miles ahead of them. A line of men coming in from the right direction might speed up things.

He couldn't see it from where he stood, but Daniel T Abernathy's house was just round the next corner. He called McGinn and the reluctant Rex to heel, and set a double time marching pace up the road.

McGinn said, 'I never complain, Sarge, but I was in the Irish Guards where one proceeded at a brisk pace, not this common Rifle Brigade thing of rushing.'

'It'll do you good.'

A couple of minutes brought them around the bend and in sight of Abernathy's house. The house was an old cottage, converted and extended as the family grew in numbers, with bedroom windows sticking out of a low roof. Colors speckled the front garden. Mrs. Abernathy grew flowers for every season of the year.

That was something he and Vera, his daughter, argued about. Louise of course always agreed with Vera. They wanted flowers where he would have run in a rig of potatoes. Leeks and parsley, maybe a few runner beans.

Two women shared his life: a daughter and a girlfriend, who worked at getting on together. Three women, if he counted his wife, though she was gone, in the head as well as physically. His wife,

Maggie, knew she had a daughter but couldn't tie that in with being married to him and sharing his bed for near twenty years.

As they got closer to Abernathy's they could see more of the house and the outbuildings. The field beyond that held a mixture of cows and abandoned fire engines. Old wartime "Green Goddesses" that were gradually sinking into the mud.

They went in the gate and walked up the path through a chocolate-box garden. It made him think that Vera and Louise were right. What if he let them have the front garden for their fancy gewgaws. The back was his.

He rang the electric bell. The last time he called it was an old brass knocker.

A man opened the door. Mid-afternoon and he wore slippers and a pair of flannels that had never seen a contrary cow.

'I need to use your phone' said Barlow.

'Who says I have a phone?'

Barlow didn't bother replying. Merely jerked his head in the direction of the feed-cable running between the house and the telegraph pole on the county road.

'And would you be paying me for the call?'

Barlow said, 'Daniel T, the last time I saw your car, the tax was up.'

Daniel T stepped back to let Barlow into the house. 'Maybe I do have one then. And it's *Mister* Abernathy when you're working, *Mister* Barlow.'

'Come the revolution,' muttered Barlow by way of thanks and made his call to the station.

Daniel T disappeared into the back of the house, shouting at the wife to put the kettle on and "hide the biscuits, Barlow's here". McGinn indicated that he was going to let the dog off the lead for a couple of minutes and headed around the back of the house.

With the light fading, Barlow knew he couldn't delay, but a gulped cup of milky tea would be very welcome. The WPC who took his call noted down his message to Foxwood, including details of a possible grave half-mile SSE of the gap in the hedge.

'Where's SSE, Sarge?'

'Ask an old soldier, love.'

Daniel T came back out of the kitchen. 'When you're ready,

the tea's wet and the wife's buttering some barmbrack.'

Mrs. Abernathy's barmbrack was home made. Barlow always made a point of buying it at church fetes.

'A decent woman there, she always makes a man welcome. Not like some I could mention.'

'Well you were in "The Rifles" said Daniel T and nodded to a photograph of himself on top of a tank with sand dunes behind him.

'You only joined the Royal Irish because you hate walking,' said Barlow and started to follow Daniel T into the kitchen.

From somewhere at the back of the house the dog burst into savage barking. McGinn yelled in alarm.

Chapter 6

Barlow was haring around the side of the house before his mind caught up with his actions. He vaguely remembered stumbling on the hall mat as he ran out the door. McGinn had yelled only once. Rex continued to bark.

It finally registered with him that the dog's pace had increased as they approached Daniel T's house. It didn't seem likely, but could they have stumbled on the fugitive?

McGinn was in the cobbled yard struggling one-handed to control Rex. The other hand held his pistol.

Rex foamed at the mouth as he fought to charge into an outhouse. The outhouse was an old farmhouse converted into a bull pen. From it came the sound of pounding hooves and the bellows of an enraged bull.

'What?' Barlow shouted over the noise of the bull and the barks of Rex.

'The bitch nearly sliced me from stem to stern.'

Barlow went from cold fear to blood-boiling anger at McGinn for taking unnecessary risks. 'What were you doing in there in the first place?'

'I was never near it. She ran in there, some woman with a dirty great big knife.' McGinn held up his arm for Barlow to inspect the sleeve. The material had a four-inch tear. 'That's how close she came to knifing me.'

At least they could stop chasing through the gathering dark. That woman, whoever she was, had probably been stamped into the ground by that… *animal.*

Barlow peered cautiously over the half-door. He jumped back as the bull's horns slashed at him. He found himself out of breath, his heart hammering.

Daniel T appeared. He had taken his time to exchange his slippers for wellington boots and pull on a stockman's coat over his good clothes. 'Don't you go annoying our Wee Willie.'

The brute dwarfed Daniel T.

Barlow kept a wary eye on Wee Willie. It looked capable of clearing the half-door and coming at them in the yard. 'I thought Jerseys were supposed to be gentle?'

'Cows, yes, the bulls are something else.'

'Aye.'

Barlow drew his pistol. 'There's a woman trapped in the far corner, and I need her out alive.'

Daniel T put himself between Barlow and the bull. 'You're not going to shoot Wee Willie.'

'Give me another option.'

All the same, at the sight of Daniel T the bull's stomping had quietened and the angry roars wound down to heavy breathing. Daniel T went up to the shed. After a few calls the bull came to the door and stood shaking its head.

Daniel T rubbed its nose and didn't seem to notice the horns slashing the air around his face. 'Poor Wee Willie, did that big bully of a policeman frighten you?'

'The woman,' whispered Barlow.

'All in good time,' said Daniel T in the singsong voice he employed talking to the bull.

He gave its nose a final rub. 'If you're a good boy I'll let you out into the field for a while.' The bull snorted and its horns slashed harder. 'I will, I will,' said Daniel T. 'Just for a few minutes.'

He stepped back from the bull and shrugged apologetically at Barlow. 'I hope he goes out.'

'What do you mean hope?'

'Wee Willie's frightened of the dark. He fell into a sheugh as a calf and was there all night. The poor wee fellow nearly died.'

Barlow eyed the "poor wee fellow" warily. 'Whatever.'

Daniel T disappeared around the corner, calling to the bull all the while. After a minute metal banged on metal and a door at the back of the shed creaked open. Daniel T's voice came louder, encouraging the bull out. Barlow could only hope that the woman didn't head that way as well. The dog didn't like anyone who attacked McGinn and cattle hated dogs. Things could get messy.

The bull stomped and snorted but finally went out into the field. The metal door clanged shut and a bolt rammed home.

'You're safe now,' shouted Daniel T, taunting Barlow as if

he'd been frightened of a week-old calf.

Barlow slid back the bolts of the door. McGinn was at his shoulder, the dog held firmly by the collar. Barlow stepped in, warily. He could see a woman crouched in the far corner.

Unless someone lay buried in the thick bedding of straw, she was alone. Gaunt and pale from malnourishment – half-starved, he reckoned – wearing little more than a thin cotton dress. She was tall for a woman, blonde-haired, and filthy. He reckoned the reek in the shed wasn't all from the bull.

A knife gleamed dully in her hand. She held it up, threatening them, her mouth set in a snarl.

'I'll put the dog on her,' said McGinn.

'You'll do no such thing,' said Barlow. He made it sharp. 'Go back to the house. There's a cup of tea waiting for you.'

Nervous, wishing to delay things however little, he scratched the dog's head. 'Towser ...'

'Rex,' said McGinn.

'There'll be a bit of barmbrack for you as well.'

He holstered his pistol. Then he took off his gun-belt and handed it to the surprised McGinn.

Chapter 7

Barlow had to repeat the order for McGinn to go for his cup of tea.

'Your funeral,' McGinn muttered as he and Rex retreated across the yard.

Rather than let the woman see sky and possible freedom, Barlow switched on the light and pulled the doors shut behind him. He opened out a canvas stool that Daniel T used when spending time with Wee Willie, sat on the stool and stretched his legs out, by the way relaxed.

He made every move slow, with a wary eye on the woman and the knife. The point of its blade remained aimed at his throat. Not the dirty great big knife claimed by McGinn but a serrated steak knife with pointed tip.

'It's a grand day for the time of year,' he said.

It was hard to put a year on her or anything else. Thirty plus or minus, was the nearest he could estimate her age. There was something foreign about her – East German, East European…

'I'm guessing you've had a hard time, love, but that's over now. A hot bath, a bit of food…' he nodded towards her bare feet. 'Those seen to at the hospital, and you'll be right as rain.'

Her eyes had flickered at "hot bath" and "food". That meant that she had some English.

'I don't know where you come from, love, but we do things different here. Any man who touches a woman finds himself in court. And if it's a wife and she won't make an official complaint, we make a point of getting the husband for something else.'

He kept talking, nonsense mostly. When he ran out of other subjects, he told her of the problems of sharing a house with a teenage daughter and an itinerant girlfriend. 'She brings her spare clothes in a shopping basket and takes them home again to wash. Not so much as a handkerchief goes on our line.'

And yet, funny, Louise didn't mind being seen out in public with him, or having him as her escort for parties or functions. Everyone knew they were an item and all that implied. But openly living with him, seen to be sharing his bed, she saw as somehow different.

He wasn't getting too far with this one either and he could hear the snuffles of Wee Willie at the field door, almost begging to get in out of the growing dark. The woman's face creased in puzzlement as she struggled to make sense of his words. At least she now held the knife almost casually, pointing at nowhere in particular.

Time slipped by. Wee Willie's snuffles became more distressed. Occasionally his head butted the door as he tried to get back into his shed. The door shuddered at every butt. It had been constructed to open inwards: designed to keep a bull from breaking out, and not one anxious to get back in. Occasionally the woman's eyes looked towards the door. Like him, she knew that a panicked bull charging in out of the dark might not be too friendly towards strangers.

'Love, I don't want to be rushing you, but it's getting on. I've a man in hospital and my quiet week has already gone to buggery.'

Maybe it was the change in tone, maybe she understood him better than he thought because she smiled.

He made a point of looking startled when he checked the time on his watch and made as if to stand up. 'I'm not one to be complaining, love, but I missed my lunch and there's a lot to be done before I head home for tea.'

'Mens,' the woman said. She rubbed her stomach and imitated a sigh.

She had some English. That had to help.

'I'm guessing you wouldn't mind a bite yourself.'

He tried not to tense as she stood up and came towards him. She limped even on the rough softness of the straw bedding. He let her get halfway across before creaking to his feet. He made a play of rubbing a stiff back. 'It's my war wounds.' Though in truth his "war wounds" amounted to a case of hypothermia leading to pneumonia.

Barlow held out his hand for the knife. She shook her head and held on to it. Her hair swung heavily with the shake. She pushed it away from her face with a look of distaste.

He reckoned he could disarm her if he wanted to. Then he noted how the woman stood poised, not for flight, but danger, and decided it safer not to provoke her in any way.

He opened the door into the yard. It was fully dark now. He

could see the outline of McGinn and Rex against the yard light. They wouldn't take too kindly to the woman still holding the knife.

An engine roared, lights swept the yard and a warning bell clanged.

Before Barlow could move or speak, the woman had the point of the knife at his eye.

Chapter 8

The point of the knife rested against the edge of Barlow's left eye. Not pricking, he noted, not ready to slide into his brain. It took him a couple of shuddered breaths before he came to that relieved conclusion.

'I only shave in the mornings, love, unless I'm going out for the evening.' Nonsense maybe, but she seemed to relate to nonsense.

McGinn stood frozen in the lights of whatever vehicle it was, with Rex beside him, poised to attack on the order. The warning bell still clanged. Moving his arm a lot slower than his heart rate, Barlow pointed in the direction of the vehicle. The knife tightened against the edge of his eye socket as he drew a finger across his throat.

McGinn got the message and passed it on. The bell stopped clanging and there was silence. Even Wee Willie had stopped butting the door. From up the road Barlow could see other vehicles approaching, their blue lights flashing.

So who's the idiot?

He made his voice scathing. 'McGinn, who's that other idiot in the yard?'

'The ambulance. I sent for it in case….'

'Thanks.'

The woman was now poised for flight. Maybe she planned to keep him between her and McGinn until she could slip away into the darkness. Maybe even risk sharing the field with the distressed Wee Willie. She'd never outrun the dog, she had to know that.

Barlow made the decision for her. He shuffled his feet forward until she had to come with him, the knife's serrated edge making dents in his skin.

A couple of shuffles and they could finally see the ambulance for what it was: a chunky, yellow-bodied truck with more windows than a terrace house. The ambulance driver and his helper busy pulling out a stretcher.

The woman laughed, a short spurt of amusement, and then tensed again, wondering if it was a trick.

At long last Barlow's heartbeat eased down. He turned slowly to face her. ‘Ambulance. Hospital.’ That, at least, had to be international. He hesitated to lean into the knife while he pointed to her feet and tried to explain about treatment. Frustrated at her lack of understanding, he touched a greasy strand of her hair. ‘Shower.’

She shook her head. The word meant nothing.

Then he remembered the time way back, during his wartime service when he and Edward Adair searched for unexploded bombs. Edward always relieved tension by playing on his royal “Wrong side of the blanket antecedents, old boy.” It never rained when they were wading through mud, feeling with their bare feet for unexploded ordnance. “One merely experienced…”

‘A douche,’ said Barlow.

She laughed again, probably at his attempt at French, and finally the knife was offered to him, handle first.

Bloody footprints showed where she had walked across the straw. Rather than have her suffer any further he carried her to the waiting ambulance. Behind him, the door into the field slammed open as Wee Willie finally forced his way into the shed.

Chapter 9

Inspector Foxwood gave Barlow a lift back to Tommy Weir's farm. 'That's quite a thing you did there, Sergeant.'

'McGinn's an old woman, sending for the cavalry like that.'

'That's as maybe.'

They left it there: Foxwood driving, Barlow sitting content in the passenger seat. Foxwood liked Barlow's results, but never dared look too deeply into how he achieved them. Barlow respected Foxwood the man, though he thought him mealy-mouthed around senior officers.

They pulled into Weir's farmyard and parked among the clutter of cars that now occupied it. Torches showed where men were making their way through the field and trees to the site of the grave.

'You've started already, Sir?'

'When Leary and his men looked there were more leaves covering the body than soil. A male, good suit, very good according to Leary. Tie still knotted and in place; a wallet with money in it.'

'Been there quite a while then?'

'Upwards on six months.'

'And not easy found,' Barlow said. He moved in his seat, his elbow touching Foxwood's. The touch might have been an accident; it could have been a hint. 'So McGinn deserves a commendation then. All that extra work he put into Rex paid off.'

'Noted,' said Foxwood as they got out of the car.

Barlow drew in the scents of the night, the burn of frost already in the air. A light glowed in what had to be Weir's sitting room and a pall of wood-smoke hung over the house.

'Any luck there?' asked Barlow.

'Mrs. Weir came to the door in the end. She's grieving too much over Tommy to be bothered with people calling.'

The sitting room blind was down. Barlow could see a shadow thrown against it by the light.

'You had a quick look around?'

Foxwood's sensed something in Barlow's words and his voice tensed. 'Not without a Search Warrant, she made that quite plain. Mr.

Harvey's seeing to that. It should be here anytime.'

'Aye,' said Barlow.

He stormed across the cobbled yard to the front door, lifted his foot and kicked. The door burst open.

Foxwood gasped. 'Sergeant!'

Outside the house was crumbling from neglect. Inside was spotlessly clean. The sort of house where Barlow could safely drink a cup of tea – so long as he was sure she hadn't spat in it first.

The sitting room door flew open. Barlow expected to see the wizen stick that was Mrs. Weir. Instead, Geordie Dunlop's body filled the opening.

'You knocked?' he asked.

Mrs. Weir stood behind Geordie. Little more than her head and a shoulder showed as she shoved at Geordie, trying to get past him and at Barlow. 'Out, out, out,' she screamed.

'Aye,' said Barlow. He got over his surprise. 'How did you get in here?'

Mrs. Weir screaming, 'You've no right,' vibrated in his ears. It had to be worse for Geordie who stubbornly blocked her way.

'Wasn't there a panic on. Some old fool of a sergeant in trouble and people hoping he'd be dead by the time they got there.'

Barlow let the insult go and stayed silent. He knew Geordie, there'd be an excuse. As well as shouting, Mrs. Weir was also kicking at Geordie to get past. Fortunately for Geordie, she wore only felt slippers.

The excuse came. 'We heard Tommy was dead and the wife sent me up with a cake, fresh baked.' He smirked. 'She's a special one in mind when it's your turn.'

'I hope you choke on the first bite.'

He wished Mrs. Weir had choked on a slice of Tommy' cake.

It had been a long, trying day. Barlow hadn't had a cup of tea since breakfast. That and Mrs. Weir's screaming gave him just the right edge of temper to go storming through the house. However, Foxwood was hard on his heels, and already breathing indignation at him for kicking-in the door.

Barlow raised his head and his voice. 'Get down here.'

There was only silence from above.

'Leonidas Chaney Weir.' He drew breath and let rip even

louder. 'Leon, I'm not in the mood to play games. You get your backside down here NOW!'

At the mention of her son's name, Mrs. Weir went silent and disappeared back into the sitting room.

Footsteps sounded above and a man appeared, stepping delicately down the cracked linoleum on the stairs. First brown winkle-pickers showed, then tight blue trousers and, finally, a white shirt with polka-dot cravat neatly tucked in, and a mustard waistcoat worn as protection against the cold of the house. The man was aged about thirty, thin without being gaunt.

'Mr. Barlow,' said Leon, ever so politely.

Barlow grabbed Leon's forearms and squeezed. Leon went white and screamed in shock.

'For heaven's sake, Sergeant,' said Foxwood.

Spots of blood dappled the left sleeve of Leon's white shirt. The spots quickly spread and ran into each other until the shirt sleeve hung heavy with blood.

'Cut yourself shaving?' asked Barlow and pushed Leon towards the astonished Foxwood. 'Hot pursuit of a fugitive, Sir: kidnap, illegal detention, assault. Question rape.'

He'd had his fill of work and of other people's problems for the day, and he still wasn't finished. He hustled Geordie out of the house and headed for McGinn's van.

Chapter 10

Constable McGinn was waiting at the van. From the back came the rumbling snores of a contented Rex.

Barlow swung into the passenger seat. 'Hospital.'

Geordie rapped the window. 'Would you give me a lift into town?'

'Go home the way you came.'

'I thumbed a lift to get here. There's still some decent people in the world who'll do a man a favor.'

'Get in the back,' Barlow said.

'He'll sit on the dog and hurt it,' said McGinn, and rushed to push the recumbent Rex to the side.

The van lurched down on its springs as Geordie got in. 'It licked me,' he said. 'Nice doggie.'

Barlow said to McGinn. 'Does that dog kill on command?'

'No.'

'Pity.'

At that Barlow stretched himself comfortable. The engine purred, the van lurched from pothole to pothole down the laneway, carefully, so as not to risk hurting Rex. Then they were on the county road and he could let his mind drift.

The van stopped. Barlow got an eye open and saw the bulk of the Waveney Hospital looming over the van. Lights blazed from every ward.

McGinn said, 'I'll come back for you when I've the dog settled for the night.'

'Good man.'

Geordie tapped the diamond–mesh wire separating the driver and passenger from the dog. 'Drop me as close as you can to the Bridge Bar.'

'Always willing to oblige a regular customer,' said McGinn.

'You're getting out here,' said Barlow.

'You wouldn't do that on a man?'

Barlow twisted around until he could see something of the bulk of Geordie. 'You fought in the Spanish Civil War?'

‘I’d heard their rioja was something special.’ He sucked his lips loudly in sweet memory. ‘The consistency in excellence is remarkable. I remember….’

Barlow interrupted what threatened to be a long story. ‘Which side did you fight on?’

‘Both. It was either that or be shot.’

‘With the Russians, I’m told.’

‘Georgians, they don’t like being called Ruskies.’

‘Okay, out, I’ve a job for you.’

The van springs groaned as Geordie bumped his way out the back door. He leaned back in to wish the dog a fond farewell. McGinn looked sour when Rex’s tail drummed hard on the tin sides.

Barlow muttered, ‘If this gets out, all our regulars will be queuing up to make friends with the brute.’

Barlow and Geordie went into the hospital together. Their booted feet clattering on the terrazzo floor ensured Barlow could talk bluntly.

‘You and Tommy Weir?’

‘You know me, Mr. Barlow.’

‘That’s why I’m asking.’

‘Mere business acquaintances,’ said Geordie.

Barlow had to be sure. ‘I hope so. What’s going on up there is a hanging job.’

‘I give you my word, Sergeant Major.’

Barlow believed him. Geordie never lied when talking to his wartime Sergeant Major.

He quickened his pace because he could hear heated voices coming from the Emergency Ward. One voice, it had to be the foreign woman’s, kept screaming, ‘No no no.’

They burst in. The foreign woman was sitting up in bed, the neck of a smashed urine bottle in her hand, ready to swipe it at anyone who came near. Doctors and nurses, Constable Wilson and WPC Susan Day were struggling to calm her, all talking at once.

‘What’s all this then?’ said Barlow in his best gulder.

Silence. The foreign woman looked relieved to see him. He almost didn’t recognize her. Someone had helped her shower and found her a hospital nightdress and towel-dried her hair. The nurses had bandaged her feet. Bloodstained ointment oozed through the sulphide dressings.

She's a good looking woman, he decided, and very determined to kill anyone who came close.

A doctor said, 'We tried to give her an anti-tetanus jab, and she went crazy.'

'Ah well.'

After what the woman had been through, Barlow didn't blame her. There had to be a lot of sedating going on recently in her life.

Geordie poked Wilson on the chest. 'You're the young copper Barlow hasn't contaminated yet.' He put an arm around Susan. 'And you, darlin', arrested me so charmingly that last time.' He put a hand to his cheek, remembering the kiss she gave him as she put him in a cell.

Susan played along. 'Any time, Mr. Dunlop. Just pop into the station and I'll be happy to oblige.'

Now Barlow knew what to do. 'Wilson, off with your jacket and roll up your shirt sleeve.'

'Sergeant…'

'Get on with it, man.'

Wilson took off his jacket and rolled up his sleeve. Barlow was tempted to rip the clothes off him just to speed things up, but he waited. Finally Wilson was ready. The doctor held up the syringe and squirted air out of the needle.

Wilson collapsed over the bed and slid onto the floor.

The woman in the bed squeaked with fear and slashed out with the broken urine bottle to keep everyone back.

Barlow hoped Wilson was dead, because if he wasn't he'd kill him himself for giving her something to really panic over.

Wilson was already groaning, coming too. Barlow felt things come under control – his control – again. The doctors and nurses were smiling in relief. One young nurse giggled and was frowned silent by the Sister.

Susan hunkered down over Wilson, dabbing at the sweat on his face with her handkerchief. She looked up at Barlow. 'He's afraid of needles, he told me.'

'Get up, you better not be.'

Geordie slid off his jacket. 'I'll do it.'

Barlow made his tone insulting. 'You're like me, full of the stuff already.'

Geordie developed a limp as he moved out of the way to let the medical staff drag Wilson clear. 'Barlow, your words hurt me more than that blast of buckshot.'

If it hadn't been for Geordie stepping between her and the gunman, Barlow's daughter, Vera, would almost certainly be dead.

Barlow fixed his face in a derisive sneer. 'You'll be easier caught the next time you run.'

Susan had her jacket off and her sleeve rolled up. Barlow made her and the doctor stand where the woman could easily see the liquid going in.

Susan was rolling down her sleeve again when the woman finally smiled and lobbed the broken bottle to the end of the bed.

Barlow sat on the edge of the bed beside her. She didn't resist when he took her hand in his. Now he had time to look closely he saw the face of a good-looking woman, with worry lines indicating a hard life behind her. Even so her mouth had a crinkle of laughter lines and the blue eyes staring at him were assessing, not judgmental.

Moving slowly, standing at arm's length, a doctor gave her the injection in her other arm. Barlow deliberately kept his hold on her hand relaxed; she could pull it free any time. The woman never moved. Finished with the injection, the doctor retreated.

Barlow motioned for Geordie to join them. 'Try some of your Russian chat-up lines.'

Geordie said, 'I only got off with the horses, I didn't fancy the men.'

Barlow didn't even bother sighing.

Chapter 11

The paperwork left *sine dei,* if he had the right expression from listening to some smart alec barrister show off in court, Barlow called in to see Constable Gillespie.

Gillespie looked comfortable. He had a private room to himself. Soothing hands had propped him up while he read that evening's Belfast Telegraph. An empty cup and a plate were evidence of him sharing the nurses' break-time. He looked healthy enough, though the green-tinted paint they put on the walls gave everyone a bad pallor.

'You're suffering, I see,' said Barlow.

'It's only cracked,' said Gillespie.

'I'm here about your leg, not your head.'

'It's stitched and bandaged. They'll put on a walking plaster in a day or two.'

Someone had left Gillespie a bag of grapes. Barlow helped himself to a handful and felt a burst of instant energy. 'All this fuss over a couple of scrapes.'

Gillespie glowered as the grapes disappeared down Barlow's throat. 'You're only supposed to eat the ones you bring yourself.'

Satisfied that Gillespie would live to go fishing and shooting again, Barlow pulled up a chair and recounted the events of the long day. So far they had two dead bodies and an apparent kidnap victim, a suspect in Leon Weir and only speculation to link the various crimes. Like him, the only conclusion Gillespie could come to was a shrug.

The story told and the grapes finished, Barlow lobbed the empty bag into the waste bin and stood up.

'So the leg doesn't hurt or anything?'

'What do you think?'

After a lifetime hearing Gillespie moan about flat feet, bad back and a weak chest, this was a new one. He framed his sympathy by way of an offer. 'These places with their central heating, they make a man dry. A bottle of beer sneaked in…?'

'You don't have to stop at one.'

‘And your study books.’

Gillespie scowled.

Barlow nodded his ‘Good night.’ He headed for McGinn’s van, and home.

Chapter 12

The front of the house was in darkness though a light glimmered through the frosted glass from the direction of the kitchen. Not good, Barlow decided, because Louise liked the comfort of the sitting room. Nor was her car in the drive. Maybe if he rang her she'd come over. After a day like this he needed the comfort of her body.

Toby, the dog, rumbled a growl as he went through the front door. There was nothing unusual about that.

He went into the kitchen. 'Sorry I'm late,' and had to work at keeping his words relaxed.

Vera sat in Barlow's chair, with Toby relegated to the fireside mat. She only did that when she wanted to tease him, or when she was upset or annoyed. This time over Gillespie being hurt, he guessed, because it could easily have been himself.

'Are you all right, love?'

'Fine, dad,' she said, and stood up and gave him a hug before pulling back. 'It was on the news, finding that man's body in the river.'

'Was it now?'

He couldn't help the terse reply. He did enough thinking about work when he was there without bringing it home.

She said, 'They even had television reporters talking to Mr. Harvey about it.'

Knowing District Inspector Harvey, Barlow was sure Harvey had told the story as if he himself had all but found and recovered the body. All the same, it wasn't so much what Vera said as didn't say that intrigued Barlow.

'Nothing about kidnapped women or bodies in the woods or a Jersey bull that's afraid of the dark?'

She laughed as if he'd made a joke. 'Not a mention.'

That puzzled him. With the reporters already in town, they must have known that Harvey had ordered the detectives off the Tommy Weir case to investigate another suspicious death.

But that was work, or rather Harvey's idea of work: self-publicity. Barlow concentrated on what was important. A wife would talk about retirement and a safer job. A daughter could only worry. He'd have to talk to her about his day but right then he couldn't find the words.

Vera turned away. 'I'll get your tea. It'll be dry, but you've eaten worse.' She hurried off into the scullery.

Toby had already taken possession of his chair. Vera had set a place for him at the table. He sat there and fingered the change in lifestyle that Louise has brought with her: a side plate, napkin and a butter-knife. Sometimes when he was on his own, he'd eat from a tray at the fire.

'Remembering the good old days,' Vera said when she caught him at it.

More like miserable, lonely old days, but he had spent twenty years of his life that way and the memories clung to him.

Propped against the sauce bottle was an envelope with his name on it. He recognized Louise's handwriting. He picked up the envelope and held it unopened. Whatever was in it, Vera already knew.

The letter was short:

John,

My sister's husband has been in a crash. I have to go to her and I don't know when I'll be back.'

Louise

Not even a "Love" or and X or O

There was a newly installed telephone extension in the kitchen. He found it so much nicer to say good night to Louise from the comfort of his armchair instead of shivering in the hallway. But aware that Vera in the scullery could overhear everything said, he went into the hallway and rang Louise from there.

She answered on the second ring, as if she'd been sitting by the phone expecting his call. 'It's bad, John, bad.'

'What happened?'

'It was night time, he hit some sort of deer.' She rushed out what had to be part excuse. 'His business, Thank goodness my sister stayed involved so she knows what to do. But it's a fulltime job on top of everything else, and then there's the children.'

'Aye,' he said. He could fight anything; argue against anything except children and their care.

'That's the one in South Africa?' he asked.

'Cape Town,' she said.

It sounded somewhere near the end of the world.

There was a tightness in her voice, a refusal to let tears come. He realized that the whole thing had been too much for her. The sacrifices for their relationship had all been on her side.

'If you have to go,' he said.

'I have to.'

So there it was. Once in South Africa she would have family and a home. They'd been at her for years to come out and build a future for herself instead of living in genteel poverty.

He knew it was over, whatever it was they'd had between them. And done nice and politely, like the lady she was.

'You'll need money for the ticket.'

'My sister's seen to that. There'll be a ticket waiting for me at the BOAC desk in London.'

'So when?'

'Tomorrow morning, first flight out of Nutts Corner.'

Their voices nice and level. They used more emotion talking about the weather. Will it rain? Will it shine?

'Do you want me to take you over? I could do it and still make work.'

'I've booked Johnny Scullion.' Her voice changed and he knew the call was coming to an end. 'I've things to do before…. She fought down the quaver in her voice. 'Thank you for everything, John Barlow. You made me believe in myself again.'

'You gave me happiness,' he said, wanting her to reconsider. But she had already hung up.

TUESDAY

Blank Page

Chapter 13

Barlow went to bed and lay wide awake and restless. He finally slept after Vera got home from a night out with the girls. At least he hoped it was the girls and not the back seat of some fellow's car.

He woke at the usual time, curled into the sheets and inhaled a trace of Louise's scent. It was Tuesday, the day the bed linen was changed and washed. He'd pretend to forget and hoped Vera would as well. That scent was the last thing he'd ever have of Louise.

Shaved and showered, he scooped his keys out from under the pillow, their hiding place at night, and went on to work. He'd have breakfast later.

Early as he was, Detective Sergeant Leary was in before him. That had never happened before. Barlow went to investigate.

The little detective's seethe of anger hit him as he went in the door.

DS Leary sat at his desk, tea un-drunk. For once the desk was clear of its usual clutter of files. Even more unusually, the biscuits were still in sight. Once Leary sensed Barlow on the prowl the biscuits disappeared.

'Who ate your wee bun?' Barlow asked.

'Bloody Harvey. Bloody Special Branch. Bloody "D Notice".'

Barlow closed the door behind him. The other detectives weren't in yet so he and Leary couldn't be overheard. 'A "D Notice"?'

A "D Notice", the "Defence Advisory Notice", was a request made by the Secretary of Defence, requiring the media not to report certain facts or incidents. In Barlow's opinion, it only happened when the British Government didn't want the general public to know something that the Russians and the Chinese already knew all about.

Leary motioned for Barlow to take a seat. 'Much of yesterday didn't happen. There's no body of a missing Civil Servant lying it Blacks' wood.'

Barlow called up an imaginary wine gum and had a slow chew on that while he thought things through. 'So he was missing, now he's found. What's so secret about that?'

Leary scowled. 'You tell me, which is more than they're doing. All they want to know is what we found other than the wallet.'

'Like what?'

'I don't know, but they put me over it twenty times.'

Which gave him another worry. 'The foreign woman, what about her?'

'They've "D'd" her as well.'

Barlow pulled up an imaginary Sour Drop and had a good suck. It was turning into that sort of day. 'Do they intend to "disappear" her as well?'

Leary actually pushed the biscuits Barlow's way. 'No, but they don't want her story getting out. They're afraid of starting up that old "white slaves" chestnut again. Every newspaper reporter in the country would be tramping over Weir's land looking for an exclusive.'

Maybe they should, Barlow thought, but he kept it to himself.

From somewhere near the Enquiry Office they heard a sharp little voice raised in indignant query. District Inspector Harvey was in.

Leary pulled an innocuous file from a drawer and opened it. 'We were discussing the Gibson case. Yesterday's happenings never came up and if….' He over-emphasized the next two words. 'Malcolm Knype wasn't dead already I'd kick him from here to Timbuctoo.'

Now Barlow had a name to work on. He nodded and left.

Chapter 14

'You, Barlow, into my office.'

'Good morning, Sir,' said Barlow.

Harvey grunted and went on. Inspector Foxwood was following Harvey. He gave Barlow a nod and his eyes flickered towards the ceiling. At the best of times, Harvey was trying. In that mood, it was going to be a long day for everyone.

Once in Harvey's office, Barlow came to attention before the portrait of the Queen on the back wall. He then stood easy, towering over Harvey and his choice of a desk. Modern laminated wood in a Victorian era room with plaster cornicing and flock wallpaper.

Harvey settled into his over-padded chair. 'Barlow, that foreign woman person and the body found in Blacks' wood. You never heard of them. They do not exist.'

'That's impossible, Sir. I don't understand.'

Harvey first read out the terms of the "D Notice" Then the law relating to "D Notices". Upwards on jail for life if anyone said a word out of place, even gave a hint of the existence of a "D Notice."

Aha, thought Barlow. The television, the radio, the chance for glory gone.

'That's a shame, Sir. You sounded really good in those interviews.'

For a moment Harvey looked pleased. 'Did I? Well thank you, Barlow.'

'It's a pleasure, Sir.'

And it was. He had managed to miss every interview of Harvey's, and intended to avoid that day's papers.

As quickly as he'd become pleasant, Harvey went back to being his usual self. He reached for a beige folder, a fresh one to add to the stack of complaints against Barlow.

Before he could speak, the phone rang. Harvey grabbed it and gave a terse, 'Yes?'

The "yes" quickly dissolved into a puddle of ingratiation. 'Sir Anthony? Here? Oh yes, yes, send him in immediately.'

Sir Anthony Chard lived in Ballymena but worked in Belfast.

His job, apparently, though he was too discrete to be specific, was to liaise between Hillsborough Castle and the Cabinet Office in London.

In Sir Anthony's well-regulated life, him turning up without an appointment smacked almost of bad manners. It had to be about the "D Notice", and that in itself was very curious.

Harvey checked that his tie was straight, stood and polished the tips of his shoes on the back of his trousers.

The ooze of servility disappeared when he again focused on Barlow. 'Out! I'll deal with you later.'

Barlow nodded as if it had been a friendly promise to meet up again. The door opened before he reached it. A constable escorted in Sir Anthony and an underling. Both wore pinstripe suits. Around town, off duty, Sir Anthony favored an off-white jacket and a battered Panama hat.

Sir Anthony's hand was out immediately. 'John Barlow, as usual a pleasure.'

'Sir Anthony,' said Barlow.

They shook hands and Barlow formally introduced him to Foxwood and Harvey, though he was sure the men had met at social events.

'Sir,' said Foxwood.

'It's an honor to have you here, Sir Anthony,' said Harvey.

Barlow sidled towards the door.

Sir Anthony called after him, 'Sergeant, this concerns you as well.' He turned to Harvey. 'With your permission of course.'

Harvey's lips smiled but his eyes burned in Barlow's direction. 'Certainly, Sir Anthony, as you wish, Sir Anthony.'

Barlow took station at one side of the door, the un-introduced underling at the other.

Chapter 15

Once settled in a seat Sir Anthony joined his hands as if in prayer and tapped the fingertips against his lips. 'This "D Notice", most unfortunate, but necessary for the ultimate security of the country.'

'Of course, of course,' said Harvey.

Barlow wasn't so sure. That "unfortunate" from Sir Anthony's diplomatic lips implied division of opinion, of censure and dispute.

Sir Anthony added. 'It also engendered other foreseen but regrettable consequences.'

'You can depend on me, Sir Anthony, I'll see to it that none of my officers speak out of turn.'

He'll be lucky, thought Barlow. There's no bigger gossip than a policeman, and the wives are like Town Criers.

Harvey added. 'One slip, and I take no prisoners.'

Sir Anthony held up a hand to quell Harvey's flow of promises. 'That, I regret to say, is one of the foreseen consequences.

'The prisoners,' he further explained to a puzzled Harvey.

'Oh?'

'The as yet unidentified foreign lady will be moved to… shall we say a secure location, the hospital records expunged.'

Sir Anthony looked Barlow's way and gave the slightest of nods. Barlow took it that he wanted some hard questioning instead of Harvey's oily agreement to everything.

Barlow said, 'With respect, Sir Anthony, we need a statement from the lady and, of course, she will be required as a witness when the Weirs stand trial.'

'Regretfully, Sergeant, that is impossible.' Sir Anthony extended his hands. 'Out of my hand's entirely.'

'So we let Leon Weir go? Drop the charges for: kidnap, false imprisonment and sexual assault, possibly rape?'

'I am afraid so.'

Harvey looked horrified. 'Barlow, how dare you question Sir Anthony's orders.'

Barlow ignored Harvey. He was getting so many conflicting thoughts that he didn't know where to start.

Sir Anthony held Barlow's gaze for a moment, then his face flickered a contraction. It could have been irritation. Barlow took it as a warning to be silent and bit down the next question.

The interview now over, Sir Anthony stood up and addressed his final remarks to Harvey. 'However, the murder of Thomas Weir appears to be an unrelated issue. The investigation into his death will, of course, continue to be carried out by your officers. Our department will be pleased to assist where we can.' Harvey was already nodding agreement when Sir Anthony added, 'In the meantime.'

He indicated his underling with a careless flick of his fingers. 'Gronville here, perhaps he and Sergeant Barlow might liaise on the practical aspects of the investigation.'

Harvey didn't know whether to be annoyed at a lost opportunity to make contacts at Hillsborough Castle, the seat of power in Northern Ireland. Or proud to be seen as above such a lowly contact as Gronville.

Barlow wasn't so sure about Gronville's unimportance. He had seen Sir Anthony stop his regular postman in the street and introduce him to a visitor. Not introducing Gronville was some sort of ploy.

He watched the man out of the corner of his eye. He was slim, mid-thirties and fit. Maybe ultra-fit. Gronville stood at easy attention without the fidgeting he might expect of a civilian. He had to be a Marine or a member of the re-formed SAS regiment.

Sir Anthony reached the door and Barlow before Harvey could extract himself from behind the desk. He dropped his voice. 'John, the party on Friday night, bring Vera.'

So the man knew that Louise was gone, had maybe advised her to how do it.

Barlow buried his hurt and humiliation. 'Thank you Sir Anthony, Vera will be delighted at the invitation.'

What he needed was time and a quiet cup of tea in the kitchen while he figured out what Sir Anthony was really up to.

Chapter 16

District Inspector Harvey saw Sir Anthony to his waiting car, Gronville stayed back to speak to Barlow. If Sir Anthony had gone on without Gronville then, in Harvey's opinion, he was a person of no importance. Harvey went back to his office and left Barlow to deal with Gronville.

"Dealing" involved the two men sitting across from each other in an interview room and doing as much looking as talking. Barlow could only guess what Gronville thought of him. Presumably the man had access to his file and intended to conduct his part of the interview on the basis of Harvey's assessment.

Barlow didn't order tea for them, though he himself could die of drouth. He wanted Gronville to add "petty" to Harvey's stupid and uneducated, insolent and over promoted. Gronville sat alert in his chair. Barlow deliberately slouched.

'How do you want to arrange things, Sir,' he asked. The "Sir" coming out with all the insolence alleged by Harvey.

'Leonidas Cheney Weir released immediately. Then, later this morning, you will bring the woman to a location chosen by me.'

This wasn't a junior civil servant trying to organize things. This was a man used to planning an operation, who gave orders and expected them obeyed promptly and precisely as instructed. More than that, Gronville's polished accent had a relaxed ring to it. The accent of a man born into the ascendancy class, rather than acquired.

And he hated the derogatory way Gronville referred to "the woman". Okay, nobody knew her real name but the reports referred to her by the catch-all sobriquet of "Jane Smith."

Barlow asked, 'And from there on, what happens to Jane Smith?'

'Not your concern, Sergeant.'

Barlow remembered Jane Smith's panic the night before, over the injection and how she took his word for things. 'Sir, anyone whose name appears in my daily journal is my concern.'

Gronville's head came up, the nearest thing the man did to appearing startled. 'Ah yes, your notebooks, Incident Reports and so on. They are to be collected from all the officers involved and placed in a sealed envelope for retention by me.'

Was there a pause there between the "by" and "me"? Barlow thought so and wondered who else was involved– military or civilian – and at what level?

The whole thing worried Barlow, especially Gronville's lack of concern for what Jane Smith had gone through. He knew something of how the SAS regiment worked. Operations authorized and expedited: some inside the law; some out, no questions asked. "Wet jobs" killings, were not the norm but might be authorized through appropriate channels.

Which made him wonder what category Jane Smith came under.

He dropped any pretense of politeness. 'About Jane Smith. She appears to have been the victim of attempted rape – or worse.'

'I say again, not your concern, Sergeant.'

'Oh it is, and you're not getting her until I've got a formal statement off her. Then there is the question of the assault with intent on Constable McGinn and Leon Weir.'

'Weir hasn't made a complaint, has he?'

'No.' This came out reluctantly. DS Leary's interview with Weir had been a series of questions, each question followed by a long silence. The man wouldn't even say if he took sugar in his tea.

Gronville snapped to his feet, his lips tight with irritation. 'You've had your orders. You will carry them out.'

Barlow folded his arms and stayed slouched in his chair. 'Or else what?'

'I'll speak to District Inspector Harvey. He'll see that my orders are obeyed.'

'And so will I,' said Barlow. He stood and stared hard at the angry man. He sensed a lack of control. More than that, anger at a subordinate, one of the common herd, daring to cross him.

Barlow wondered how much it would take to make the man throw the first punch. But then Harvey would blame him, start another one of those complaint files.

To be sure that Gronville started nothing Barlow flexed his shoulders to emphasize his advantage in breadth and weight. 'When the murderer or murderers of Tommy Weir appear in court….'

'Not a chance,' Gronville said.

'.... the fact that we haven't taken a statement from a potential witness to the murder, maybe even an accessory to the fact, it's going to look bad.' He leaned into Gronville's face. 'Generate the sort of publicity that could ruin the District Inspector's career.'

Barlow sat down again and motioned for Gronville to do the same. 'So when I hand over Jane Smith, it will be to some appropriate and easily identifiable senior person, not some minor Civil Servant.'

Gronville glared at the "minor".

That stung, thought Barlow.

Gronville stood on and stared, blank-faced, at Barlow for a long, long time. Barlow gave up the slouch, which he kept for his padded chair at home, and stared back.

Gronville said, 'You will release Leonidas Cheney Weir, immediately.'

'And?'

'You will remove the woman from the hospital this afternoon. Say four-thirty, after the visiting hour. I will tell you later where to meet Sir Anthony, assuming you consider him an appropriate and important enough person.'

With that, he walked out of the room.

Barlow sat on, feeling that somehow he had been outmaneuvered.

Chapter 17

Barlow stayed on in the Interview Room. He even went to the bother of producing his notebook and opening it at a blank page. He ached to do one of his lists: of people involved, of what he knew and what he guessed. But he had to give the notebook to Gronville with all the rest. The last thing he wanted was for Gronville to know anything of his thoughts.

He creaked to his feet. 'Bollocks and bother.' He still had to start that day's routine duties – and that long-delayed cup of tea sourced.

Grit cracked under his feet as he walked up the corridor. WPC Day appeared. Rather than tell her to brush the floor he let his tongue hang out and he panted hard.

'I take it you're not looking for sex,' she said and detoured into the kitchen. The sound of water thrumming into the kettle followed him into the Enquiry Office.

DI Harvey was there, personally supervising the release of Leon Weir. Sergeant Pierson buzzed around making a mound of work over a routine event. Barlow stood back and let them get on with it.

Much as Barlow hated to admit it, DS Leary was a good interviewer. He could get even the most hardened criminal to talk and yet Leon had refused to give more than his name and address. It reminded Barlow of the old army axiom for captured soldiers: name, rank and serial number, nothing else.

Leon waited while the two officers fussed through the release process. He stood relaxed, not in the stiff stance of Gronville, and yet there was no unnecessary movement, no sign of impatience to be gone.

Leon hadn't been in the army but he had disappeared for a number of years. Working in England, according to the mother. Working at what she didn't know or wouldn't say.

Leon's hands were slim and unscarred, not the hands of a laborer. And he certainly hadn't learned his dress sense while working on building sites around London. There could be a criminal record somewhere in England. Leary was looking into that, or at least had been until the order came to release the man.

Rather than waste time on pointless speculation about Leon, Barlow phoned the hospital and asked to speak to the Duty Sister in the Emergency Ward.

He knew the voice immediately. It was the grey-haired one. He kept forgetting that he owed her at least one parking ticket for being smart with him. Sometime back, she had sent the best-looking nurse in the hospital to apply cream to burns on his backside.

His writing hand twitched. 'Some day,' he muttered. 'Some day,' and knew he wouldn't.

He said, 'I'm ringing about the Jane Smith.'

'Krista Riekstinš is doing well,' said Sister.

'Who?'

'The woman you brought in last night. Her feet are in bad shape and there's some infection, but nothing to be concerned about.'

Krista. He liked that name, it suited her.

'How did you get her name?'

'I pointed at Geordie and said "Geordie. Then at myself and said "Ethna", and so on. And she's from Lithuania.'

'Let me guess. You found a map of the world and she pointed.'

'You're reasonably bright for a policeman,' she said and hung up.

By then Harvey had gone, Leon had gone and Sergeant Pierson was standing, bursting with an important message.

'Mr. Harvey wants to see you. Right now, no excuses accepted.'

Barlow chewed on an imaginary Clarnico Mint Cream on the way to Harvey's office. He kept the memory of Clarnico mints for special occasions. He liked their gritty crunch and could pretend it was Pierson's throat.

Chapter 18

Harvey had the buff folder back on his desk, and this time it lay open. It contained a single typed sheet of paper.

'Barlow, this morning I received a serious complaint about you.'

'Indeed, Sir?'

'From a Mr. Abernathy.' He consulted the file. 'A Daniel T Alexander Abernathy. Quite incensed the gentleman was.'

For a moment Barlow wondered if Harvey was joking. But Harvey didn't do jokes.

'His son, William. Last night you terrorized the young boy.'

Daniel T's only son was called Alexander. Alexander was a thirty years old and ran the Abernathy Light Engineering Company.

'Sir, are you sure…'

Harvey glared. 'You will not interrupt me, Barlow.' He went back to reading off the report. 'You caused the child great distress by threatening to shoot him….'

'You mean Wee Willie?'

'Silence!'

'But Sir…'

Harvey's finger stabbed at Barlow's face. 'Another word, Barlow. Another word.'

He consulted the report again. 'William spent the whole night lying in a corner and wouldn't come out. The only thing he would take was a drink of water. Not a bite, Barlow, not a bite has the child taken since, and Mr. Abernathy is worried sick about him.'

Barlow didn't know whether to be amused or irritated at Harvey's total misunderstanding of Daniel T's call.

Harvey tidied the page into the file and closed it. 'I personally intend to interview Mr. Abernathy and the child.' He put the file in a drawer and snapped it shut. 'A traumatized child, Barlow. Let's see how long you can keep your career, let alone your stripes.'

Barlow didn't mind Harvey acting the idiot in the office, but not out in public. 'Sir….'

'I warned you, Barlow. One more word and I'll add

insubordination to the charges.' He gestured towards the door. 'Out!'

Barlow stared hard at the Queen's portrait. It's not that he blamed the Queen personally, but her ministers keep promoting plonkers like Harvey.

He clicked his heels together and left.

Chapter 19

The clock hands stretched towards lunchtime. Barlow found the routine of that day hard going. Harvey's demand for the completion of reports not due for another week only added to his frustration. So far as Barlow was concerned, the only effective thing he had done that morning was to warn Inspector Foxwood that Harvey planned to take a statement of complaint from a bull. He left Foxwood worrying how to, tactfully, put Harvey right.

Mugs of tea came at regular intervals. There was even a Trisha's Pantry bun, courtesy of the detectives. He ate it, sure that day at least that no one had spat on it first.

His head churned names in an unending circle: Krista; Malcom Knype, the dead Civil Servant; the Weir family; Geordie.

One thing Geordie had said stayed fixed in his mind. When speaking of the Spanish Ouija, Geordie had said "consistency in excellence". Definitely not a Geordie Dunlop expression. If Geordie respected the word of his wartime Sergeant Major, he adored his old Commanding Officer: Major the Honourable Edward Adair, GC, MC. Gentleman and town drunk. Barlow needed to have an urgent word with Edward.

Eventually the clock hands reached twelve-thirty and Barlow could head out on an early lunch break.

Without saying, Louise had left the spare key for her car on Barlow's hallstand. He had put it on his keyring, intending to give the car a short run every week to keep the battery charged. Now, today, it would be useful to allow him do about a dozen things in the short hour.

Instead of going to his house on the Ballymoney Road, he headed out of town to Louise's house on Leighmohr Avenue. She had left the car on the driveway rather than put it in the garage, as if she guessed he'd need it soon.

He had known that the old bitches in the blue-rinse brigade had made it difficult for Louise, with her dating him. Snide remarks could cut deep as a knife and hurt more. He stood and looked at her house, which took up nearly as much space as his house and front garden combined. 'Sorry, darling.'

Any more than that would sound like an excuse.

He'd keep the car in his own garage until he received instructions what to do with it. This big white house, where he'd drunk champagne on the back patio and mixed on first name terms with people like Sir Anthony, and swore his love for her in a Wicca marriage of a year and a day – he'd not be back. Nor would he go to Sir Anthony's party. He'd tried that life and enjoyed the strangeness of it, but it wasn't him and Louise had known that as well.

He drove into town, collected Toby and headed out to Curles Bridge.

Chapter 20

Edward was "in" and "receiving". Edward sat on a wooden bench outside his house. Edward held stubbornly to the opinion that if a man arose every day before ten, then he couldn't be a hopeless alcoholic.

The wind had a bitter bite to it so Edward sat well wrapped up in his old army greatcoat while he took in the winter sun. Edward's "house" was a wood and tarred-paper hut in the shadow of Curles Bridge.

'My dear chap,' he said by way of greeting when Barlow pulled up beside him.

Barlow told Toby to go drown himself in the river and sat on the bench beside Edward.

Edward said, 'One sees that one is in uniform and therefore one assumes that one is working and one is not in a position....'

'Nothing to drink, thank you,' Barlow said before he got totally lost in all the ones.

'So not a social call then.' Edward touched his arm briefly. 'You and Louise, my dear chap. So sorry.'

Barlow wondered if there was anyone in the town who doesn't know that Louise had gone. He didn't mind people laughing at him for being rude, or ignorant, or stupid. But not Louise.

'Are you still in the drink trade?' he asked Edward bluntly.

'One's employment with the Ballymena Brewery Company has been terminated by mutual agreement.'

Edward had taken a temporary job with the brewery when his sister was home on a visit from Australia. Geordie's family had stolen a lorry load of whiskey from the brewery. A loss not covered by insurance because the management had failed to take reasonable security precautions. And this had caused the brewery serious cash-flow problems. Rather than see old soldiers put out of work, Edward had claimed it was an inside job, that he had opened the window and turned off the alarm.

Barlow had saved Edward from jail by getting the Dunlops to return the whiskey, but the insurance company refused to renew the cover while Edward remained with the firm. Worse, he could no longer continue to live with the office manager, his fiancé, Mrs. Anderson.

So back Edward went to the hut on the banks of the Braid River. At least he remained clean and shaven and, that day at least, his eyes weren't red-rimmed from excess alcohol.

'You and the Weirs?' asked Barlow.

'Really, my dear chap, there is a certain confidentiality…'

'Edward, I haven't time for niceties.'

The explanation came out in a circumlocution of evasions and long-winded words.

The Weirs had been distilling poteen for years. Nothing big and they never used ingredients that might kill or blind customers so Barlow had ignored the enterprise. Then came Geordie with a bright idea. Geordie had seen how valuable a lorry-load of water turned into alcohol could be. The bigger breweries dominated the local whiskey market, but vodka was a coming drink among the younger generation. Now if Geordie and the Weirs between them could produce a lorry-load of vodka, then they'd be rich.

Edward finished by saying, 'Of course they required someone of discernment and judgement for the purpose of establishing quality control. Give their beverage a certain je ne se quoi that would be appreciated by the discerning customer.'

'That's rich coming from someone who'd drink turpentine if there was nothing else handy.'

Edward smiled and nodded his head as if receiving a compliment. 'My dear chap.'

'I'm here to tell you to keep clear of the Weir place. Not that you've any reason to go there now Tommy is dead.'

Edward didn't reply

Barlow looked at him suspiciously. 'It was Tommy you were dealing with and not that son of his?'

'One is selective with whom one associates.'

So the brew-master was the mother. He'd got that wrong. Most wives made do with the egg money.

It was police business but he felt he had to ask. 'When you were up there, did you ever see anything, sense anything not right?'

Edward frowned; possibly because the sun had disappeared

behind a cloud. 'That poor lady? No. Then one hasn't been in attendance in over a week.'

'And?'

'One could always tell that Leonidas anticipated our departure with pleasure.'

That didn't surprise Barlow. Leon probably never wanted Edward and Geordie around in the first place.

That at least gave him a timeframe to work on. Krista Riekstinš had been at the farm for less than a week before she escaped. The unknown was, where had she come from and where did she think she was going?

As for Malcolm Knype, he'd been dead for six months. Long before the stolen whiskey had given Geordie another idea of how to make money.

Barlow stood up and called for Toby to come. 'The Weirs and Geordie are bad news. Stay clear of them.'

'One has obligations.'

Sometimes he could shake Edward. 'Illicit vodka is Customs and Excise business. I won't be there to water-down the charges, and it will be the High Court in Belfast, not your cousins in the local Magistrates' Court.'

He drove off, pleased with that "watered-down" bit.

Chapter 21

No matter what he did after lunch, Barlow couldn't hold the clock back. The second hand jerked inexorably towards four-thirty and his appointment with Sir Anthony. All around him, constables went smartly about their business. He sensed this because when Barlow went quiet and talked quiet no man dared cross him. No one wanted to risk the wrath of temper that he could hardly contain.

Handing Krista Riekstinš over meant a loss of control of the case when there was still a mound of unanswered questions running around in his head.

Who was Krista? Where did she come from and how and why had she ended up a prisoner on Weir's farm? What was going to happen to her? What plans had the Gronville's of this life concocted for her, and how come unspecified Departments in government were taking an unhealthy interest in her and in the death of the unfortunate Malcolm Knype?

He chewed savagely on a concoction of imaginary sweets and never came up with a taste that suited his mood. *Astringent.* He'd seen that word once in the paper and had to look it up.

Nearing four o'clock, Susan ostentatiously tiptoed up to him with a cup of tea. 'Any time you're ready, Papa Grumpy Bear.'

'I'm all sweetness and light,' he said.

'Of course you are.'

Susan and Wilson were going to the hospital with him. Susan because Krista was a woman, and Wilson to drive. Whatever happened Barlow needed to be free to react. He fought down an urge to check his pistol even though he knew it was loaded and there was spare ammunition in the pouch. He ached for the peaceful old days under the previous District Inspector when he could leave his pistol in his locker and take a wander downtown.

Something was changing, something that he couldn't put his finger on. It was like a heartbeat in the town, in Northern Ireland as a whole. A heartbeat that insisted on speeding up.

He sank the tea gratefully, settled his cap on his head and joined Susan and Wilson in the car. Stretched comfortably in the backseat and pretended not to notice Susan's hand on Wilson's thigh.

'There's no rush to get there,' he told Wilson, who was staying well inside the speed limit. Even so, they arrived at the hospital with plenty of time to spare.

Barlow made Wilson park tight to the steps at the front door. 'Don't forget, the woman's feet are raw.'

The woman. Somehow, putting it that way, distanced her, made Krista an object to be discarded rather than a person he felt he was about to betray in some way.

Susan went direct to the ward. Barlow stayed back and convinced the white-haired sister to give him a package of bandages and ointments for Krista to take with her. Infection was still a serious possibility if she didn't take care of those feet.

When he arrived at the ward, he found Susan standing guard at the door. 'Go and see Gillespie for a minute, Papa Bear.'

She didn't seem to mind Geordie staying on to chat her up.

He nodded, understanding. The girls had organized a whip-round at the station and raised enough money to buy Krista fresh clothes and some toiletries. From behind the door, he heard a sob that could have been gratitude.

Gillespie sat propped up in his bed. He scowled when Barlow handed him a heavy volume of police regulations. 'You're a sadist.'

Barlow made his smile sardonic. 'If we get you a stool, you could do a shift in the Enquiry Office. Unless of course you've a chit for piles as well as everything else.'

Satisfied that Gillespie was okay, the wounds starting to itch so healing nicely, he went back to Susan. Krista was already in a wheelchair, with Geordie and a porter arguing over who would wheel her to the waiting car.

Geordie leaned into the porter's face. 'You can take the wheelchair back in.'

It was pure intimidation, Geordie's bulk and reputation as a fighting man, encouraged the porter back off. Barlow ignored them and checked the woman in the wheelchair to make sure it was Krista. A touch of lipstick and make-up had changed the grey-faced person of the previous night into someone people would look at twice. No eye-shadow he noted. There was enough dark shadows from exhaustion still under her eyes.

He shook her hand to assure her of his friendship and complimented her outfit – a green patterned dress, with a cardigan draped over her shoulders. He was sure she didn't understand a word he said, but she seemed to pick up on his complimentary tone and smiled.

While he was at it, he tried to explain what would happen to her. Or rather, that Sir Anthony would accept responsibility for her continuing wellbeing, and he trusted Sir Anthony. 'Now there's a gentleman of the old school.'

He plonked the bag of medical dressings on her lap and led the way to the lift. He felt the joy of being a big sergeant, bulling ahead to clear a path up the corridors. For some reason, right then, he needed that boost of confidence. The Gronvilles of this life and unknown Civil Servants making decisions that compromised his official competence – now there was a Harvey word if ever there was one – made him realize how little more than a nod could see him on the street with no job to go to.

At the front door, he made the group stop while he did a reconnaissance. A man and a woman were walking together down the drive. Locals. Give him a minute and he could put a name to them. A man he had never seen before hung around the gate. *Probably waiting for a lift.* Satisfied, he waved Geordie and the porter on.

The wind caught Krista's cardigan and lifted it off her shoulder. Susan bent to secure it and then fell over Krista. The porter staggered back. Before Geordie could stop it Susan's unexpected weight pulled the wheelchair off the top step. The chair toppled over and the two women rolled onto the ground.

Krista crawled out from underneath the chair towards the safety of the hospital building. The porter leaned against the door, blood pouring from his shattered arm.

The sound had faded but Barlow could still hear the boom of a rifle over the blustery wind.

Susan lay still.

Chapter 22

Susan had bumped her head and knocked herself silly. Barlow's mind locked on that thought even as his eyes saw blood gush from her uniform.

Wilson was screaming her name.

Barlow found his pistol in his hand and didn't remember drawing it. Across the green of the hospital lawn, way beyond the Nissen hut that housed the Outpatients' Department, was the lava-stone boundary wall separating the hospital from the cemetery. The head and shoulders of a man dropped out of sight behind the wall. The couple on the drive had stopped and were looking back. The unknown man at the gate was walking towards the town.

The point of Barlow's pistol went between the boundary wall and the walking man. 'Geordie,' he yelled.

In wartime it was the only order Geordie ever needed and it was enough now. He pushed Wilson aside, scooped Susan into his arms and sprinted for the Emergency Ward. 'You're going to be all right, darlin'. You listen to Big Geordie, it's barely a scratch.'

Barlow hated himself. Hated being the big policeman: taking control, giving orders, always doing the right thing. *My wee Susan.* He wanted to be there with her, to hold her hand and convince himself that she was going to be okay.

Wilson was out of it. He was stumbling up the steps, following a diminishing trail of blood. Susan was dead or would be before they reached the Emergency Ward.

Barlow checked the car; Wilson had taken the car keys with him. Barlow's feet took over and he found himself hurtling across the lawn, heading for the angle between the cemetery wall and the road. He heard a car engine rev and the screech of tires. The gunman was gone.

He changed direction. 'Hey you, I want a word with you,' he called after the walking man.

It was the way he would have organized the attack himself: have a man do spotter from the front gate. His walking away the signal that the target had appeared. All the gunman had to do was hoist himself up the wall on the cemetery side, take his shot and jump down again, slip out the side gate and away. Simple. Straightforward.

Except that Susan had bent over Krista as they took the shot. What he couldn't understand was why people wanted Krista dead.

He was on the pavement now. The unknown man well ahead, walking at a brisk pace.

'Hey! You!' Barlow shouted.

The man continued to walk.

'You!'

This time the man looked back. Any normal human being would have frozen with fear at the sight of an armed policeman charging towards them. This one reached under his coat.

'Dare you,' Barlow yelled at the possible threat of the man producing a gun.

The man's hand reappeared and he started to run. Barlow couldn't go any faster, he was already at full stretch but he was gaining as the man veered off the Cushendall Road into the new housing estate of whitewashed houses and red-bricked flats.

Barlow's finger was tight on the trigger. He ached to put a flurry of shots around the man's legs to bring him down, but there were people about, children playing on the green and a heavy .45 bullet could smash through those brick walls into someone's home.

Out of the housing estate now, across the Old Ballymoney Road into The People's Park. Barlow's chest was straining with the effort but he'd die of a heart attack before he gave up the chase.

The park had a lake on one side of the path. On the other side a football pitch with a match in progress. Barlow pulled out his whistle and blew. Long blasts that used up the remains of air in his lungs. If the slope hadn't been downwards, he would have been on his knees. As it was, he lost ground but the football match had stopped. The players and the spectators running out to block the fugitive.

The man did have a pistol. He drew it and waved it threateningly at the crowd. They hesitated, stopped. Someone threw a boot as he passed, and missed. The crowd shouted encouragement at Barlow as he forced himself on towards the main road dead ahead.

The man was running well, maybe even gaining a little. Barlow edged away from the lake. If he could get the man between himself and a stand of trees, he'd risk a shot.

It didn't happen and they were already at the water fountain and nearing the gate onto the road. A car pulled up, the back door opened. A man wearing a hood pointed something at Barlow.

A flash of pain.

Darkness.

Chapter 23

Dying was painful. Barlow's head hurt, his chest was on fire. His mouth gaped wide but no air was going in.

He managed to force an eye open. A crowd had gathered, a circle of faces surrounded him.

'Are you all right, Sergeant?'

What was he doing lying spread-eagled? He remembered the hooded man pointing the rifle at him. He could feel his heart pulse the blood out of his dying body. His vision tinged with a growing darkness and he couldn't breathe because his lungs were filling with blood.

The eye closed again.

'He's unconscious,' said someone.

'Dying,' said someone else.

Someone slapped Barlow's cheek. He forced both eyes open.

An ambulance man hung over him. 'Where are you shot?'

Indignation made him catch his breath. It hurt nearly as bad as breathing.

'Where there's blood,' he said.

His voice sounded near normal, even to him.

'There is no blood,' said the ambulance man.

Barlow touched the burning agony in his chest and felt a lump right over the pain. It had to be an aneurism ready to burst.

'Try there.'

The ambulance man unbuttoned his jacket. 'No, no blood.' Unbuttoned the shirt and pulled up the vest. Barlow buried a scream in his throat as fingers pressed skin. 'But you've got a dirty great big bruise – the fingers pressed again, causing another near-scream – there, and probably a couple of busted ribs.'

'There has to be. I was shot.'

In patting himself down, looking for the lump, Barlow's finger snagged a tear in his jacket pocket. The lump in the pocket had stopped the bullet. His wallet.

He remembered his panic over blood gushing out of his body, filling his lungs and felt the biggest sissy.

By now they had him on a stretcher with a blanket tucked around him. He was glad of the blanket because he was cold. Willing hands loaded him into the ambulance. It was nice to lie there and if he didn't move the pain would ease. He closed his aching eyes against the light.

The ambulance man tapped his nose. 'You stay awake, you banged your head when you fell.'

The ambulance bell was like a saw going through his head, the bumps in the road had every jagged bone-end rubbing together. They arrived at the hospital. He already felt better now he knew he wasn't going to die.

Policemen crowded around as the ambulance door opened. 'Are you okay, Sarge?'

'Aye, that's why I'm lying here.'

He shouted instructions as they carried him into the Emergency Ward. 'Look for a man five-foot eight or nine, dark hair, plain grey trousers, sports jacket. The bugger's armed. And a Wolseley car, four-door, fairly new, black. And here…' He handed over his wallet with the bullet buried in it.

Constable McGinn hung over him. 'Is that your deathbed statement?'

'I've already got Gillespie. I don't need you to get lippy.'

Chapter 24

Barlow spent the first hour in the Emergency Ward arguing with everyone and losing most of the battles. No they didn't need to cut off his uniform, that was evidence, and they could clean his boots while they were at it. Ribs cracked but not broken? No damage to the skull? Just tape up his chest and he would be on his way.

The white-haired Sister stood over him. 'You're staying here so we can keep an eye on you.' She dangled his own handcuffs before him. 'We can do it the easy way. We can do it the hard way.'

He'd never yet won an argument with her but she was willing to negotiate. He spent two hours lying in a bed proving that he wasn't going to die of a brain hemorrhage. Sister even brushed down his jacket and cap. Someone had lobbed it into the ambulance after him, and someone, maybe the same man, had stuffed his pistol back into its holster. He was glad of that. He had need of that gun.

The worst part was dealing with a tearful Vera.

'It's my stars,' he assured her. 'They said I would have a bad year, but we're in the teeth of Christmas and next year is predicted to be a cracker.'

Her own stars, as predicted by one of Louise's friends, were the same. She went home comforted.

On his way out the door of the Emergency Ward, Sister handed him a strip of tablets. 'I know you Barlow, if we give you something heavy you won't take them. But these, once you feel tired they'll get you into a doze and the body will take over from there.'

'I thought I wasn't supposed to sleep.'

A wheelchair, not walking, was part of the deal. Sister herself wheeled him into the ward where Krista sat curled into herself like a wounded animal. Even hours on from the shooting her breathing came shallow and jagged and she seemed thinner than ever.

No Geordie, no translator. He needed to talk to her and yet he didn't dare have anyone overhear what he had to say, especially Sister who stayed with them.

Krista had some English. He could only hope that she would understand something of what he was trying to tell her.

‘Krista, I don’t know what’s going on or who is trying to kill you ...’ First, he pointed at her, ‘…but you…’ He put his hand over his heart. ‘…have got to trust me.’

Did she understand him so far? He thought so.

Encouraged, he pushed on speaking slowly so that she could take in the individual words, and make sense of them. ‘You do not leave this room. You do not go with anyone, anywhere, unless I am here as well. Do you understand?’

He didn’t think she did.

He tried again. ‘Stay!’ He stabbed a finger at the bed. ‘Here, unless…’ He tapped his own chest. Too close to the bruise and he winced in pain. ‘…unless I come. Me. Okay?’

Krista nodded at that.

Sister said, ‘Leave it to me, Barlow. And I’ll make sure the night shift understand that as well.’

It was the best he could do in the circumstances. From Krista’s ward, Sister wheeled him to the room where Susan had been laid out, and tactfully left him there, saying she had to get back to work.

They had dressed Susan in a fresh uniform brought from the station; a blanket covered the lower part of her body. She could have been dozing. Even in death, her lips had a curl of humor.

Gillespie stood honor guard. Best uniform on, medals gleaming on his chest.

Barlow knew if he stood that he’d probably fall over. Yet he felt guilty sitting, when Gillespie supported himself on crutches.

He leaned over and touched Susan’s hands. They held a ragged teddy bear. Her original Papa Bear. ‘I bullied her to study for those exams, but all she ever wanted was an armful of children.’

‘She only studied when she could play footsie with Wilson,’ Gillespie said.

They were silent. Barlow remembered the bounce of Susan’s hair as she walked and her voice wondering where they put all that tea.

Barlow broke the silence first. ‘What about her family?’

‘They’ve been. God help them, they’re in pieces.’ Gillespie tried to lighten the atmosphere. ‘You should have seen their faces when they walked in and found Geordie kneeling beside the bed.’

‘I can imagine.’

A nice family: straight-laced and God-fearing. They couldn't understand Susan wanting to be in the police, let alone having a soft spot for the "regulars." Barlow remembered her in action: sneaking cups of tea into the cells for her favorites or spending time talking to men who deserved the door slammed in their face. At the same time, she was no softie. In the middle of a drunken ruckus, a man took a swing at her. She left him with dislocated shoulder and a limp.

'All that training,' she'd said, dusting down her clothes and pretending not to be shaken.

'That unarmed combat course came in useful after all,' he'd said.

'No Papa Bear, the dance hall any Saturday night.'

Barlow held down his sobs. He could trust Gillespie not to blab but his chest hurt too much. The ribs would heal and the bruise go away but his wrung-out heart would never recover. He'd let Susan down, and cost her her life. He'd been too busy spending the day being annoyed instead of sitting down and thinking things through.

Eventually he dried his face and rang for a nurse to wheel him away.

Before the nurse came, he said to Gillespie. 'Hold onto those crutches. I'll need you and them tonight.'

Chapter 25

Barlow let McGinn ease him out of the wheelchair and steady him going down the front steps of the hospital to the waiting van. At the house, he again had McGinn help him into the kitchen, where Vera fussed him into a chair and wanted him to go straight to bed. It had to be a good act because Toby got out of Barlow's favorite chair without a snarl.

Before McGinn left, Barlow pressed coins into his hand and asked him to return to the station by way of the Bridge Bar. 'Geordie will be there. Tell him the drink's on the Sergeant Major.'

'Whatever,' said McGinn.

'The Sergeant Major,' repeated Barlow and had Vera see McGinn out.

Somehow, at home with the front door closed against the world and Vera fussing in the scullery, getting him something to eat, he started to feel better. Could feel strength trickle back into his limbs. Toby insisted on sharing the chair.

'No peace for the wicked,' signed Barlow and made room for him.

He balanced a writing pad on his knees and had a good think to himself before he started to write.

First a list of names of people involved:

THE GOOD: Krista Riekstinš
Sir Anthony Chard

THE BAD: Leon Weir
The gunman
The running man
The getaway driver

After some hesitation, he created an "UNKNOWN" list. The first name he entered there was Gronville. Mainly because he disliked the man and didn't want to be prejudiced. After a bit of thinking he added the names of people involved in the investigation, however indirectly. Finally, Krista's name as well because, for all he knew, she could be the European version of Ma Baker.

UNKNOWN: Captain/Major Gronville
Mrs. Weir
Daniel T Abernathy
Krista Riekstinš

He had done a lot of lists in his life. This was definitely the worst. Half of them had no names and the "UNKNOWNs" was little better than people of interest.

Without consciously willing it, his pencil rested against Sir Anthony's name. That unheralded call to the station. What had the man said?

He turned to a fresh page and thought back.

Sir Anthony had landed in Harvey's room. He insisted that Barlow stayed and never introduced Gronville. And his almost first remark: "Sergeant, this CONCERNS you as well."

Barlow wasn't sure. Was he adding an emphasis that wasn't there in the first place?

All the same, many of Sir Anthony's remarks seemed addressed to himself personally.

He wrote down the words and phrases as they came to him, leaving gaps between the lines, allowing him to put what Sir Anthony had said, in the right order. He started with a question mark at "Concerns" to remind him of his doubts:

Concerns?
This "D" Notice, very unfortunate
Security of the Country
Foreseen but regrettable consequences
The foreign lady… moved to a secure location
Hospital records expunged
Impossible (for Krista to give a statement)
Out of my hands entirely
Totally impossible, I regret to say

Cooking smells were coming from the scullery. He'd no idea how he was going to cope with a heavy meal, other than sick it up again.

He added "Ultimate" to "Security of the Country." Then he put what he thought were key words and phrases in capitals.

CONCERNS?
This "D" Notice, very UNFORTUNATE
ULTIMATE security of the Country
Foreseen but REGRETTABLE CONSEQUENCES
The foreign lady… moved to a SECURE location
Hospital records EXPUNGED
IMPOSSIBLE (for Krista to give a statement)
OUT OF MY HANDS ENTIRELY
Totally impossible I REGRET to say

Had Sir Anthony been trying to warn him that someone planned to kill Krista? If only he'd listened properly, remembering that Sir Anthony had been a diplomat and trained to consider the effect of every word before he spoke.

He tried not to think of Susan and the nickname she had ready for her first child. "Baby Bear."

He knew he should have taken precautions. Slipped Krista out the backway. Secured the area properly. They wouldn't have dared do anything.

His instructions were to handover Krista to Sir Anthony.

What would have happened to her then?

Only one line "Ultimate security of the Country" didn't have a word highlighted. He looked at it again. Did that mean "For the security of the Country" or "The Security Services of the Country"?

The Security Services, he reckoned, people like Gronville who seemed to delight in violence. They were the ones who wanted her dead.

He remembered the spotter at the hospital. Armed and all as he was, he chose to run and risk capture rather than get into a gunfight with a policeman. Against that, the man who had pulled the trigger, and shot Susan instead of Krista, had been careless, at the very least amateurish. Or maybe the sort that didn't mind killing. Liked it even.

But why had they chosen to shoot Krista in public? Once he'd handed her over to Sir Anthony, they could have killed her at their leisure. Buried her deep in some army base where she'd never be found.

Which gave him two more problems, which he wrote down:

Why didn't they bury Malcolm Knype properly?

Would Sir Anthony have stopped them from shooting Krista?

Which gave him a third problem:

Did Sir Anthony even know about the proposed handover?

The feeling he'd had in the station, that somehow Gronville had out-maneuvered him. The man had sat and planned Susan's murder right there in front of him.

Chapter 26

Vera appeared with a heaped plate of steaming-hot mince and potatoes. 'I knew you'd be starving when you got out, Dad, so I cooked this earlier.'

She looked so pleased with herself that Barlow forced himself to smile his thanks. What he really wanted was a big mug of tea and a runny poached egg on toast.

He moved over to the table and took a forkful of mince. To his exhausted mind it could have been cardboard. 'Delicious,' he said and pointed for her to hand him the phone. 'It's a bit hot. I'll make a call while it cools.'

He took another mouthful and made appreciative smacks with his lips before dialing Sir Anthony's home number. His wife answered.

'Lady Chard.' Really he should call her by her Christian name, Katherine, but this was business.

'John! John are you all right? On dear, that poor girl.'

'Aye,' he said.

'And I must apologize. We haven't called yet with the family, but Anthony is in London. There was a meeting, it's been planned for weeks, and he had to be there.'

Which meant that she was one hell of a good actress or Gronville had set him up.

He assured Lady Chard that he was fine and no, she didn't have to tell Sir Anthony to phone him, it could wait.

He was just hanging up when the front door bell rang. Vera answered it. He heard a gravel voice speaking politely and the tramp of heavy feet in the hallway. An anxious looking Vera reappeared with Geordie in tow.

Barlow pretended to swallow food before speaking. 'I hope you wiped your feet on the way in.'

'Dad!'

'He's not a visitor, he's an imposition.'

All the same, he indicated for Geordie to take a chair at the table.

Vera went off to make them a cup of tea and to hunt out a plateful of biscuits.

As soon as she was out of sight, Geordie nodded at the heaped plate of food in front of Barlow. 'You're not fit to eat that, are you?'

He pulled the fork out of Barlow's unresisting hand. The fork started to go in a continuous motion between the plate and his mouth.

Geordie mumbled through a mouthful of food. 'Any time the Sergeant Major bought me a drink there was a dirty job attached to it.'

'Why change the habit of a lifetime?' said Barlow and started to explain his idea.

Vera reappeared with the tea. She looked suspiciously at the empty plate on Geordie's side of the table.

Barlow said, 'He took the scraps I'd left for the dog.'

He went back to the start and told Vera what they planned to do. She was intrigued and delighted to be involved in the planning. 'But Dad, you're hardly able to put one foot before the other.'

'We'll take the car. There'll be very little walking,' he assured her.

''So long as I come with you,' she said.

'Now wait a minute.'

She wagged her finger under his nose. 'You're not fit to drive; you're hardly fit to sit there as it is.'

She was right. Times like this he missed the little girl who had believed every word he said. There again, who wouldn't be proud of this sparky young lady.

'I'll do the driving,' said Geordie.

'With apologies to Mr. Dunlop,' she continued. 'But Dad, you will be associating with a known criminal. Does he have a license and he certainly isn't insured to drive Louise's car.'

Geordie groaned. 'Two Barlows on my case. Maybe it's time I went straight.'

'To hell,' agreed Barlow.

Blank Page

WEDNESDAY

Blank Page

Chapter 27

They sat around and waited until two o'clock in the morning when everything would have settled down in the hospital. With a bit of luck even the night staff would have their heads down for a quick kip. Barlow did a lot of dozing and felt better for it. Geordie entertained the wide-eyed Vera by telling her tales of his life as a professional villain.

When it was time, not only Vera but Toby came as well.

'It's not a trip to the seaside,' moaned Barlow.

'He needs a walk,' said Vera.

Barlow gave up at that point. Arguing would only use up what little energy he had and it would get him nowhere. Anyway, taking Toby along gave Vera some sort of protection. When it came to protecting her, that dog would rip the throat out of a lion.

Toby got into the back with Geordie, Vera drove down into town as if they were running Geordie home then curved back north out of Ballymena into Broughshane, then onto the Cushendall Road by way of Ballygarvey. From there the hospital was a straight run down into town. Nobody followed them though there could have been watchers out there in the dark. It depended on the number of men Gronville could call on. Not that many, reckoned Barlow. Two, three at most, which would make a neat four-man section.

So they were up against four men in the field: Gronville and the gunman he intended to deal with personally. The other two men? Soldiers obeying orders without question. Not that was an excuse under law.

Then there were the faceless men in London. Men who couldn't risk their names or their dirty deeds coming out in a public trial.

Instead of driving in the main gate, he told Vera to use the entrance nearest the town. That took them up a seldom-used driveway between the Council Estate on one side and the medical Annex wing on the other. The next bit was complicated driveways and dead ends, and things had changed. It might be nearly forty years since he'd lived there but Barlow's stomach was in knots as they passed the Workhouse, now renamed The Braid Valley.

They parked in the shadow of the Waveney Hospital itself. On Vera's suggestion they let Toby out first to run around. While they waited, Barlow handed out gloves. Harvey would know he was involved in Krista's disappearance but he had no intention of making it easy for the man.

After a few minutes Toby came back. Barlow got out and heaved Toby into the car beside Vera. 'If he hasn't brought back someone's leg there's no one around,' he told her.

He wished she hadn't insisted on coming but she was safe if she stayed in the car with the dog.

He found it bad enough walking down the side of the building but the sight of the steel fire escape towering above them made him bite back a groan. They went up slowly, 'So as not to make a noise,' he told Geordie who dogged his footsteps. By the first floor he was sucking air through his mouth and still couldn't get enough.

'Too many fries,' Geordie told him.

'Shut up.'

He struggled up to the second floor. Some of the wards threw out light that made them visible against the grey concrete wall. They could be nightlights, maybe the nurses busy with ill patients. If someone spotted them they'd have some explaining to do.

He gave himself a minute to catch his breath and then tried the Emergency exit door. It was locked. 'Damn.'

He tapped it once. Waited. Tapped it again.

The door opened. Gillespie stood there, balanced on his crutches. 'You're late.' He gave Barlow a good look up and down. 'You look like death warmed up.'

'Don't you start.'

They had to go back down to the first floor and Krista's room.

Gillespie got back in his wheelchair. Geordie pushed him and Barlow carried the crutches. They headed up the corridor to the nearest lift. The wooden crutches were heavy and wore down Barlow's tired muscles. He was tempted to leave one and pick it up later but decided that Krista couldn't cope with only one.

They walked quietly, aware that a nurse could appear at any second. If that happened, Gillespie would be ordered back to bed and them escorted off the premises.The return journey would be a different matter.

Chapter 28

The hospital was quiet without being still. At an almost subconscious level they could pick up voices and the whirr of machinery. The lift bell tinged as they reached it. It went past them and stopped on the floor below.

Barlow counted thirty seconds, enough time for someone to vacate the lift and walk away, and then pressed the button. The lift clanked up to the second floor.

'A bit of greasing needed there,' Geordie said.

'Shut up.'

There was a lot more clanking as they got into the lift and closed the metal door. All they could do was hold their breaths and hope no one came nosing to see who was around at that time of night. The lift stopped at the first floor. Gillespie went first because he had an excuse to be in the hospital, if not out of his room.

'All clear,' he said.

They walked even quieter than before. Gillespie's wheelchair developed a squeak. Or maybe it had been there before and Barlow hadn't noticed. Someone coughed as they passed their room. In the distance a bell rang and footsteps hurried.

Krista's room at last. There was a trickle of a nightlight from beneath the door. She could be awake and in any form of undress but this was no time to be polite and knock. Barlow pushed on in.

Krista was in bed and dozing but she started-up with a gasp. Barlow put a finger to his lips for her to be silent. Two quick breaths and she relaxed.

He went over and took her hand. 'I know you don't understand me, love, but we're going to get you out of here.'

Geordie helped Gillespie out of the wheelchair; they would need it for Krista. Her street clothes lay on the second bed. Barlow reached for them.

Footsteps sounded in the corridor outside. Confident, authoritative steps. Someone was coming and there weren't that many wards to choose from.

A man's steps. That didn't seem right on the women's wing.

Maybe male nurses were on at night, but not in the women's ward. Acting more through caution than instinct Barlow motioned the other two men to join him at the second bed. Gillespie stretched out on the bed itself. Barlow and Geordie sat on its edge so that their feet wouldn't show below the drawn curtain.

The footsteps stopped. A hand tapped Krista's door. Barlow saw the movement of air along the curtain as the door opened.

A man's voice said, 'Thank goodness you're awake, Miss. I'm sorry to disturb you at this time of the night, but we forgot to give you your vitamin injection.'

Barlow listened hard. The man was speaking quietly. What he wanted to do might perhaps be reasonable, even at that time of night, but the voice was English.

The door clicked shut. The man's footsteps were now in the room. Metal rattled on metal as he put something down.

Barlow drew his pistol and ripped the curtain aside. The man stood squirting liquid out of a syringe to expel any air. He could have been a nurse. He wore scrubs, and a hygiene mask dangled below his chin. Age about thirty, Barlow reckoned, and if he had any fat around his waist, he hid it well.

In the moment Barlow spent assessing the man, the man reacted. The syringe became a threatening weapon and his spare hand disappeared behind his back.

Barlow cocked his revolver. 'Both hands to the front.'

The hand reappeared empty, the syringe no longer a threat but something waved about aimlessly. The voice sounded panicky. 'What are you doing here? You shouldn't be here this time of night. Who let you in?'

'Name?' asked Barlow.

'Jordan. Nurse Jordan.'

Barlow didn't know what was in that injection but it was going nowhere near Krista. He nodded at a kidney dish that had appeared on the bedside locker. 'Well, Nurse Jordan, I suggest you put that syringe back in its dish.'

Jordan looked at the syringe as if he'd forgotten about it. 'But I've got to give it to her.'

'Dish.'

Still Jordan hesitated. 'But it's only a vitamin shot.'

‘Guns are noisy. I could always break his neck,’ said Geordie.

He stood beside Barlow, flexing his muscles. Gillespie balanced on one crutch and held the second in front of him like a sword.

Now Jordan acted indignant. ‘Sister will hear about this.’

He slapped the syringe into the kidney dish. Before he could turn away, Krista grabbed the syringe and drove the needle into his thigh.

They all froze, Jordan with his mouth open.

Let it be vitamins, Barlow prayed.

Jordan’s face lengthened in horror. ‘No, no.’ He folded to the ground. His body twitched and contorted into a fetal position, heels drummed on the floor. Then he lay still.

Chapter 29

Rather than do anything he'd regret, Barlow took time to try and make sense of things. The whole week had been running out of his control but witnessing a murder was something else. Krista might get off with a charge of manslaughter but it was murder plain and simple.

They'd all known that Jordan – if that was his real name – was lying when he claimed the syringe held only a vitamin shot and the look on Krista's face as she depressed the plunger was raw revenge. Nothing less.

He couldn't blame her, she'd been through hell recently, but...

That "but" was him, a policeman, sworn to uphold the law. But what law? A law that let government agents execute people without even the pretense of a trial. If he arrested her and took her down to the station, she was as good as dead. And if he didn't, how many other people would she kill? Could she have killed Tommy Weir and dumped him in the river?

He didn't think so, the timing was all wrong.

He still held the pistol, pointed now at Krista. He put it away. The movement jerked everyone else out of their frozen stance.

Krista hopped out of bed, away from her clothes and towards Jordan, but she had forgotten her tender feet. She cried out in pain when they hit the floor. Barlow shouldered her back onto the bed and scooped up a pistol jammed into the back of Jordan's trousers.

He threw the bundle of clothes at her. 'Get dressed.'

She got out of bed, a lot more slowly this time. With the nightgown flung to the floor, she wore only pants. Something Barlow noticed as a matter of fact. He was still too shocked at Jordan's death to feel embarrassed.

'Gillespie, I want you back in your bed, now.'

'But the wheelchair? I was supposed to….'

'Steal another one somewhere. We've got to get out of this place.'

'And fast,' said Geordie. He glared at Barlow as if it was his fault. 'If we're caught, my record will see me locked up until Kingdom Come.'

Krista was already pulling on her cardigan. Barlow pressed a hand against his damaged ribs to cause pain. Anything to keep upset at bay. That was the cardigan Susan had leaned down to adjust when the gunman fired.

'Okay, move out.'

They crowded around him as he cracked the door open and listened. Silence. Really the non-silence of a sleeping building.

He went first, and ached to do it gun in hand, but didn't dare in case he gave some doddering old fool a heart attack. Even so, he kept the holster flap unbuttoned. There had to be at least one of Jordan's friends out there as backup. With a bit of luck, he'd be waiting at the front of the building.

The crutches stomped, the wheels on the wheelchair squeaked at every turn. Geordie developed a sniff and the corridor stretched forever. Even that last step to the lift and the button to summon it took inordinately long.

Inordinately? An unusual word to come into his head. He had time to think about it while the lift arrived and Geordie opened the doors and reversed Krista in.

Inordinately? Vera used it once, something about me being stubborn.

Somehow they were all crowded into the lift and it was moving. He realized his mind was drifting and shook his head hard to bring himself back into focus.

'Are you all right?' asked Gillespie.

'Aye.'

The lift stopped. They slid the doors open and found no one in the corridor.

He didn't even want to think so far so good. It was like tempting fate.

They tried to keep their speed down but the Emergency exit drew them. Thump-bang of the crutches. The near-continuous squeak of the wheelchair. At Gillespie's ward, he pulled everyone to a halt and pointed to the door.

'In,' he ordered Gillespie.

'I'm fine.'

'You've got a wife and kids.'

'Are you going to run back with the wheelchair?'

He'd planned to steal the crutches to help Krista along. Now they didn't dare take anything of Gillespie's otherwise they'd know he was involved in Krista's disappearance.

He tapped Krista's shoulder and pointed at the Emergency Exit sign. 'Walk. You walk?'

Geordie held the wheelchair steady while he helped her step out of it, and felt the intake of breath as her injured feet pressed against the hard floor.

'Atta girl.'

He shoved the wheelchair into the room and jerked his head at Gillespie. 'In.'

'You're right,' said Gillespie, but stood on.

With no time to argue, Barlow got on one side of Krista, Geordie on the other. They supported her weight as she limped up the corridor. It wasn't that far to go but her steps were small and reluctant.

Behind them, a bell rang and the lift shuddered into life.

Chapter 30

Someone had called the lift. Every chance they were coming to the second floor. Barlow and the rest had reached the Emergency Exit but it would take time to manoeuvre Krista onto the platform and shut the door.

Barlow heard the thump of Gillespie's crutches. He looked back. Gillespie was heading down the corridor towards the lift. Geordie pushed through the Emergency door. The lift door clanked open at the same time. They manoeuvred Krista onto the metal platform. She breathed hard. If the hard floor hurt her, then standing on metal struts had to be ten times worse, yet she never moaned.

Barlow looked back as he pulled the door shut. Gillespie was standing blocking the lift. A woman's voice, high with indignation, carried in the silence.

Gillespie said, 'Ah, come on nurse. I can't sleep and I'm gasping for a cup of tea.'

The woman's voice continued: stern, authoritative.

'And there's me thought you a wee angel.' Gillespie said, pretending disappointment. 'You're sounding more like the wife every minute.'

Barlow got the door shut. Hopefully Gillespie would be able to lock it later.

Out on the platform he felt that they were standing in artificial daylight. Every window in the building across the way seemed to be aiming its light at them. He could even see people moving about. It only took one of them to look their way…

He peered over the railings. It was long way down, thirty twisting steps at least. Krista couldn't cope with that on her raw feet and he wasn't fit to lift her.

'Geordie.'

'I didn't think you wanted me here for my looks,' said Geordie. He had learned well from Gillespie over the war years. It came out as a put-upon moan.

'I'll go first,' said Barlow. He went down a couple of steps to give Geordie room to grunt Krista onto his shoulders in a fireman's lift.

'Great idea. If I slip, you'll give me something soft to land on.'

Barlow stayed two steps ahead of Geordie and Krista. One hand on the railing for support in case Geordie did slip, the other touching the butt of his pistol. SAS men never operated on their own. Someone had to be out there, wondering what was keeping Jordan.

Going down he found so much easier than the climb up. He only had to hold up a leg and his buckling knees did the rest. He found himself trying to take the next step on a concrete path.

At last.

Geordie wheezed down beside him and twisted sideways to lower Krista gently.

Gronville stepped from under the final turn of the fire escape. 'She's mine.' One hand held a pistol, the other reached to grab Krista.

Geordie swung around as if startled, and tried to head-butt Gronville. Barlow's kick caught his knee, but wasn't crippling. Krista's fingers stabbed at his eyes. Gronville cried out, staggered back and fell, holding his hands to his face.

He had dropped his pistol. Krista spat words at Gronville and grabbed for it. Barlow hauled her back, Geordie booted it away into the darkness.

'Disable him,' he ordered Geordie. He pulled the struggling Krista towards the car, keeping an arm tight against his own pistol in case she tried to reach it.

Geordie slammed a heel down on Gronville's groin. Gronville screamed.

'Like that?'

'Like that,' agreed Barlow.

Krista said something to the two of them, something obviously disapproving.

'Whatever,' said Barlow.

At least she had stopped struggling. Even so, he made sure he was between her and the now moaning Gronville before releasing his hold.

The scuffle and Gronville's scream had drawn figures to surrounding windows. Even so, Barlow took time to draw breath and think ahead.

The two-man SAS teams were made-up of other ranks. They

were the *doers*. The Rupert, the officer, in this case Gronville, was there mainly to make policy decisions. That meant that a third man, Jordan's team mate, was still out there in the darkness, probably stationed at the front of the building. He was bound to investigate the cause of the scream. The sooner they were away the better.

Barlow and Geordie got on either side of Krista and hurried her around the corner to the waiting car.

Vera was outside the car, the growling Toby close by her side. 'I heard someone scream.' Her voice trembled.

'Nothing to do with us,' said Barlow as they eased Krista into the back-seat.

He and Geordie would deny everything if they had to. He didn't want to put Vera in the position of having to lie as well.

Once they were all in the car Vera drove back the way they'd come.

'No lights,' Barlow told her.

'We could hit someone.'

'We'll send a wreath.'

Better that, he reckoned, than drawing gunfire from a trained soldier.

He sat back in his seat and appreciated not having to do anything for a few minutes. All the climbing and heaving had ignited a fire in his damaged chest. The pain had faded to glowing embers by the time they reached the house. They all got out.

He handed the car keys to Geordie. 'Take a long drive.'

Geordie hefted the keys in his hand. 'Where to?'

'The Enniskillen lakes and back by Limavady.'

'I've no license,' said Geordie.

'He's not insured,' said Vera.

'If he's stopped we'll say he stole the car.'

Chapter 31

It was past noon before Barlow finally got his eyes open. Reluctantly.

Duty didn't matter, technically he was off on the sick, and Pierson would be in charge. Nevertheless, he had to be there for the men at the station. The loss of Susan would hit hard and there was the funeral to arrange. Pierson was bound to make a mess of things.

Once out of bed he made it to the window. The car sat in the drive which meant Geordie had got back safely. Which was great. Almost certainly Gronville had someone watching the house. Hopefully, when they saw Geordie arrive back they'd assume that he'd taken Krista to some distant safe house. How to keep her alive long-term was something else, but he had an idea. More than that, something kept nagging in his brain. Whatever it was wouldn't come.

He dressed in his good suit and RUC tie and went into the kitchen. Really, he wanted to be in uniform and carrying a weapon. Normally he hated the weight of a pistol against his side, today he felt naked without one.

He had locked both his own pistol and Jordan's automatic in a secure box. He planned to take Jordan's automatic with him and leave it in the station. In Gillespie's locker to be precise. Gillespie wouldn't be nosing in there for the foreseeable future.

He found Vera in the kitchen, sitting in his chair, reading a magazine.

She jumped to her feet. 'You shouldn't be up.'

'And you should be at work.'

'I'm upset at you being shot, aren't I?'

She tried to make a laugh of it, but her lip trembled. He hugged her to him. Her upset hurt him. 'Our luck will change with the New Year, remember?'

'It's only October.'

'We'll get there.'

He held her until she started to pull away. He didn't often get a chance to hug his big daughter. Eventually she went off to make him his porridge and scrambled egg. Toby made room for him when he sat in his own chair. 'Too kind,' muttered Barlow, but let Toby stay. If Toby hadn't been in the car, Gronville might have put a gun to Vera's head and used her as a bargaining chip to seize Krista.

Breakfast over he went to see Krista. Her room was to the back of the house. Even so, he slid in the door in case there was a watcher out back. Krista was in a lot of pain with her feet. All the walking had reopened the wounds. Blood had even transferred from the bandages to the sheets. What they had by way of a first aid kit in the house wasn't enough. He couldn't be seen buying bandages and ointments but there were plenty in the station. He'd lift some from there.

He perched on the edge of the bed and talked to her for a few minutes. Nonsense maybe, and the woman probably didn't understand one word in twenty, but he had to make her feel safe. Before he left he pretended to look out the window, then shook his head and said, 'No, no no no no.'

She nodded back. She'd already worked that out for herself.

He'd got a hug from his daughter and Krista was safe, the car sat in the drive ready to whisk him to the station and the sun was shining. A good start at least to what was going to be a trying day.

His luck continued at the station. Inspector Foxwood had relegated Pierson to the Duty Rosters and had taken personal charge of the funeral arrangements. Barlow stepped aside when he met Constable McGinn in the corridor. McGinn had a swagger to his step. As a wartime Drill Sergeant, he was now in charge of organizing the parade. Not only would they march properly, dare any man have so much as a fleck of dust on his uniform.

Susan could have been Barlow's personal loss the way McGinn stopped and shook his hand, as did every other man in the station. In a way it was. This young girl straight out of training, who refused to be intimidated by his growled, 'And who are you?' He'd lost his heart to her that very first day.

Detective Sergeant Leary was out, processing a new crime scene at the hospital. Krista Riekstinš was missing and a strange man found dead in her room. Barlow professed shock and interest in this new mystery and pumped for information. The dead man, Jordan, wore a nurse's uniform but he definitely didn't work in the hospital. They suspected that Jordan wasn't his real name and they were treating his death as suspicious. There was a report of a fight somewhere in the hospital grounds during the night. They were looking into that.

Barlow thanked God that he'd thought to tell Vera to keep the car lights off. Someone was bound to see the number-plate and remember enough of it to cause problems.

Chapter 32

Barlow wished the Detectives "all the best" with their enquiries into the mysterious body in the hospital, and followed the worst silence in the station. The office that Susan had shared with the other WPCs. Faces were blotched, eyes red. They crowded around Barlow and the tears started again. The pain of them pressing against his damaged chest hardly mattered as he fought back his own tears.

With everyone spoken to and consoled, including Harvey, and Jordan's automatic safely deposited in Gillespie's locker, Barlow retreated to a desk in a hidden corner. Normally, when it came to paperwork, he sat at the old deal table in the kitchen, but Susan had spent too many hours sitting across from him.

What he wanted to do was recast his list to see how things stood. Krista was still both Good and Unknown. Gronville now definitely one of the Bad and the Running Man definitely wasn't the late Nurse Jordan. He'd have recognized him straight off. For some reason he didn't think he was the gunman either. Not that he could put a shape or build to the man who had shot both him and Susan. It was more a feeling, an instinct.

THE GOOD:	Krista Riekstinš
	Sir Anthony Chard
THE BAD:	Leon Weir
	Captain / Major Gronville
	The gunman
	The running man
	Nurse Jordan (decd)
UNKNOWN:	Mrs. Weir
	Daniel T Abernathy
	Krista Riekstinš

That gave him five names in the 'Bad' section. An odd number when the SAS operated in teams of two.

Something Gronville said that first day came into his head. "Weir hasn't made a complaint, has he?" Nobody had talked to him about Leon Weir and yet Gronville knew Leon or at least how he would react.

Barlow found his hands clenching and unclenching. He wanted to take Gronville by the throat and shake the truth out of him. Gronville was operating outside the law, had almost certainly orchestrated the murder of Susan and the attempted murder of Krista, yet there was no way he could even bring him into the station for questioning.

The Bad list now had only four names left alive and active: Leon, Gronville, the gunman and the Running Man. Could Leon be…? Was he the gunman who had shot Susan?

In the station Leon had acted like a captured soldier: name, rank and serial number, and there were all those missing years when he was supposed to be working in England.

At what? Where? Someone had to know.

Barlow had a good chew at an imaginary Imperial Mint while he studied the list. Every possibility that came into his head was pure conjecture on his part. He needed to go talk to people. But first he had to visit Susan's family. Good people, Church going people. Christians in the nicest sense of the word. They mightn't blame him for her death but they had trusted him to keep her safe and he'd failed.

Chapter 33

Susan's family were all at home, all crowded into their little sitting room. Barlow sat and juggle a cup of tea and a plate of sandwiches while he assured them that Susan had died almost instantaneously, was unconscious from the moment the bullet struck and never suffered. Their sympathy for him for his near death in chasing a suspect hurt more than the pain in his chest.

The Coroner had not yet released Susan's remains. A bedroom had been prepared as a shrine to hold the coffin. The Papa Bear teddy bear was back home taking pride of place in the display of photographs and little mementoes. Playing the tough, unemotional sergeant wore Barlow down. He was glad to escape.

Wilson had been there, sitting with the family, being part of them. He had shrunk into a suit that fitted him only days before.

He followed Barlow to the front door. 'Sarge, they've stood me down, put me on sick leave.'

'And you want to be out there, strangling the first suspect you come across?'

'Yes,' said Wilson. Wilson never lied.

'DS Leary has enough crime scenes to be going on with, without you starting more?'

Wilson started to look hopeful because Barlow hadn't said no.

Barlow shoved him in the direction of the car, 'In,' and took him back to the station where Wilson rushed off to put on his uniform. Meantime Barlow sought out McGinn and gave him his full orders.

When Wilson reappeared he got an edited version. 'I want the two of you and Towser…'

'Rex,' said McGinn.

'Whatever, to hang out around the Tin Bridge. When Geordie appears, follow him and see where he goes.'

Wilson seethed. 'But we know it wasn't Geordie. If anyone could have saved Susan ...' His voice stumbled to a stop because he had stood frozen with shock even as Geordie scooped up Susan and rushed her to the Emergency Ward.

Barlow gave his shoulder as squeeze. 'Trust me, son.'

As he walked off, McGinn muttered sotto voce, 'This is going to be a fun outing.'

Barlow nodded at that. Maybe McGinn didn't need Wilson, but Wilson needed the aura of calm that surrounded McGinn.

Right then Barlow could have done with a cup of tea and a sit-down but he still couldn't bring himself to go into the station kitchen. Instead, he got into the car and headed over the Tin Bridge onto the Antrim Road. He turned into Victory Park, which held a cluster of temporary wartime prefabs. Geordie's house was the fifth along.

As soon as he got out of the car, the local dogs gathered in a snarling pack. One or two made a dart at his ankles.

'Dare you.'

Curtains fluttered in the surrounding houses. Many of his best customers lived in Victory Park. They and their families had set up a spy network that the British Secret Service could only dream of. He had thought of having Krista stay with Geordie and his wife.

He rang the doorbell and waited. After a short pause an ageing woman opened it. She wore slippers and a wrap-around apron.

'Connie,' said Barlow and waited to see what sort of greeting he would receive. More than once he had to duck a barrage of flying shoes and crockery.

Connie grasped his hand in both of hers. 'That wee girl, God love her, but she didn't deserve that.'

'You're right there.'

He found himself ushered down the hallway into the kitchen. No change there, he noted, other than more plants than ever dripping off every worktop. Geordie was up and dressed and enjoying a fry.

'My breakfast,' he said used an egg-smeared knife to point to where Barlow was to sit.

'It's near teatime,' said Barlow but made no objection to Connie cracking two eggs into the frying pan for him.

'You can't eat an egg on its own,' she said and added slices of soda bread, followed by strips of bacon, 'for the taste.'

Vera was bound to have a big tea waiting for him at home, but he'd never yet won an argument with Connie. Anyway, the smell coming from the stove was too delicious to refuse.

He didn't bother keeping his voice down. Geordie kept

nothing from Connie and she'd hardly tell you the time of day. 'Any trouble with the car last night?'

'No but it's a long drive on your own.'

Geordie pointedly yawned.

Barlow pulled out his notebook and pencil. 'Just to keep our stories straight. That Russian stuff. What exactly did Krista say to Jordan?'

'You mean…?' Geordie had the sense not to finish that statement.

Barlow kept his pencil poised over the notebook. 'Yes.'

'Well first she called him a bastard.'

'Right.'

'Then "I'll see you in hell" or something close.'

Barlow wrote the words into his notebook and then tackled the plate of food Connie put before him: soft-fried eggs sitting on two halves of fried soda, with bacon draped over both. 'Woman, you should do this professionally.'

The meal finished Barlow sipped at a second cup of tea.

'What are your plans for tonight?' he asked Geordie, keeping his voice casual.

'Find that English bastard and sort him out proper.'

'He's got friends. Important friends.'

'So?'

'You attack Gronville and all those suspended sentences will be enforced.

'So?'

Barlows glared at Geordie. Connie was looking their way, a hand over her mouth.

'So you find Gronville and you make sure he attacks you.'

Geordie cheered up at that. 'Now that's an idea.'

There was no easy way to put this so Barlow said it bluntly. 'You end up on the deck with him standing over you, and not a mark on him.'

'What!' Geordie's roar rattled the display china. 'I can take that man and wring his neck, one-handed.'

'And do time for assault while he gets off. But what if Gronville ends up down at the station, charged with assault?

Geordie stormed to his feet, fists bunched and threatening.

‘What sort of fool do you take me for?’

Barlow sat on. ‘I never said you were a fool, merely an idiot.’

Chapter 34

Between tiredness from a late night and exhaustion from the nagging pain in his chest, it felt good to ease himself into a car rather than throw his leg over a bike.

In fact, Barlow was beginning to wonder if his finances would stretch to a car of his own. Vera was now earning decent money but the new house cost more in rent and heat and light than the old mill house.

At the station, he had parked the car in the station yard so that he could slip a First Aid pack into it without being seen from the road. Getting it into the house was another problem. If he was a betting man, he'd wager that people were watching either him or the house or both. If he looked, the chances are he wouldn't spot them and they'd know that he was suspicious. Gronville, based on Harvey's assessments, thought him thick bordering on moronic and it made sense to keep that illusion going as long as possible.

Instead of going straight home, he drove up through the town and parked outside Matthews Home Bakery. It was near the end of the day and choice was limited. Still he managed to select a box of buns, but remembered to refer to them as pastries. Vera's gentrification was starting to take effect. He didn't know if this was a good thing or bad.

'And a bag of flowery baps.'

As an apparent afterthought, he asked for a whole wheaten-round. It went into a separate bag. Back in the car he put the bags in the passenger footwell, swopping the wheaten-round for the First Aid kit in the process. The wheaten-round he shoved under the seat and out of sight. The smell of the wheaten-round made him salivate like a St Bernard. Hopefully, he could slip it into the house later.

Then home and the pleasure of easing into his own chair and drawing breath for a few minutes. The lights were on, the curtains drawn against the now dark outside. Vera made herself busy running between making the tea and watching the television. Krista had made it into the living room and was sitting with her feet propped up on a footstool. The day's rest had done her good. Her face had gone from grey to colorless.

Barlow hated himself for the pain he was going to cause her but those feet needed seen to.

He filled a basin with hot water and mixed in Dettol. As always, he marveled how the clear Dettol turned cloudy grey when mixed with water. He got Krista to put her feet in the water. She sucked air when the Dettol soaked through the bandages and stung her feet. Working slowly, he teased the bandages loose and threw them on the hearth. The Sulphur dressings proved more difficult, clots of dried blood had entangled themselves in the mesh. The wounds needed checked for infection and cleaned, so they HAD to come off. Cuts reopened as scabs came away with the dressings. Vera disappeared into the scullery and didn't come out again. Krista kept her eyes squeezed shut. The odd whimper escaped from the back of her throat.

'I'm sorry,' Barlow kept saying, hating himself for what he was doing to her. At least there was no smell of putrefaction. Sweat dripped off him from the effort and the strain. He tried not to let it fall onto her feet.

The last dressing came free. Now Barlow wanted to be sick. There was damage done by Krista running barefoot through the countryside, but the worst injuries, the stitched injuries were straight lines.

Barlow sat back on his knees, hardly believing what he was seeing. Someone had slashed at her feet with a knife. Tortured her.

Earlier in the day Krista had put on lipstick. The red glared against the translucent white her cheeks had become.

Barlow eased her feet back into the basin of water. He took her hand in his. 'Did Leon do that? Leon?'

'Leon.' She made a slashing motion with her hand. 'Leon.'

He pressed her hand to his lips. 'I swear to you Krista, I don't care who is protecting Leon, he will pay for this.'

Chapter 35

The call came at nearly nine o'clock. It roused Barlow out of a deep slumber brought on by Connie's soda sandwich and Vera's special tea. The curtains were drawn, the television on and a coal fire glowed at his feet. Vera sat flicking through a magazine. Krista wasn't in the room.

'Where's Krista?' he asked over the loud trill of the phone.

'She's gone bed.'

He could understand Krista wanting an early night. The woman was in a lot of pain from her raw feet. The painkillers they had in the house were Dinky toys compared to what she needed.

He answered the phone. 'Barlow.'

Behind him Vera muttered, 'Good evening, Sergeant Barlow speaking.'

The voice on the end picked up on her correction. 'Good evening, this is Constable McGinn.'

Barlow grunted an acknowledgement and McGinn laughed.

'Sarge, we've got Gronville down at the station. He's one unhappy gentleman.'

It worked. 'Is Geordie all right?'

The delay in the reply coming worried Barlow, took the edge of his pleasure.

'We got him checked out before we sent him home.'

He hadn't wanted this. A couple of blows, not much more. 'How bad is he? I mean …'

'He took a kick to the head. He's fine, but he says he's going to kill you.'

He'd sensed that Gronville had a hair-trigger temper. But a reaction like that? He would have to be careful.

He hurried into an overcoat against a mizzle of slushy rain and drove down to the station. Things were working out as hoped. The humiliation of his arrest heaped pressure on Gronville. Let him see that the other side could fight back. Not only that, his bosses wouldn't like the fact that someone had made a fool of him.

He remembered Sir Anthony's hint of factions within the

security services. Gronville's humiliation might even make his side reconsider their decision to kill Krista.

There was the question of something missing. Something unspecified. The security men wanting to know if Leary had found anything other than the wallet. Even Sir Anthony wanted it found. Whatever "it" was.

If only he could communicate with Krista, find out what had happened to her and why Leon had tortured her. Almost certainly over that missing parcel, letter, whatever. There again, what made Leon think that she knew where it was? Apparently, Malcolm Knype was the last person who had it. Did she know Knype? Work together? Associates of some sort? Lovers? Lovers possibly because Krista has been around a few corners, had the sort of life he'd dread for Vera.

There was one sure thing. Finding something apparently as important as that missing whatever could put a lot of people on Krista's side, guarantee that they would protect her.

That thought brought Barlow to the station. He parked up and went in, surprised at how tired his legs felt. The sleep in the chair had recharged his batteries but the prospect of an early night in bed was enticing.

The subdued hum of things winding down nicely for the night suddenly went up a gear. His arrival seemed to have that effect on people.

Not only McGinn waited for him in the Enquiry Office, Inspector Foxwood stood there as well.

Foxwood kept up a restless movement from foot-to-foot as he vented his disquiet. 'Barlow, this is serious.'

'So I understand, Sir, this could easily have been murder case.'

'Major Gronville claims that it was self-defense.'

So it's major, is it?

'Major Gronville claims that Geordie attacked him. And the dog bit him. He's asking for a rabies shot.'

'Aye, the dog will need something after getting Gronville's blood in his system.'

McGinn exploded a laugh. Foxwood gave a reluctant smile as he produced Gronville's statement taken under caution.

According to the statement Gronville was staying in the Castle Arms Hotel. After a decent dinner he decided to go for a constitutional. He had just reached the Pentagon, at the Minor Town Hall, when an inebriated ruffian accosted him and became verbally abusive. Eventually the man swung a punch and he, Major RN Gronville, found himself forced to defend himself against an unprovoked attack. At which point an ill disciplined and out of control Alsatian dog attacked him from behind and bit him in the calf of the leg. The extensive lacerations required immediate medical treatment and were already showing signs of infection.

He handed the statement back. 'All those big words, Sir.'

'The man's well practiced in bamboozlement,' added McGinn.

Barlow nodded in agreement. 'It comes with the rank of inspector and above.'

Foxwood glared at the two of them as he produced two more statements: one made by McGinn, one by Wilson. Their statements were almost identical copies of each other. They were on patrol and had stopped at the Pentagon where they could observe people coming into town by three main roads: the Galgorm Road, the Cullybackey road and the Ballymoney Road. George Dunlop stopped to pat the police dog, Rex. Mr. Dunlop was in a pleasant, cheerful mood and did not smell of drink.

Soon after Mr. Dunlop left they heard an altercation and observed Mr. Dunlop talking to a gentleman they later identified as Major RN Gronville. The two gentlemen appeared to be having a disagreement. Mr. Dunlop had his hands by his sides when Major Gronville kneed Mr. Dunlop in the groin. Major Gronville then struck Mr. Dunlop in the face knocking him to the ground where he kicked him: first in the ribs and then in the head. Concerned that Mr. Dunlop might suffer more serious injuries, Constable McGinn had released police dog, Rex, with instructions to "seize."

They arrested Major Gronville and escorted him to the station. Mr. Dunlop refused to go to hospital but agreed to come with them to the station. At the station, Mr. Dunlop refused to make a statement without his solicitor being present.

'Old habits die hard,' remarked Barlow and continued reading.

The Police Doctor treated Mr. Dunlop's injuries, after which a police car ran Mr. Dunlop home.

Barlow didn't dare do more than nod his satisfaction at a job well done. Inspector Foxwood looked suspicious enough as it was.

He handed the reports back to Foxwood. 'Gronville will be lucky to get away with a charge of ABH. It could easily have been manslaughter.'

Foxwood frowned at the statements as if reading them for the first time. 'Geordie PATTED the police dog? If I even look near the brute, it snarls.'

'But then, Sir, you're an officer.'

Foxwood refused to rise to the bait. He put the statements in one of Harvey's buff folders. 'My office, please, Sergeant.'

Foxwood set off down the corridor. Barlow hung back. 'McGinn, what about the District Inspector?'

'He's coming in. He had to make a couple of phone calls first.'

Barlow could imagine what sort of phone calls. Harvey at his cringing, apologetic best.

'Have you taken Gronville's fingerprints yet?'

'No. We usually do that when we give Police Bail.'

McGinn had got the message. Barlow trekked after Foxwood.

Chapter 36

Foxwood shut his office door securely behind them. He sat on the edge of his desk and folded his arms. 'Right, Barlow, what are you up to?'

'Sir?'

'When you're around, things don't just happen. Like McGinn and Wilson just happening to be there when Gronville attacked Geordie.'

Barlow could trust Foxwood with the truth, but only so far.

'Sir, I'm merely making enquiries into the events surrounding the death of the late, unlamented Tommy Weir.'

'Which is DS Leary's case.'

'The detectives are snowed under a number of suspicious deaths. I'm only trying to help.'

'And you think Major Gronville is involved in Weir's death? A serving officer with a very prestigious regiment?'

Barlow knew he had no proof of anything against anybody. Only an instinct that cages needed to be rattled, people put under pressure.

'Sir, I formed the opinion that Major Gronville is taking an unhealthy interest in a lot of things that shouldn't concern him.'

Having hinted at Gronville's involvement in Krista's disappearance and maybe even in Susan's death, he decided it safer to backtrack. 'I'm off on the sick.' He rubbed gently at the bruised and cracked ribs, and sucked in a breath that wasn't all playacting. 'I've this feeling about things and how they are all related.'

'What things?'

'Well, Tommy Weir for one thing, and Malcolm Knype in that grave I found.'

Foxwood's head jerked up, his manner intense. 'How do you know his name was Malcolm Knype?'

'The fairies told me,' he said and smiled to show it was really a joke. There was no way he was telling on Leary and, hopefully, Foxwood didn't really want to know. As long as the inspector could deny involvement or knowledge, he tended not to question his methods.

He'd guessed right because Foxwood changed the subject. 'You're off on the sick and accountable to no one. So if you go rogue…'

'Never, Sir.'

'Ignoring the strictures of the "D Notices".'

Barlow liked that word "Strictures" It was the sort of word he could throw back at Edward.

Foxwood smiled. 'Barlow, I know you're not a man who likes sitting around and I appreciate your offer to help out the detectives. But I think it best we keep it between ourselves.'

Obviously Foxwood didn't want Harvey to know what was going on.

'As you wish, Sir.'

He was turning to go when Foxwood motioned him back and into a chair. 'Barlow, those *fairies* have another piece of information for you.'

Barlow sat, grateful to get resting his legs. He remained wary because Foxwood had given in too easily to him investigating Weir's death.

'You heard about the body being found in the hospital ward?' Foxwood asked.

'It was on the news.'

'And Krista Riekstinš has disappeared.'

Barlow imitated a start of surprise, and then grabbed his chest against a real stab of pain. 'How? When?'

'The dead man was dressed as a male nurse.'

Barlow had to remind himself that he knew nothing. 'Somebody local wanting to play at being a real doctor or something?'

'No, a stranger.'

'So how did he die and where's Krista?'

All these questions took an effort to think up. He knew he should have stayed in bed and out of the way of Foxwood and his ilk.

'He died of an antihypertensive overdose.'

'A what?' didn't take any play-acting.

'A calcium based drug, and not one that came out of the hospital Pharmacy either. In fact the Pharmacist had never even heard of it.'

'That's funny. I mean where did…' Barlow stopped and drew breath. He'd nearly said the man's name: Jordan. 'I mean, where could anyone get their hands on something like that?' He pushed his brain to think further. 'What was he going to do with it? Kill Krista? I'm guessing she was people trafficked and they wouldn't want her talking, but to kill her?' He made his voice pitch high in disbelief. 'People don't do that sort of thing.'

'And worse, I'm afraid Barlow.' Foxwood threw his hands out in a self-depreciating gesture. 'Don't forget, I've spent most of my career in London.'

'I'm told Knightsbridge is a pretty rough posting, Sir.'

Foxwood glared. 'It had its moments.'

Barlow knew wasn't asking the right questions and pushed his brain to switch off his image of Krista killing Jordan before he dared speak again. 'So this pretend nurse comes in to give – Just in time, he remembered that Foxwood hadn't mentioned the injection – her a drug that will kill her. For some reason she is suspicious and fights back, and in the middle of the struggle ...' He paused as if working things out in his head. 'You're not likely to accidently shove a handful of tablets down someone's throat. It had to be an injection.'

Foxwood nodded at that. Looked almost disappointed that Barlow hadn't fallen into the trap.

Foxwood said, 'It was an injection, as you guessed, right into the femoral artery. Death had to be almost instantaneous.'

Barlow found himself nodding in agreement and changed it to one of understanding. 'After that Krista took off.' Again he played puzzlement. 'She couldn't have got very far on those feet, unless….'

'Unless what, Sergeant?'

'The man, what's his name. Oh, you don't have a name for him yet. This man, he was hardly likely to walk or to come on a bike. So I'm guessing he'd left a car handy and she found it.'

'Spot on, Sergeant.'

Barlow gave a mental *wheee* of relief.

Foxwood stood up, making it plain that the interview was over. 'A car without any lights on was seen leaving the hospital between the night staff last looking in on Krista and the body being found. She's gone, probably over the border. We've asked the Garda

Siochána to keep an eye out on their side.'

'Good idea, Sir.'

At that Barlow made good his escape. Only to run into District Inspector Harvey and Gronville. Harvey wasn't quite bending the apologetic knee but he almost certainly had received orders from on high to release Major Gronville, immediately, and without charge.

'What are you doing here, Barlow?' demanded Harvey.

'Inspector Foxwood wanted a word, Sir.'

Harvey grunted. Gronville stared at Barlow, unblinking.

McGinn came rushing up holding out a stiff sheet of paper. 'Major Gronville's fingerprints, Sir.'

Harvey took the fingerprint sheet off McGinn. Gronville already had his hand out for it. Harvey handed it over. Barlow watched as Gronville tore the paper into halves, then quarters and then eights. There could have been a glimmer of triumph in his eyes as he put the pieces into his pocket for burning later.

McGinn flicked a wink at Barlow. Gronville might have got a sheet of fingerprint paper with his name on it. The chances were that the fingerprints belonged to McGinn himself.

Why Barlow wanted Gronville's fingerprint taken, other than to humiliate the man further, he didn't know. It was all about applying pressure. If he kept pushing, someone or something might give. Meanwhile, it had been a long day.

He went home to bed.

Blank Page

THURSDAY

Blank Page

Chapter 37

Barlow woke up at eight o'clock, his mind alert, already planning the day ahead of him. It took longer for his body to begin moving. His big toe hurt, his neck hurt and everything in between creaked and groaned.

It's all in the mind, he decided though it didn't feel like that as he forced himself out of bed and under the shower. At least the water was warm thanks to the back-boiler in the kitchen fireplace. It seemed funny to be dressing in flannels, a check shirt and a colored tie when he intended to spend the day on "business." He draped his sports coat over his arm and went into the kitchen. Krista was already there: the curtains still drawn against any watchers and the television on very low. He supposed the moving pictures helped keep her mind from her worries. Small things, like did she have a future?

He pointed. 'Feet?'

'Okay.'

They weren't, she had to be awake half the night with the pain, and there was a glow to her cheekbones that he didn't like. Those feet required proper medical attention and she should be on heavy antibiotics. Every hour she stayed with him risked septicemia setting in. She must know that herself, but she was very stoic, never complained.

He brought her a cup of tea to be going on with and let Toby out for a run around the garden while he cooked them up porridge followed by scrambled egg on toast. One egg and one flowery bap each. He'd have loved more and she needed fattening up but the cupboard was pretty bare and they couldn't be seen buying food for three people.

The wheaten-round still in the car, if only he could figure a way of slipping it into the house.

At near nine he climbed into the car and headed over the tin bridge and down Railway Street into the industrial area of the town. He decided to call first at the Abernathy Light Engineering Company. With a bit of luck Daniel T would be there and it would save him a trip out into the country.

He'd been down Railway Street hundreds of times over the years but never had reason to call with Abernathys. The workshop was an old lava-stone building with bricked up windows and a yard secured by high walls and army style razor-wire. The gateman was an old soldier, a former military policeman, a man he shared the odd pint with. Even so, he had to produce his Warrant Card before the gateman lifted the barrier and directed him to a parking spot beside the front door.

Barlow's professional antennae twitched. Heaps of rusting iron and slabs of steel lying about the place hardly seemed to warrant that level of security. It made him wonder what he'd missed seeing over the years.

The Receptionist, again, was ex-military though he knew nothing about her other than that she had married a local man. Another ex-soldier. An armorer with the Logistics Corps.

The Receptionist made a call. Daniel T was in and would see him. After a short delay, she escorted Barlow to a windowless room where Daniel T waited. Not Daniel T's normal office, Barlow guessed. This room was too carefully furnished. A Daily Telegraph lay folded on the desk, the dark-brown jacket that hung off the chair-back clashed with Daniel T's selection of tie for that day. A spreading pot-plant sat in the corner. No way would Daniel T spend money on frippery for his office. Not when he could get better out of his wife's garden for nothing.

The office didn't feel right: not enough dust and a somehow organized untidiness.

Barlow sat across from Daniel T and made himself comfortable. 'Mr. Harvey asked me to call.'

'About what?'

'You made a complaint about Young William.'

'Who? Oh you mean Wee Willie.'

A tension went out of Daniel T. He looked haggard, nothing like the cheerfully grumpy man Barlow had crossed words with on the Monday.

'He's fine,' said Daniel T looking towards the door as if wishing Barlow gone. 'Don't worry about it.'

'I'm relieved to hear it.' Barlow sat back in the chair. 'So what do you do here other than cut metal into funny shapes and stick them back together again?'

'Internal steel work, aluminum casing.' Daniel T's eyes remained fixed on the door.

Barlow made his voice sound enthusiastic. 'That's fascinating. I didn't know anyone in the town was doing something like that.'

'Well you do now.' Daniel T made a show of looking at his watch. 'If there's nothing else?'

There wasn't, not really. The call was merely to put a tick against Daniel T's name in the "Unknown" box. Now Barlow's instincts were twitching like mad.

'No, I just wanted to make sure Wee Willie was okay.' He stood up and stretched, made as if to leave and then hesitated. 'You know I started life as a carpenter with Terry Esler.' He shrugged self-depreciatingly. 'Sometimes I still hanker for the smell of the old workshops. Would it be possible to have a quick look around on the way out? I mean, if you've the time?'

'If you want,' said Daniel T.

He waited while Daniel T phoned the Receptionist and told her that he'd be out of the office for a few minutes that he was showing Sergeant Barlow around the workshop. After that, Daniel T talked about the products they made: a mixture of ad hoc protective casings for industrial machinery and metalwork to go with the new fitted kitchens that were now all the rage.

In the midst of his talk, he had to raise his voice slightly over a warning bell and metal clanging.

'It's hard to beat the old Belfast Jaw-tub,' Barlow said.

Eventually Daniel T led him down a corridor and through a steel fire door into the workshop. Guillotines sliced giant sheets of aluminum into the required size, rollers shaped the curves and polishing machines added luster to the final product. Unlike the mess in the yard, the materials were stacked neatly against the walls or on shelving. Scrap metal was stored in bins, the floor brushed and not a cobweb in sight.

Everything army style, Barlow decided. As were the employees, he noted. Everyman he recognized was ex-army, armorers almost to a man.

He took his time, not rushing but not holding men back either as he greeted old acquaintances and watched as they worked their machine. After years of having to begrudge every penny leaving his pocket, the binning of metal off-cuts seemed like a waste. Though not too much and not too big, he noted.

'We sell it back to the smelters,' Daniel T explained.

Something else intrigued Barlow, though he didn't mention it. At the back of the workshop was a large metal door. A door that needed winding gear to raise and lower it. The warning bell and the clanking of metal had immediately followed Daniel T's apparently casual phone call to the Receptionist. Barlow was suspicious, but of what he didn't know. However, Abernathys could wait until the Krista problem was resolved.

One guillotine sat positioned near a wall. For some reason it looked different from the rest. Older and showing stains of ancient oils. Barlow took an elliptical path in its direction. A heavier slicing blade he noted. To deal with iron and steel, he guessed. To prove his conjecture he looked in the nearest waste bin and saw chunks of what had to be steel. Most of it tubular.

Right then the Receptionist came racing up. 'Daniel T, your wife. She thought they were going to kill her.'

Chapter 38

Barlow froze for a moment, not sure that he'd heard the Receptionist correctly. Someone, people, "they" had threatened to kill Daniel T's wife?

He needed descriptions, details. Obviously if the wife was ringing, then the men had gone and she was okay. Daniel T was already sprinting out the office door, the Receptionist hard on his heels. Barlow went after them.

Daniel T took the call from his wife in Reception. Mostly he listened. Barlow could hear a distressed voice, the panicked words garbled.

He grabbed the Receptionist's arm to get her attention. 'Give me a line next door.'

He ran back into the office. The phone tinkled as he went in the door so he had a line. A bell sounded somewhere in the workshop. It gave a staccato of urgent rings.

He dialed the station direct. When Wilson answered he told him to put him straight through to Inspector Foxwood.

Barlow drew breath before he spoke, he had to get this right first time. 'Barlow here, Sir. There's been a raid on Daniel T Abernathy's farm. I've no details yet and the wife's okay but the men were violent. Send cars to the farm from every direction. The men are to make a note of the registration number of every car they pass. Stop anything with two or more men in it, and tell them to keep their pistols handy. Those boys play rough.'

He realized he had delivered the message more by way of an order than a suggestion to a superior. He'd apologize later, meantime he went back into the Reception area. This time a tall, broad-shouldered man was there as well. Daniel T's son. The alarm bell still pulsed through the building.

The son carried a pistol. Two more lay on the reception desk.

Barlow slammed to a halt, shocked. 'I hope you've got a license for those.'

'Yes,' said the son.

'I'll see the license later. In the meantime, this isn't Dodge

City. Put those guns away.'

The son ignored him and sprinted out the door. The Receptionist picked up one of the pistols, racked a bullet into the breech and put it on safety. Nothing uncertain about her movements, he noted, and she hefted the heavy pistol with practiced ease. She also stared him back with complete disdain.

The Receptionist was hardly likely to start shooting unless someone came at her. The son was a different matter. Barlow ran for his car, jumped in and spun it backwards in a tight semi-circle to face outwards. The son was already speeding out the gate, the gatekeeper straining to hold the barrier up even as he struggled into body armor.

Daniel T appeared, pistol in hand. Barlow threw the passenger door open. 'In.'

Daniel T jumped in. Barlow had the car through the barrier and onto Railway Street before Daniel T could shut the door. He was breathing heavily, his shirt dank with fear-induced sweat.

Railway Street lay to the south of the town. Barlow decided to head out the Moat Road. A bit of a detour, he knew, but it saved fighting his way through the traffic.

He threw Daniel T his notebook and pencil. 'Note down every car registration I shout out.' He took time to glare at Daniel T. 'And put that gun away before I shove it somewhere you won't like.'

Chapter 39

Traffic was light on the Moat Road and Barlow knew every car he passed: mostly farmers and their wives heading into town for the cattle mart, and to do a bit of shopping. Even so, he called out the registration numbers. It kept Daniel T busy and got him into the habit of doing what he was told.

Eventually the traffic thinned out and he had the car rattling along between the hedgerows. No matter how fast he went Daniel T's body strained for him to go faster.

When he thought the timing right, Barlow asked, 'What's going on?'

'I don't know. Honest.'

'Daniel T, flannel is for dusting bric-a-brac.'

'I don't know.'

He's lying, Barlow decided and the only way to find out was to start with the obvious. 'What are you doing with Browning semi-automatics? Those things don't just hurt people, they blow holes in them.'

'We're arms dealers.'

Barlow was on a bend before he even realized it was there. The wheels burned smoke as he hauled the car clear of disaster. 'All these years and you never thought of saying?'

DI Harvey had to know. And the old DI who, apparently, had trusted him with everything to do with the station had held back that piece of information. He knew he was being ridiculous feeling hurt at a dead man's lack of absolute trust in him.

'All legal,' said Daniel T, trying to control his worries for his wife by talk. 'Army surplus. We take it, fix it up and flog it on. Every rifle, every round of ammunition is properly accounted for.'

'And the stuff you buy abroad?

'Same thing.'

He sensed an evasion in that answer. The truth, the whole truth, yet an edge to the words.

Barlow knew that he was in no position to question Daniel T about the international arms trade. To him it was a dirty little business. In third world countries, people might be dying of starvation but their leaders always found the money for arms.

'So what's going on?' he asked.

'I don't…'

'Come off it!'

'It's just a wee business, now all this.' Daniel T was near tears.

'Dead bodies and people being murdered.' Barlow spat the words in his face. 'What did you think people were using your guns for, walking sticks?'

He'd have loved to stop the car and wring the truth out of Daniel T. And he wanted another look at those circular bits of metal in the waste bin, but they were already turning into Daniel T's farmyard. He stood on the brakes and the car slid to a halt.

The wife was in the yard, her face buried in her apron, crying. The son stood beside her, constantly turning, watching. His pistol held two-handed, ready for trouble. Daniel T jumped out of the car and raced to take her in his arms.

Barlow deliberately took his time getting out of the car and in walking up to the son. Northern Irish people were exempt from National Service and he'd always wondered why the son had taken a short-term commission. Now he knew why.

'Report.' He made it crisp and authoritative, the superior officer demanding answers from a subordinate.

'House and outbuildings clear. Two men. Mother saw them drive off.'

The men were gone. Maybe it was the son's attitude, maybe an instinct of things coming to a head, but Barlow ached to have his own pistol in his hand. He hadn't brought it with him, not on a day when he only planned to talk to people. A pistol would drag down the pocket of his jacket and stretch the material.

He could already hear the distant clatter of the police car bells. They were only a minute away. Mrs. Abernathy wasn't fit to give any sort of coherent statement. Rather than stand doing nothing he decided to have a sniff around.

The house was out of bounds until an armed unit had given the "all clear" and Forensics in the rotund shape of DS Leary had checked for prints. Not that he was likely to find any, those men were professionals. They'd come, terrorized Mrs. Abernathy with minimum violence – she was still on her feet, wasn't she? – and left. He checked his watch, it was barely nine-thirty. In and out fast, professionals. It had to be people acting under Gronville's orders. There couldn't be two gangs of ruthless men haunting the area, or could there? Certainly some sort of conflict was going on.

Those men were looking for something? Yet why did they distrust Daniel T when he was one of their own.

Doors to outbuildings lay open. They'd even searched in them.

The thought of Wee Willie appearing in his doorway and nothing between them but open yard gave Barlow the shivers. He sidled up to the bull house and swung the door shut with a satisfying clang. Rammed the bolt home. He could tell from the light in the shed that the other door into the field lay open as well.

As was the gate leading from the farmyard to the field. That smacked of someone being vindictive. However, instead of piling into the yard and maybe escaping down the road the cows stood huddled at the far hedge. Only now was one of them daring to make a move in his direction. Was it his imagination or was there a whiff of gun-smoke in the air? Certainly there was nothing better designed to panic cattle than gunshots. At the field gate he spotted the track of feet leading to the abandoned fire engines. They'd even looked around them.

Which meant that someone, and it didn't take any guessing as to whom that was, would have to take a look as well.

Behind Barlow, the first police car swept into the yard.

Chapter 40

Inspector Foxwood jumped out of the car and glared in Barlow's direction.

Barlow knew that he owed the inspector an apology. At the same time he felt drawn to the fire engines. It was definitely safer to check them before Wee Willie appeared out of the ruck of cattle.

He went back to speak to Foxwood. 'Sorry, Sir. That phone call, I was totally out of order.'

'Don't let it happen again, Sergeant.'

'No, Sir.'

'Report.'

Barlow told what little he knew, without any suggestions or guesswork. Foxwood nodded when he mentioned that the Abernathys were arms dealers, so he knew about that little enterprise.

Finally he said, 'Someone's been in the field, as far as the old fire engines. If it's all right with you, Sir, I'll go take a looksee.'

'As you wish.'

Foxwood's cold attitude grated, but he deserved it. He snapped to attention and then headed out of the yard into the field. The cows were drifting his way, curious as to the excitement in the yard. There was still no sign of Wee Willie.

The fire engines sat close to the boundary with the county road. Against a ditch with a straggly hedge laced with barbed wire. He reckoned he could be over the hedge and long gone before Wee Willie got near him.

The fire engine doors hung ajar. Barlow used his pencil rather than risk contaminating the metal with his fingerprints. Even before the first door swung wide, his mouth was open.

They weren't old fire engines that Daniel T couldn't sell. They were the shells of fire engines: roof, bonnet and sides. Someone had cut everything else away, including the floor. Facing Barlow was a twenty-five inch field gun, minus its barrel and breechblock. During World War ll, it was the only weapon capable of outgunning the feared German Tiger tanks.

Barlow heard a step behind him and spun round, wary that it

might be Wee Willie. Daniel T's son had followed him into the field.

Barlow jerked a thumb at the artillery piece. 'You have a license for that?'

'Yes, two of them here and more to come. The barrels are down at the factory for refurbishment.'

The cows were closer, spreading out as they approached. He couldn't see Wee Willie among them, but kept looking. 'I hope you don't plan to sell them locally.'

'They're for Israel. The British government don't want to be seen supplying the Jews with arms, Arabs, oil and all that, so we're the deniable middlemen.'

Barlow knew he was wasting his time there. The son didn't seem worried about him finding anything around the guns. He went back to the farmyard to find a lot of policemen hanging around looking busy, doing nothing.

Foxwood wasn't in sight, he had to be in the house with Mrs. Abernathy. Tact told Barlow that he shouldn't take control outside without permission, not with a couple of senior sergeants standing around as well.

I'll do my next call, he thought, and headed for his car. With a bit of luck he could manoeuvre it out through the tangle of police cars in the yard.

Daniel T came out of Wee Willie's bull house.

'Is he down the field?' he asked the son.

'No,' said the son.

'That's all we need.' Daniel T sighed. 'He's worse than a mongrel dog with a bitch on heat.'

Barlow froze. Wee Willie missing? He could wreak havoc, kill people. Foxwood had to be informed, people alerted. Policemen, currently standing around with nothing better to do, sent to scour the surrounding country for the bull.

Normally he would have roared out the orders but the way things were, those orders should come from Foxwood direct. Anyway, he needed an excuse into the house to talk to Mrs. Abernathy, and this was as good as any.

Chapter 41

Barlow knocked the back door, then the kitchen door and finally the sitting room door as he made his way through the house. He had to make his way around things pulled out of cupboards and drawers and left strewn. All the same, the mess wasn't too bad. No broken crockery, he noticed, and the display cabinet of fine china and family Sterling silver left untouched.

Foxwood was in the over-furnished sitting room taking a statement from Mrs. Abernathy. There were still tears but now her words made sense.

Barlow tapped the open door. 'A word if you please, Sir.'

Equally polite in their newly brittle relationship Foxwood said, 'Certainly, Sergeant,' and came out into the hallway, closing the door behind him.

Barlow explained about the dangers of Wee Willie loose on the countryside, finishing with, 'He's a bad bugger, Sir. He'd toss you as quick as look at you.'

'Okay, right, would you.... No, I'll deal with it, you're off on the sick.' Foxwood hurried off. At the door into the kitchen, he looked back. 'Go home and rest. See you Monday.'

As soon as he was out of sight Barlow slipped into the sitting room. 'Are you okay, love?' he asked Mrs. Abernathy.

'I'm okay, Mr. Barlow. I'm just... you know.'

'You're fair shook, and who wouldn't be.'

He sat down on the settee and leaned forward. 'These men, can you describe them?'

She shivered. 'He put a gun to my head. I knew he wanted to pull the trigger.' She wiped away a fresh flow of tears. 'He was the one who didn't speak. Never a word, but his eyes....' The tears flowed harder.

Barlow waited patiently until the flow stopped. At the same time he was anxious to be finished and gone before Foxwood reappeared. 'Do you know if they took anything?'

'No, nothing. I don't think so. There was this box, package thing they were talking about.'

‘What box, what package?’ he asked but she only shook her head, not knowing.

Barlow couldn’t understand why people thought Daniel T has something to do with the missing package, but Mrs. Abernathy obviously knew nothing about it.

He could hear Foxwood’s voice, still giving orders as he came back into the house, so he pushed on quickly, asking what he needed to know.

The quiet man was thin. Thinner and taller than the other one, she told him. They wore coveralls over their clothes and masks to conceal their faces.

‘The man who spoke, what sort of accent did he have?’

‘English,’ she said and nodded her confirmation when he queried this. ‘Not Cockney, but sort of London.’ She appeared happier talking about the English man than the one who never spoke.

From her description he could be the watcher at the hospital gates, the man he had chased through the town. The second man, the one who never spoke, was probably the same man who had tried to kill him in the People’s Park. A killer over anxious to pull the trigger. Almost certainly, the same man had killed Susan, taking a shot that no sane gunman would have risked.

Foxwood came back into the room. Barlow made sure he heard him tell Mrs. Abernathy, ‘I’ll get you that cup of tea,’ as if that’s what they’d been talking about.

He slipped past Inspector Foxwood, whispering, ‘I’ll tell someone to bring you a cup as well, Sir, and a bit of her famous barmbrack bread’

Chapter 42

Barlow drove back into town at a speed where he could trust the car to behave while he did a bit of hard thinking. A chew on an imaginary wine gum didn't bring any clarity to the ideas floating around in his head. Nothing of what was going on made sense at that point.

His list of names didn't have a tick against Daniel T's meaning "dealt with." Daniel T needed talked to like a Dutch uncle. That would have to wait until later, when things had calmed down and Foxwood and company had headed back to the station.

He checked his watch. The day was flying and so far he had only managed to add to his confusion. Daniel T Abernathy an arms dealer? That was a new one in his book.

The call at Abernathy's workshop was supposed to have been a five-minute call on his way to see Captain Charles Denton. Denton, starting with little more than Barlow himself, had forged ahead by the use of guile and a fortuitous marriage. Like Abernathys, most of the employees at the brewery were old soldiers or the sons of old soldiers. Probably the nearest thing the brewery had to a weapon was Clarissa Denton's tongue when she found things not up to her standards of hygiene.

Barlow swept in the brewery gate to a casual wave from the gateman, parked and tried to do his usual run up the stairs to the offices on the first floor. Pain slowed him to a sedate climb.

Edward Adair's fiancé, Mrs. Anderson, held him back wanting to know how he was and gave him a hug before showing him into Denton's office.

'Good morning, Captain,' said Barlow.

'You call me "Captain" you're looking for something,' growled Denton. But he was already on his feet, both hands out in greeting. 'Sometimes, Barlow, I think you've more guts than sense.'

As Chairman of the Local Policing Board – with the bulk and build to go with the status – Denton was entitled to know what had happened when Susan was murdered. Barlow kept his report brief and changed the subject as soon as he could.

'Charlie,' he said, rather than "Charles", and did it deliberately. This was favor time. They went back to primary school together and Denton owned his commission and his future success partly to Barlow putting in a word for him at the right time. 'I need a couple of things and I don't want you asking any questions because you won't be getting any answers.'

'Try me,' said Denton, more curious than cautious.

Barlow pointed. 'I need your Dictaphone and a couple of blank tapes.'

Denton eyed the Dictaphone with distaste. 'Clarissa thought we should move into the electronic age.'

'So you don't mind if I keep it for a few days?'

'No. What else?'

Barlow knew Denton wasn't being rude. The man had so many businesses running that he had to move swiftly from subject to subject.

Barlow had trouble keeping anxiety out of his voice. What had happened at Abernathys made him worry for his daughter's safety. 'I want Vera out of the house for, say, the weekend.'

'No problem. Clarissa's in town. I'll get her to pick her up when she's done shopping.'

Barlow held his hands up. Mentally he was holding back a furious Vera. 'It needs to be an invitation of some sort coming from Clarissa.'

Denton frowned working out the logistics in his head. 'If it could wait a day. What if we get her to babysit tomorrow night? We're going to a party in Sir Anthony's.'

Barlow gritted his teeth in frustration. He'd forgotten all about the party. 'So are we, Vera and myself.'

He was grateful when Denton nodded as if accustomed to seeing him at the grandest house party the town had to offer. 'Leave it to Clarissa. She'll think of something.'

Barlow tucked the Dictaphone under his arm and left, content. After what happened at Abernathys he wanted Vera well away from the house. Things could get very nasty if Gronville even thought that he had Krista stashed there. He'd spend tonight on guard, gun in hand, just in case anyone tried anything.

Chapter 43

Major Edward Adair, GC MC was "at home" in his hut under Curles Bridge, and "Receiving." Barlow told him, 'Get in the car.'

'My dear, chap,' Edward said in a reproving voice, but complied.

Barlow was easing the car up the slope onto the main road when Edward enquired. 'One assumes that one has need of ones services?'

'I think I preferred it when you were permanently sozzled.'

'Sticks and stones, my dear chap. Sticks and stones.'

'Mrs. Weir, widow of the late, unlamented Tommy Weir. I want to talk to her.'

'Difficult.'

'Not if you're with me. You're her blue-eyed boy at the minute.'

Edward investigated something obstructing his feet and found the wheaten-round. 'Ah, breakfast, how considerate.'

He tore off a large chunk and started to eat. Barlow supposed he could buy another one without causing undue suspicion. Anyway, a full mouth kept Edward quiet.

He chose a route through the town that would bring him to Weir's farm without passing Daniel T's on the way. Somewhere in the lower part of the town, he sensed that someone was following them. The traffic was light, even so he couldn't spot which car it might be.

Those boys are good, he told himself as if he didn't know that already. He drove on through the town to the Broughshane Road and out beyond the town boundary. Once they were on the Woodside Road the feeling of unease disappeared.

Edward twisted around in his seat to stare out the back window. 'This road runs straight uphill and never has any traffic.'

It didn't surprise Barlow that Edward had sensed them being followed. It was something he had passed on to Barlow during the war. Edward had taught him to use his senses to find unexploded bombs, when to defuse a bomb and when to run for his life.

All the same, the follower had to know they were heading for either Abernathys or Weirs.

Barlow wished he'd thought to bring his gun with him. Especially when they bumped off the rough track into Weirs' farmyard. Leon stood in the farmyard, hands on hips, obviously expecting them.

Barlow felt an overwhelming urge to drive over Leon, and then reverse over the body to make sure he'd done a proper job of killing him.

Edward touched Barlow's arm. 'Easy, Sergeant Major.'

Barlow stopped the car, put on the handbrake and switched off the engine. He sat on, forcing himself to focus on what he wanted to achieve at the farm. He found he was trembling.

'Thank you, Major.'

He and Edward got out of the car.

'What do you want?' Leon asked, his eyes fixed on Barlow. Not on Barlow's face but at the spot on his chest where the bullet had struck.

'Is the good lady, your mother at home and "Receiving"?' asked Edward.

'No.'

Mrs. Weir appeared at the front door of the farmhouse. The hens rushed over to her, hopeful for scraps of thrown food. She ignored them and stood humped into herself, arms folded over her chest, as if cold. She could well have been cold. The dirt on the farmyard shone with ice crystals and crunched underfoot.

'I told you to stay inside,' Leon said. Then he rounded on Barlow. 'Is this an official visit or are you just here nosing?'

Barlow pointed to the police tape crisscrossing the doorframes of two of the outbuildings: the outhouse where Leon had held Krista captive and another building across the way that had to be the distillery. 'Those makes it official.'

He stepped past Leon, broke the police tape closing off the distillery and went in. The building had been a workshop at a time. Pegs to hold machine parts and tools, still stuck out of the walls and hooks fought for place among the cobwebs stretched between roof beams.

'That's one way of getting your protein,' Barlow told Edward who had followed him in.

'A variable brew with little finesse. The quality of the grain acquired remains suspect,' Edward informed him.

Barlow nodded and walked the line of distillery equipment: from the rotating drum where the barley germinated to the copper stills that produced the final, drinkable brew. Bags of barley seed and what had to be a quarter ton of sugar lay stacked against one wall.

The one thing missing, Barlow noted, was fingerprint dust. The men from Headquarters who had taken over from DS Leary obviously had no interest in identifying and prosecuting those involved in the illegal distillery.

'Which is a good thing for certain people,' Barlow informed Edward.

All the same, it was a much bigger and much more sophisticated operation than he'd ever suspected.

Back at the distillery doorway, he looked at Leon still standing sentinel in the yard and at Mrs. Weir shrunk against the house wall.

He spat on the ground in Leon's direction. The next time he came here he'd be carrying his gun. With Leon around he felt vulnerable without it.

Chapter 44

Barlow had to pass Leon on the way to the house. Leon's eyes challenged his every step. There was something about his eyes that Barlow couldn't put a word to. Mrs. Abernathy had struggled the same way, trying to describe the man who never spoke.

Which made Leon the fourth man in Gronville's unit: Gronville and Leon, the late Mr. Jordan and the Running Man.

Barlow couldn't get Running Man right in his head. Running Man had more than one opportunity to shoot him during the chase from the hospital, and hadn't.

Presumably the same man had managed to terrorize Mrs. Abernathy without even bruising her. Which was more than he could say about Jordan. Even with witnesses looking on, Jordan was willing to inject Krista and kill her, knowing that his organization would protect him. It was possible, even highly likely, that Leon had the same guaranteed protection.

He had no way of finding out what Leon had got up to when supposedly working in England, but it had to be dirty. And dirty enough for some organization to find a use for him. What was that word Daniel T used? Ad hoc: on a one-off basis, now and again, as needed. So how many other Susans had Leon killed? Butchered.

He dug his mind out of his thoughts when he reached Mrs. Weir. It was the day after Tommy's funeral. He doubted if many had gone to the service: a few relations, the odd neighbor. For Susan's funeral on Friday – tomorrow, he realized – the church would be packed.

'Can I have a word, love?'

The last time she'd screamed at him, wanted to claw him out of the house. Now Mrs. Weir seemed almost glad to see him, her eyes full of hurt. She was quick to take Edward's arm and allow him to escort her into the house.

Nice one, Edward, thought Barlow. If he himself had asked, they'd never have got over the doorstep. Not that the Weirs could have kept them out. Someone had made a botch job of fixing the front door.

Leon came hard on his heels. 'Mother's not fit to be questioned.'

'I'm here to pay my respects.'

'Visitors then.'

Barlow ignored him and followed Edward and Mrs. Weir into the sitting room. This room was obviously her escape from the reality of living with the late Tommy. Handmade covers hid the ravages of generations of Weirs on the furniture. Thick cushions protected against protruding springs. Worse, from Barlow's point of view, was the obvious absence of any serious searching of the house. A week's dust circled ornaments in a cabinet. The detectives should have pulled it out for a look-see behind.

Edward sat with Mrs. Weir on the settee. Barlow selected a chair opposite her, from where he could keep an eye on Leon hovering in the doorway.

He thought he should start with the positive. 'The thing is, Mrs. Weir, that whiskey still in the yard. The official line is that Thomas was the brew-master so no one is likely to be charged with any offence.'

He didn't mention HM Customs & Excise. If they got wind of the still, they'd seize the equipment and sue Tommy' estate for an estimated loss in excise duty. The family were likely to lose the farm.

'So I suggest you sell the copper for scrap and feed the barley seed to the chickens.'

Mrs. Weir became animated. 'But I need the money. How else am I going to live?'

'Aye,' Barlow said, peeved that the woman couldn't take a hint. His feelings for her was dislike coupled with sympathy. Maybe Tommy had been difficult to live with, but he obviously had been a stopgap between her and a son who had to be a pure psychopath.

'Mother, your Widows Pension will keep the house,' said Leon.

Maybe Barlow and Edward being there gave her courage. She spat the words at her son. 'The pension won't run to your T-bone steaks.'

'I'll see you right,' Leon said.

'You! Who has your hand out for the coins if I ask you to buy a loaf of bread.'

‘I will, mother, don’t worry,’ he said, his voice somehow threatening in its silky assurance.

She curled back into herself; all fight seemingly gone. Leon stood on in the doorway, triumphant.

‘Now, damage,’ said Barlow.

Mrs. Weir didn’t seem to understand but Barlow was watching Leon, and he did. His eyes seemed to roll pound signs.

Edward squeezed Mrs. Weir’s arm to get her attention. ‘During the search of a house by the police, floors have to be ripped up and things get broken. It is their duty under law to recompense and make good all such damage.’

Barlow added. ‘It will give you a few quid to help tide things over.’

What little hope there was faded from Mrs. Weir’s face. ‘There was nothing. That nice inspector…’

‘Inspector Foxwood,’ prompted Barlow.

‘... Inspector Foxwood was very careful. When he was in the kitchen he even made me a cup of tea.’

Barlow pulled out his notebook and sat poised on the edge of his chair, pencil hovering to take notes. ‘Other than replacing the front door, I’m sure there’s a few things, if we just take a look around.’

Leon snorted. ‘What he means, mother, is that he wants to search the house himself.’ He stepped clear of the doorway and gestured effusively. ‘Feel free, Sergeant. Feel free.’

Chapter 45

Leon's offer for Barlow to search the house for himself was a gloat at someone wasting their time.

Barlow got to his feet. 'I will then, thank you.'

He knew that Inspector Foxwood had done a superficial search of the house. Drawers and cupboards searched, furniture tipped up to check underneath, pictures looked behind, mattresses rolled back to display the base. Yet the tone of Leon's words held some sort of challenge: see if you're a better man than me.

There had to be something that Leon didn't want him to see. But to be sure of finding out he'd need two days and a squad of men with nail-bars and sledgehammers to take the whole building apart. That sort of permission would never come, and Leon knew it.

What Barlow couldn't understand was why some wee man got done for not having a light on his bike? Yet Leon is allowed, encouraged even, to get off with murder?

Barlow made a show of doing a search. He pulled open the drawer in the hall table to see what was in there. That day's post of bills and circulars, still unopened, and the telephone directory. He checked down the list of names on the "Frequently Used Numbers" page. Nothing stuck out except the names and numbers of a couple of bar owners. He made a note to speak to them about the source and quality of drink they served.

The kitchen was clean, as clean as anyone could make a cracked Belfast sink and wooden worktops disintegrating under a lifetime of wet pots and pans. An unused china teapot sat on a high shelf. Under a handful of faded receipts, Barlow found a ten-shilling note and some coins. He put everything back. The ever-watchful Leon took the teapot down again and put the money in his pocket.

Barlow said nothing. That sort of thing came under "Domestic" and outside the law. With battered wives, the only thing he could do was make the husband's life hell. Leon now came under that same category. First chance, he'd charge him for anything and everything, including jaywalking.

Mrs. Weir's bedroom he barely looked into. Like everything

else he'd seen in the house, the furniture was weary and the bedclothes thin from use. She had to be cold at night without Tommy lying alongside her.

Like himself, he realized, and he still hadn't changed the sheets. Louise had gone, it seemed like forever, and not a word from her. There was no report of a plane going down, he checked for that in the papers every day. She might have written a letter rather than sending a telegraph. That would take a few days to arrive. It wasn't much but the best he had to hold on to.

He'd kept Leon's bedroom to last. He didn't dare break anything because the "D Notice" people would know he had been interfering. Nevertheless, he planned to tip a few things over and leave the bed tossed, knowing Leon that wouldn't dare complain over a bit of untidiness. Not with his reputation as a renowned killer.

Leon's bedroom came almost as a shock. It was small, only big enough to hold a single bed and a wardrobe, a chest of drawers and a head-high bookcase. Every bit of wood that showed was ebony and the wallpaper was the quality of the stuff he saw in the grandest houses.

'I'd appreciate it if you would take off your boots first,' murmured Leon at Barlow's elbow.

Barlow looked at Leon and then at the carpet: a carpet obviously not new but still pristine white. Still wearing his boots, Barlow walked into the room. He could only hope that some of the cow dung and hen droppings in the yard still stuck to the soles.

In spite of the promise to himself to wreck the room, he touched nothing. Merely stood in the middle of the room and looked around to get a sense of the man. Books in the bookcase stood upright and all filed in alphabetical order. Leon had even arranged the sticks in the fireplace in a neat crisscross pattern. Barlow checked carefully but found no sign of dust. Not even the trace of a cobweb hanging from the ceiling light or in the furthest reach of the room.

Leon indicated to draw Barlow's attention to the posters pinned to the walls: the Empire State building, the Brandenburg Gate, and the largest of them all, an odd-looking angel, pinned to the chimneybreast. 'Mementoes of my travels.'

'I'll send you one of the Waveney Hospital for your collection,' said Barlow and stalked out.

Chapter 46

Barlow found that he was again trembling with rage. He stopped in the hallway and worked at steadying himself. He would leave this house, not retreat from it, and if Leon even flickered a gloat…. His hand reached for a gun that wasn't there.

The sitting room door was open. Through the gap between the door and doorjamb, he could see Edward holding Mrs. Weir's hand as he comforted her. 'Give it a week or two, let things calm down first,' he was telling her.

Obviously they were planning to get back in business. It wasn't worth wasting a sigh on those two.

He gave the door a thump. 'Right Edward, we're on our way.'

Edward promised the "good lady" that he would call again in a few days to discuss the "logistics of the operation" and joined Barlow. They walked out of the house together. Leon stood on the bottom stair and watched them go.

The drive into town seemed to take forever. He asked Edward what he knew about Lithuania.

'One of those little Baltic States, my dear chap. A place that people are always fighting over: the Russians, the Poles, the Germans. Currently the Russian Bear is in occupation. It happened after the war when….'

Barlow let Edward talk on. It stopped him from talking nonsense and saved himself from having to think.

Once in town, Edward asked Barlow to drop him off at the Bridge Bar. 'It's past lunchtime and one has need of one's sustenance.'

He knew it was a hint that Edward expected a complimentary drink but he was too tired to even think of going into the bar. His fury at Leon getting away with Susan's murder had faded, leaving him drained. Sleep beckoned.

He roused himself to ask, 'Do you mind if I stand you a pint and chaser another day?'

'My dear chap, you are under no obligation. It's always a pleasure to oblige one of my comrades in arms.'

Even having to put the car in gear and drive off seemed a chore. 'I don't know what's wrong with me, I'm fair beat.'

Edward patted his arm. 'Of course you are. Don't you remember in wartime? It wasn't the physical injury per se; it was shock to the system that laid us low.' The pat became a tap of disapproval. 'And you haven't given yourself a chance.' He picked up the remains of Barlow's wheaten-round and stepped out of the car. Before closing the door, he ducked in again for a final word. 'Go home, my dear, chap. Rest.'

'Aye, I will. One more thing then I'm done for the day.'

From where he sat parked he could see the tin bridge and the river. One of these days, he and Gillespie should do a bit of fishing. Gillespie could use his crutch as a fishing rod.

Awkward bugger and all as he was, he missed having Gillespie around to watch his back.

Making sure that he didn't knock down an old biddy doddering across the road he turned right and headed for the police station. He found McGinn's van in the station yard.

Even better, he found McGinn in the kitchen enjoying a break between patrols. He drank McGinn's tea while he explained what he wanted him to do. The uncomplaining McGinn poured himself another cup and pushed a sandwich Barlow's way while he listened. Any question he had was about the actual execution of the task, not what Barlow was up to and why.

'When you and Towser are ready,' he told McGinn.

McGinn didn't even bother saying, 'Rex,' as he reached for his cap.

Barlow fetched a package out of the boot of his car while McGinn collected Rex from the kennels. A wind had got up from the north. It carried the odd snowflake. Rather than wait out in the cold he got into the van and put the package at his feet.

'It's going to be a bitter night,' said McGinn, joining him.

'Ever the optimist,' said Barlow.

Chapter 47

Barlow sat quiet while they wound their way into the country. He surprised himself by falling into a light doze but came to full awareness again when McGinn said, 'I think this is it, Sarge.'

"It" was a farm gate at the point where Krista had crossed the county road while escaping from the Weirs.

Barlow got out of the van, taking the package with him. McGinn collected Rex from the back and clipped on his long lead. Rex stood expectantly: ears cocked, panting with excitement. Barlow wouldn't have minded transferring some of that keenness for the job into some of his constables. Looking at the long hill stretching before them, he wouldn't have minded some for himself. Instead, he opened the package and handed it to McGinn. 'Let him smell this.'

McGinn looked in and pursed his lips in surprise. Barlow put on a stony face when he glanced up, daring him to ask any questions.

'It's been near a week,' said McGinn.

'It doesn't hurt to try.'

McGinn put the package on the ground and tore it wide open. Blood soaked bandages and dressings spilled out. Even from where he stood, Barlow could get the smell of rancid blood.

Rex had a good sniff around the bandages. Once McGinn gave the order to "seek" he went straight to the gap in the hedge leading into Blacks' estate. Before Barlow could think of a put-down remark Rex came back across the road and stood expectantly at the farm gate. All of a sudden, for Barlow, the long hill got longer and steeper.

They went through the gateway, Rex pulling impatiently when McGinn stepped back to close the gate behind them. There was no sign of any animals in the field. And no Wee Willie, thought Barlow, in relief. No way did he want to run into that brute in the middle of a huge field.

He didn't even try to understand dogs and their noses as Rex hauled McGinn up the field and to the left. At the crest of the hill stood an artificial mound now covered in mature oak trees. Back in the middle ages, it had doubled as a lookout post and a palisaded farmhouse occupied by the invading English. By day, English armor and swords controlled the countryside. By night, the native Irish roamed free and God help any stray Englishman they came across. Krista had been smart to use the mound as a vantage point to get her bearings in a strange land.

Barlow was puffing hard long before they got to the top. When McGinn suggested that they stop for a breather he could only shake his head and plough on. His legs dragged and the cracked ribs seared pain through his lung. Finally, brutally, they reached the base of the mound. He used his arm to wipe sweat out of his eyes before looking around.

The countryside fell away from them on all sides. In the distance, almost a mirage in its appearance, he could see Ballymena and closer by, the village of Broughshane. Small farmsteads dotted the land. About a house for every thirty acres, he guessed, which gave Krista a lot of places to aim for to get help.

Still short of breath, he nodded to McGinn to get Rex going again. Krista's path took them to the right, around the base of the mound. Barlow understood her reasoning. No way could she cope with a finger and toe scramble to the top, not with those shredded feet of hers. Here and there she appeared to have stopped and looked out over the countryside. About two-thirds of the way around, Rex suddenly lunged downhill. McGinn struggled not to go with him headfirst.

He dug his feet in, pulling the excited Rex to a halt. 'From here on, Sarge, I think she's heading straight for Abernathy's.'

Barlow allowed his weary legs to fold and he sat on the grass. 'Check it out as far as the county road. I'll meet you back at the van.'

Cold air chilled the sweat on his body. Even so, it felt good just to sit for a few moments in peace. In front of him he could see Daniel T's little house with its picture-perfect garden, the outbuildings and, to the side, the line of old fire engines. Currently they held a battery of 70 pounders. It seemed reasonable to wonder what else the old engines had concealed over the years.

When McGinn and Rex reached the hedge straight across the road from Daniel T's place he returned McGinn's triumphant wave and headed straight downhill to the van. McGinn had the petted and fussed-over Rex loaded into the back before the leg-weary Barlow reached it.

They got into the van and drove back into town, with McGinn pointedly not speaking. Their route chosen by McGinn took them onto the Ballymoney Road.

The thought of driving past his house, of delaying the aching pleasure of stretching out in sleep was too much for Barlow. He pointed. 'Drop me at the gate. I'll pick up my car later.'

McGinn didn't speak or nod in acknowledgement. He parked as instructed and sat staring straight ahead. 'Sarge, Inspector Foxwood is recommending me for an Official Commendation for finding Malcolm Knype's body.'

'And well deserved.'

'There'll be a different sort of recommendation if he finds out what we've been up to today.'

Barlow didn't blame the man for worrying. Retirement and a pension wasn't that far ahead.

'It'll be all over by Monday,' he promised McGinn and got out of the van.

For the first time ever he hated the length of driveway between the front gate and the front door. He let himself in and shouted, 'Vera,' and got no reply.

Without any reason to be anxious but still worried he searched the house for her. Toby growled at him from the chair in the kitchen. *No change there.* Slightly reassured he plodded around the house. The bathroom door was open, so was the door into Vera's room.

He tapped Krista's door and went in. She lay in bed with the clothes heaped around her against the cold in her bones. She held the small radio close to her ear, the sound turned low. The Light Programme, Barlow thought.

'Vera?' he asked Krista.

Krista pulled a piece of her hair straight and pretended to cut it with *scissored* fingers.

'Ah, the hairdresser, for the party tomorrow night.'

Krista nodded.

All the same, he'd rather have her home instead of wandering about town as daylight faded.

Krista seemed to have everything she needed. He went into his own room, stripped off and fell into bed.

Chapter 48

Worry forced Barlow awake. He opened his eyes into darkness. Vague shapes became clear: the brooding shape of his wardrobe in the corner, a sense of lightness where the window should be. Is, he corrected himself. Someone had been in to pull down the blind and draw the curtains.

'Vera!'

He jerked upright in the bed. She hadn't been in when he arrived home and she couldn't be home now because the house was unnaturally quiet.

He hurled out of bed, dragged on a dressing gown to cover his nakedness and went to the door. 'Vera,' he roared into the silence.

He heard his chair squeak as Toby jumped off it and the click of his nails on the linoleum.

'Vera,' he tried again, his breathing coming quick and jagged. If anything had happened to her. If Leon even touched her…

Krista appeared from the kitchen. 'Vera.' She pointed to the front door, made the motion of someone coming in. Her hands made circling motions of someone eating quickly, then waving goodbye. Finally she again pointed to the front door.

He got the message. Vera had come back, eaten her tea and then gone out again into all sorts of dangers.

He became conscious of his dressing gown not terribly well pulled together and retreated back into his bedroom. He dressed quickly, he wanted Vera found and home where he could keep her under guard until she went to stay with the Dentons.

His temper cooled as quickly as it had arisen. She wasn't to know that she had to stay in. He hadn't made it plain. She'd had enough to contend with over the past year without her worrying about Gronville and nut case Leon.

Trousers on and the braces looped over his shoulders, he hesitated. There was something about the way things sat in his pockets. He liked them just so for comfort and they weren't quite right, needed adjusted. He frowned at the curtains. Did Vera come in and draw them or had Krista used it as an excuse to be in his room while she searched his pockets?

The car keys!

Not just the car keys. The key to his gun box was on the same ring. A panicked search of his pockets failed to find the keys.

He had the vaguest recollection of pulling the keys out of his pocket and ... He lifted the pillow off the bed. Not there, where they should be. He got into bed holding they and … he pulled the bedclothes back and there they were.

That problem solved he dug into the base of the wardrobe to where his gun case lay concealed. He had also bolted it through the back of the wardrobe into the wall.

When he opened the gun case, both pistols were still there: his own and the one he'd taken off Jordan's body. Seeing them wasn't enough. He checked the action to make sure they were working properly and that nothing blocked the barrels. When closing the case again he noticed a scratch on the metal plate surrounding the keyhole. Someone, Krista presumably, had tried to pick the lock.

He hated the thought of her being in his room, searching through his things, maybe even around his body while he lay asleep and unaware.

'That lady needs watching.'

All the same, she had a lot to be anxious about. He should give her some sort of reassurance that all would be well. Getting her to use the Dictaphone would give her something to do, lift her mind a bit. Except that the Dictaphone was still in the car and the car was at the station.

Dressed, boots pulled on and his hair combed without looking in a mirror – he didn't want to see the wreck his face had become from tiredness – he trundled into the kitchen.

Krista had his tea out of the oven and waiting for him on the table. A brown stew with flowery potatoes and lashings of gravy. It was piping hot and still moist. Suddenly hungry, he ate fast. The shooting was now behind him. A couple of days with his feet up and he'd be absolutely fine.

Fat chance of that, he thought as he scraped the plate. A full stomach, a chair by the fire to warm his weary bones and a comfortable doze until bedtime seemed a good idea. Krista could watch as much television as she liked, the noise never disturbed him.

Except that he had to fetch the Dictaphone out of Louise's car and, more importantly, he needed to find Vera and have her home and safe.

The chair by the fire drew him. Maybe he'd just ring round and see where she'd got to. Have Johnny Scullion and his taxi bring her home rather than risk her walking.

He stood up from the table. Toby immediately jumped down from the chair and looked up at Barlow without even one tooth showing.

'Oh aye,'

The two-faced brute wanted his evening walk. Expected it. Anyway, it was only a short mile to the station. The walk would do him good, get oil back into creaking joints.

Krista was looking expectantly at him. There was less of that unhealthy burn in her cheeks. She looked not well, but better and needed some sort of reassurance, if only to stop her from striking out on her own.

'Krista, love, things are working out and I think I know what's been happening. Tomorrow, the weekend at the latest, and I'll be able to hand you over to a man who will protect you and see you safe.'

She looked at him blank-faced, then an uncertain smile flickered as if she understood the reassurance in his voice. 'Wee….kend,' she repeated.

'God willing.' He pulled on his jacket. 'And now I have to go out.' He made steering motions with his hands. 'Car.'

She nodded at that. 'Automobile.'

Toby was already waiting for him in the hallway. Barlow was reaching for his overcoat when he noticed the message from Vera taped to the glass door panel.

DAD
You are in for tonight
Don't even think of going out again
I'll be back at ten and you better
BE HERE

He checked his watch. It was nearing ten and Vera would be prompt to the hour. That amount of his blood was in her. God help the man who gets that one, he thought. He'd thought it often enough, sometimes with rancor, mostly with frustrated affection. Things were bad when a man ran scared of his own daughter.

He opened the door and shoved Toby out. 'Don't you dare stop for a piddle this side of the courthouse.'

Chapter 49

The night was bitter with a brisk wind that exploited every gap in his clothes. He buttoned the coat up to his neck and buried his hands in his pockets. The first hundred yards was difficult, every part of him wanted to limp or complain. After that he found his stride and walked slowly while he thought things through, starting with recasting the list in his head.

THE GOOD: Krista Riekstinš
Sir Anthony Chard

THE BAD: The gunman / Leon Weir
Major Gronville
The Running Man
Nurse Jordan (decd)

The "UNKNOWN" changed to
INVOLVED: Krista Riekstinš
Daniel T Abernathy
Malcolm Knype
The package

Mrs. Weir he left off the list. All the woman wanted was a bit of comfort and enough money to put food on the table. He added Malcolm Knype's name he because he had started the current spate of problems. The package as well because somehow that missing package was the key to everything. Find it and things would fall into place.

He was nearing the courthouse and had reached McCann's, the solicitors, offices. He let Toby off the lead rather than be bothered having to stop at every tree.

The package and Malcolm Knype definitely went together. Who else then? Sir Anthony and Gronville were looking for it, and for two very different groups of Civil Servants. Leon? One thing he was sure of. Leon's only loyalty was to himself.

Toby snarled, heckles raised. Barlow sensed the footstep behind him and half turned, instinctively bringing an arm up to protect himself. The arm partly blocked the blow but the cosh still caught the side of his head. He staggered back against a tree, fighting to retain consciousness. He was aware of men and a car showing only sidelights and a booted foot kicking Toby away. A sideswipe with the cosh hit him on the face, and then nothing.

Chapter 50

Barlow didn't mind the pain in his head, even though it hurt more than his ribs. Pain meant that he was still alive. Nor did he mind the vomit that spewed in waves out of his system. It wasn't his car that he was in. At least he hoped it wasn't.

It had to be a car. There was an engine noise, and the floor shook and he had the impression of other vehicles passing. He was uncomfortable, lying doubled over a drive shaft, his hands jammed behind his back.

One eye remained stubbornly shut, with something like a brick attached to that side of his face. The other eye, the one that worked, ground into the floor and watered like blazes from the dirt caught in his eyelashes.

He tried to bring an arm around. It moved an inch then stopped. He tried again and heard a clink of metal. They had handcuffed him.

Now he had no hope. With his arms free, he could strangle the driver or open the back door and throw himself out of the moving car.

'He's conscious,' said an English voice.

Thank God it was him they'd caught. They could have been waiting for Vera. The thought of her in Leon's power made him sick again. Somehow it helped the pain in his head, allowed him to ignore the worst of it.

Only forty-eight and he was going to die. Not easily either in the hands of Leon. His heart hammered and he whispered a prayer for deliverance.

The sick felt cold against his face and threatened to get up his nose. Turning his head away was like taking a blow from a swinging sledgehammer.

Leon's voice said, 'Do you want me to hit him again?'

'There's a big enough mess in there without you adding brain splatter.'

With that English voice he had to be Running Man.

Barlow decided it best to stay still. There had to be some way he could get out of this mess, if only he could think of it. Meantime best to lie doggo and pretend to be unconscious. That way they'd have to drag him out of the car, bringing them close. If a good head-butt didn't put them down he'd take to his heels. Running

Rather than move and let them know he was conscious, Barlow forced himself to stay still and tried to ignore the pain and cramps scything through his body. Running Man didn't speak again and Leon was the silent sort. When they hit a particularly bad bump, Barlow's body rose up and crashed down again. He couldn't hold back a groan.

He sensed they were going slower. 'Watch for the turn,' said Leon. Soon afterwards the car turned sharp right.

There were more bumps and a lot of lurching. He heard Running Man change down gear and the engine noise quieten as he made his way across a rough surface.

The rattling of his body up, down and around seemed to go on forever. They had to be off the tarmac road and on a cart track. That gave Barlow some hope. Get a couple of hedges between him and them and they'd never find him in the dark.

Something scraped along one side of the car, then the other. The scraping sound became continuous. They were in bushes, he reckoned. A couple of steps through them and he'd be out of sight. Even if the men risked using their guns, they'd never get a clear shot.

The car stopped moving, the engine died. *Died.* He wished he hadn't thought of that expression. The men sat silent for a moment. Nearby he could hear water splashing over stones. They were at a river. They'd found Tommy in the river.

Fear knocked his breathing out of control. They had to hear it, know he was conscious.

The car edged left and right on its springs as the men got out of the car. It was almost a pleasure when they closed the doors again, cutting off a biting wind. Then they opened a back door; not the one at his head, the one his feet pressed against. They looped something around his feet before they dragged him out of the car backwards. First his chin then his face scraped over the bottom of the door frame. He slammed into the ground and fresh burst of pain couldn't overcome the realization. They didn't intend to get him onto his feet. That meant…

Panic made him try to turn, to kick, but the loop around his feet held them together. He screamed in pain when one man forced his legs up over his back, making his body concave. The other man looped more and more bindings around him. He could tell the bindings were light and thin by the speed they looped and pulled. It had to be fishing line.

They intended to kill him the same way as Thomas Weir. Hog-tie and then drown him with a stone tied to his chest.

He tried to lash out again with his feet, but the looping and tying had already reached above his knees and the kick had no power. Whoever held him, raised his legs higher until only his head and shoulders touched the ground.

He screamed again and kept screaming. There could be houses nearby, someone might hear him and come to investigate.

A swinging boot buried itself in his stomach and the screams ended in a gurgle. They dragged him over rough ground to the edge of the river. He sobbed with pain and couldn't stop himself.

Running Man hunkered down and fiddled around his hands.

'What are you doing?' asked Leon.

'They'd look suspicious. How many poachers do you know have handcuffs?'

Leon didn't reply. Barlow felt his arms jerk as they unlocked the handcuffs and pulled them off. The men flipped him onto his back. Hands that had become numb hurt again under the crush of his own weight.

A heavy stone landed on his chest. Running Man twisted it here and there to get the uneven surface to balance. Right on his cracked ribs seemed the ideal spot. He gasped in relief when Running Man removed the stone and dropped it close enough to his head to make him jerk.

'Now the good bit,' said Leon.

'What good bit?' asked Running Man.

'Didn't the Major say he'd pay me extra if I made the bastard suffer before we rolled him in?'

Running Man said, 'We're talking about a good copper here. A man only doing his job.'

Leon's boot gave Barlow's ribs an experimental tap. 'We've got our orders.'

‘Orders are orders, but the kicking is personal to the Major.’

Barlow didn’t wait for a decision. He contorted shoulders, hips and anything else he could get to move. He rolled down the bank and into the river.

Chapter 51

The water was bitterly cold and his body kept trying to float upside down. Barlow struggled to stay at least on his side. The men skidded down to the water's edge and tried to haul him back. A backwash held him clear of the bank as the current carried him away.

Someone hurled the big stone. It splashed into the water beside his face. The instinctive jerk away from the splash rolled him underwater again. He struggled and contorted to get back onto the surface. It took longer the second time because his clothes now dragged heavy with water. At best, with straining, he could keep his mouth and nose out of the water. The dark shapes of the men followed along the bank, keeping an eye on him.

The men reached a fence barring their progress. One stopped and crouched and he heard Running Man snap, 'Don't shoot, someone might to hear.'

At first he'd found the cold water a relief as it absorbed the heat from his damaged body. Now the cold was different. It made his muscles heavier and harder to get them to do anything. In spite of the numbing cold they burned from effort. They could only take so much and then…

Somehow, with all the twisting and straining his hands had moved from their shackled position to his sides. He had a chance if he could get them around to his front.

He tensed his arm muscles and tried to force his hands around. Immediately his head went underwater and stayed there until shortness of breath forced him to give up straining and he fought his way back to the surface. But the hands had moved a bit. Not from all his straining, he realized, but because it was impossible to properly secure a few loops over a heavy overcoat and a sports jacket. There was slack there if he could exploit it.

The saturated overcoat and jacket weighed more than an army kitbag filled with stones for a route march. He struggled against their sodden weight and fought to remain on the surface while he scoured his wrists back and forth across his stomach. Fingers touched fingers, then knuckle to knuckle. Finally his wrists came together, his fingers stretching up outside the mesh of fishing line.

He was nearing the end of his strength. More and more the river covered his mouth and bubbled around his nose.

He struggled to stay on the surface while he worked to get his arms free. Increasingly he had to stop and concentrate on merely staying afloat. An overhanging branch scraped his face. He grabbed at it with his fingers and caught only leaves. For one moment they held. He tried to slide a hand up to grip the twig stem, but the leaves gave way, and again the current swept him on.

Something smashed into the back of his head.

It had to be the men. They'd followed him and were throwing stones to knock him out.

The next stone hit the same part of his head. So did the third and the fourth. And something else. He wasn't floating with the current. It was pulling him sideways, threatening to turn him upside down. He struggled against the thrust of the water. A stone scraped along his shoulder, followed almost immediately by a blow to his ankle.

He scrabbled with his fingers and found stone. Good solid stone with no more than an inch of water running over it. He was at the weir, the weir where they had found Tommy. He was drowning in three feet of water.

He gripped the stone hard and twisted his body until his bound feet touched bottom and he could rest against the weir.

Much as he wanted to stay and recover his breath, he didn't dare stop. At least he thought that stopping was what he shouldn't do. The chill of the water had seeped into his brain making any sort of logical thought difficult. He told his brain to order his fingers to move to the next stone. The fingers did as they were told and he pulled his body after them. Reach, pull, reach, pull, and all of a sudden the next stone was mud. Sticky, wonderful mud. He had reached the riverbank.

He knew the slope, had been there only a few days before. A mere nothing, a couple of steps up. His fingers clawed loose mud, his toes pushed until finally his chin dug into grass and he was all but free of the water.

Even then he didn't dare stop. Not with half the river caught up in his clothes and a bitter wind swirling snowflakes around him.

There wasn't a chance of being able to hop to the nearest farm for help. Maybe if he strained he could wiggle his way out of the fishing line.

He stretched his body and compressed it then stretched again. The overcoat material proved stubbornly un-pliable.

Somewhere nearby a car was heading up a laneway towards the river. It had to be Running Man and Leon searching the riverbanks for his body. The sound of the car engine carried in the silence of the night. Its distant lights let him make out the vague shapes of looming trees and bushes. He was running out of time.

He strained harder, until the fishing line bit into his hands and arms and they started to go numb from lack of blood. The car was now heading back down the laneway. The next one they tried had to lead straight to the weir and to him.

He banged his head against the ground in frustration at his stupidity and immediately regretted it. Hitting the stone in the weir had left a large bruise back there.

He had a penknife, if he could reach it. It only meant slipping a hand inside his trouser pocket. After all the straining and hauling it didn't seem a big ask.

He shoved his hands under the fishing line until he was able to pack the coat flaps around his hips and out of the way.

Getting his hand down that final inch or two into his pocket had him sucking air. At last he had the penknife gripped between his middle fingers and pulled it out. He struggled to open the blade. His breath came hard with excitement that he might live, could live. Will live, he told himself. Will live.

The blade opened. He sought and sliced every bit of fishing line he could feel. His arms came free, then his chest, finally his feet.

That car was definitely them. They'd been in at least one wrong field but they'd got it right this time.

He stumbled to his feet and staggered off into the darkness. With a bit of luck they'd think he'd gone over the weir.

Within minutes there was a light behind him, sweeping the ground, looking for signs of his passing. The light paused for a few moments, aimed at the ground. They'd found the fishing line. He had to go faster. If he didn't, they'd soon catch up with him. If he did, they'd hear him crash through bushes and be on him in seconds.

He heard footsteps sucking mud. One of the men had got ahead of him.

He stopped and listened. The man behind him was using a torch and he could roughly pinpoint his position. The man in front had no light. Both of them were coming his way, leaving him cut off. He backed against a tree and held his arms up to conceal any reflected glow off his face while he figured out which way to run.

He heard a voice say something. The voice was very close. He couldn't make out the words but a white shape shimmered before his eyes. Then a brute of a head pinned him against the tree.

FRIDAY

Blank Page

Chapter 52

The head withdrew from Barlow's chest and then smacked into him again. The blow hard enough to flex his cracked ribs. His body contorted with pain. Something slobbery wet, with the texture of a soft scrubbing brush, scoured his cheeks.

He finally made out the shape of his attacker as something more-or-less his height but several times his weight. It was Wee Willie.

The bull snuggled his head into Barlow's shoulder and *grunted. The stupid brute was lost and glad to see him.*

With his back hard against the tree Barlow could only stand and hope Wee Willie would get over his joy and back off a few inches. The last time they met, the bull wanted to gut him, now he wanted to be his friend.

Away to his left, the sound of the searching men forcing their way through the undergrowth increased. They were coming faster. They'd heard Wee Willie lumbering through the bushes and had mistaken that for him.

The light from the torches got brighter. Barlow could now see the blaze of white in Wee Willie's eyes and the curved horns that touched his overcoat.

At long last, Wee Willie backed off, allowing him to slide away from the tree. It was too late to run, even if he could force his weary legs into any sort of speed. There was a stand of bushes nearby. He decided to crawl in and hide. Not that it would do any good. The first sweep of a torch in his direction and they'd see him.

On hands and knees, he crept over to the bushes and crawled in as deep as he could go. Covered his face with the collar of his overcoat and closed his eyes. He didn't want to see himself being killed.

The torchlights of the approaching men got brighter, then darkened. Maybe they'd given up and gone away. Barlow looked and found himself eye to eye with Wee Willie, who snorted in his face as if saying, 'Found you.'

Barlow wished he had the nerve to thump the stupid brute on

the nose. 'Clear off,' he hissed.

Then the men were in the clearing, their torches sweeping in his direction. Wee Willie spun on his heels and went after nicer friends with their own lights.

'A bull,' said Leon. Being a countryman and used to cattle, he didn't panic.

Running Man had to be a townie. He shouted, 'Run,' and took off, haring back the way they had come.

Leon went with him and after Leon went Wee Willie, snorting indignantly at them for running away with his nightlight.

Barlow thought he should stay under the bushes for a few minutes until he was sure the men didn't return to resume their search. Anyway it was nice to lie there, partly sheltered from the biting wind, and give his tired muscles time to recover. Much of the pain eased out of his muscles, the cold leached away.

I must not sleep, he told himself. Mustn't…

Chapter 53

Barlow couldn't remember buying a rocking chair for home. All the same it was relaxing, his body swinging to and fro, and he didn't even have to do it himself. The next swing was hard, the one after that hurt.

He got his eyes open, and with that came all the accumulated pains of the night. Wee Willie was back, nudging at him to get up and be his friend.

Crawling out from under the bushes he found hard going. Standing impossible until he thought to grab Wee Willie's horns and use them to leaver himself upright. Hypothermia was already in his bones. If he stayed in his wet clothes he'd freeze to death and if he took them off he'd probably die quicker.

He thought he knew where he was, at least he had a good idea of what way to head. He reckoned he'd about half an hour's walking left in him, and then he'd be done. Out of luck and energy.

There had to be farmhouses along the river but thick stands of bushes and boundary hedges would have him beaten. Right then he wouldn't bet on getting his leg over a matchstick. He needed a farm gate and a tarmac road running downhill.

Wee Willie came with him, snorting at his heels like a well-trained dog. The bushes and trees quickly gave way to grassland. In the latent light he could see a hedge marking the boundary with the next field.

The land sloped up from the river. Each step was a conscious effort: lift foot, swing forward, put down; lift foot, swing forward, put down. Most of the half-hour had gone by the time he reached a hedge bordering a road of some sort and stumbled upon a small shed. The shed was unlocked, a length of string opened the latch. Something swung against the back of the door as he pushed it open. He searched in the total darkness with his hand and touched material. An old stockman's coat he guessed. No matter how dirty, it had to be drier than what he was wearing.

Sliding one foot before the other he moved deeper into the shed. Now that he was out of the wind the shed seemed almost warm.

Wee Willie's head and shoulders blocked the doorway making it almost airtight.

He knew he was still in trouble and had a long way to go before he was safe, but the hope for life felt good. He should spend the night in the shed and after that… After that was after that and would have to wait.

The floor was uncluttered, probably little more than dry clay underneath. About six foot in his toe hit an obstruction. It gave a dry crackle. He put a hand out and felt a firm but pliable wall. Hay, he guessed. An emergency supply for animals caught out on the hills in snow.

He reached up and grabbed at the highest bale. He sensed the whole wall of bales lean towards him and changed the grab to a pull and a wiggle. The bale came down and another one with it.

'I can see my obituary: suddenly by bale,' he told the bulk of Wee Willie. 'A man would have trouble living down that sort of thing.'

A third and fourth bale came easier. Out of breath from the effort, he sat on a bale while he used his penknife to slash at the baler twine securing the others.

The whole building shook and creaked as Wee Willie forced himself through the doorway.

Barlow slid past the bull, and closed and secured the door. It seemed to take forever to pull off the wet overcoat and jacket and pull on the stockman's coat. He kicked his boots off, lay down and used his feet to push the bull out of the way.

Wee Willie snorted in indignation and began to eat the hay that Barlow had pulled over himself for warmth.

'That's my bed, not your flaming supper,' Barlow told him.

Like trying to deal with Vera, he was wasting his breath.

He hoped she was safe.

Chapter 54

First light came far too soon for a Barlow reluctant to move. He was comfortable and warm. It was impossible not to be with a fifteen-hundredweight bull lying snuggled into him.

Sometime in the night he had wakened long enough to throw his coats over Wee Willie's back. Hay crackled as he reached out a hand to test the material. They were more or less dry thanks to the heat radiating off the bull.

The hay crackling had aroused Wee Willie. He snorted and lumbered to his feet, his whole body swaying dangerously over Barlow as he did so. Hooves stamped inches from him and the tail swiped across his face.

Barlow could only close his eyes and hope. He had visions of people finding him with a hoof jammed in his breast cavity. The shed creaked and groaned as Wee Willie squeezed himself around to snort in Barlow's face.

'Okay, okay, I'm getting up.'

What muscle didn't hurt belonged to someone else. Hay slid off him as he rolled onto his side. The real effort came in keeping that roll going while he heaved himself onto his hands and knees. He stopped there for a few moments to assess the damage. Wee Willie's constant nudging did not help.

'You're brave now there's a bit of daylight around,' he said and clawed up the stack of hay bales to get himself onto his feet. He stuck his feet into his boots and swapped the stockman's coat for his own clothes. Wee Willie was already head butting the door to get out.

He squeezed up the side of the bull and shoved hard at him to get him to move back and over. Wee Willie snorted and stamped a foot.

Barlow shoved harder. 'Shift over you brute and let me at the door.'

Wee Willie finally went back a couple of steps. Barlow found himself between a closed door and an annoyed bull whose head was down, the horns very prominent.

He didn't dare show the fear choking his throat. 'Don't come the old soldier with me.'

He got the door opened and found himself pinned against the side of the shed as the bull lumbered out into the field.

Outside was a mixture of grey and dark shadows. A low mist hung over the field. Wee Willie bellowed and tore up clods of earth with his hooves. Dawn had brought back his courage. He might have been glad to follow Barlow through the dark but now he wanted to reassert his authority and that could mean trouble.

Barlow slipped out of the shed and down its side. The gate onto the county road was at the other end of field, but farmers never walked where they could take a shortcut. He spotted the stile even as Wee Willie's bellows changed into a roar of rage. Barlow's run was achingly slow, nothing had warmed up yet and every muscle had a complaint. Behind him, the pound of hooves got faster, louder.

The stile was a crude affair, two planks of wood, hardly eighteen inches long, nailed to a couple of paling posts. Barlow put his hand on one of the paling posts and vaulted for his life. He hit the ground hard and, off balance, stumbled into the path of an oncoming car.

The car screeched to a halt. Instinctively he reached for his gun that wasn't there. He couldn't escape back into the field. Wee Willie was at the hedge, his shoulders going up and down as he considered jumping the hedge to continue the battle.

A head appeared out the driver's window. 'Sergeant Barlow, that was a daft place to go looking for anything but trouble.'

The hair was white, the accent local. Now he'd time to pull himself together, Barlow knew the man and the car. Old Mick Campbell from Roughan above Broughshane.

Wee Willie gave a hop that took his shoulders above the top of the hedge.

Without waiting to ask, Barlow jumped into the passenger seat of the car and slammed the door. 'You'll give me a lift.'

Mick gave a snort of laughter, put the car in gear and moved off. Pretty smartly, Barlow noted. No one wanted to tangle with an enraged bull.

They exchanged pleasantries about the weather, changeable they agreed, and stock prices. Never the same price one week to the next. Mick kept eyeing Barlow's dirt-stained clothes and the bruising on his face, the fact that he was on his own and had no means of transport. He had the countryman's manners not to ask questions.

'I'm heading into town,' Mick said.

'Maybe you'd drop me at the station.' Barlow said and answered the unasked questions with a casual shrug. 'It's been a bad start to the day and it's not going to get any better.'

'Aye, that wee girl's funeral. A pleasant wee lass to do business with.'

He had forgotten. Totally forgotten that today was Susan's funeral. He found tears in his eyes and remembered a fond memory he could tell. 'Geordie Dunlop says that Susan arresting him was the only time he felt like a gentleman.'

'The bugger took one of my bullocks.'

Barlow nodded noncommittally. Stealing cattle had been one of Geordie's schemes for making easy money. The prosecution failed to prove that Geordie was involved, but three of his grandsons were still in jail.

Which made him wonder what he was going to tell them at the station: kidnap, attempted murder, pursuit with intent to murder, aiding and abetting a crime. Conspiracy….

Leon and Running Man would have cast-iron alibis, the Establishment would see to that. With Running Man it was orders. Gronville had made it personal by ordering the kicking. And Leon? Leon had a certain reputation to uphold. Neither he nor Vera would be safe until Leon was out of the way.

Mick dropped Barlow on the Galgorm Road. Barlow walked around the side of the station. The back gate was open and no one around. He got into his car and drove home.

Chapter 55

Every light in the house was on. Vera lay asleep in Barlow's chair with Toby lying across her lap. She was fully dressed and obviously hadn't been to bed. Lines of dried tears marked her cheeks.

Toby's head came up. Instead of snarling, he woofed and jumped down to greet Barlow. Barlow patted the dog in thanks for trying to save his life. Toby licked his hand.

Vera flew into Barlow's arms. 'Dad, you're alive. Oh My God, I was so worried.'

'Of course I'm alive.'

'Where have you been? You've been out all night? And Toby came home on his own, and he's hurt.'

'He got a fair kicking, love.'

'Look at your face, dad, what happened?'

'I caught my foot on a tree root. The tree hit one side and the ground the other.'

She was crying again. For him. He shushed her tears and wiped her face dry with his thumb. The only person in the world who really cared about him, and she had spent the night sick with fear. He held her that bit closer while he finalized the story in his mind. If Vera believed him then no one else would doubt his word.

'It was that bull of Daniel T Abernathy. It escaped yesterday. Didn't I see it come down the road, heading into town just about closing time.'

'On no.'

'Well that bull is a bad one, it would go for anybody. So I turned it back or rather, to be honest, Toby did. That's when he got the dunt in the ribs.'

'Poor, brave Toby,' she said and bent down and brought the dog into her arms.

'He sure is,' he agreed, and didn't dare risk another pat. Things were getting back to normal between him and the dog. Toby was showing his teeth.

'I knew he was hurt, but I had to leave him. I couldn't risk that bull turning back again, not with the streets full of drunks.' He drew breath, this was where the real lying could unravel. 'I kept chivvying the bull on and on and it was miles before I got the brute tired enough to risk turning him into a field.

'By then I didn't know exactly where I was. There was a hut in the field, so I sat it out there until dawn. Mick Campbell from Roughan gave me a lift back into town.'

He stopped speaking, relieved that he'd managed to end with the truth.

'You could have been killed,' she said.

'Well I wasn't.'

'You alone with that bull?' She shuddered. 'I avoid the Fairhill like the plague when the cattle mart is on.' She pulled back from him. 'You smell like a cow and there's cow sh… manure in your hair.'

She put Toby down and pushed Barlow into his chair. Toby tried to jump up but missed his jump because of the damaged ribs. Barlow caught him by the hips and scooped him onto his knee.

'You sit there,' said Vera, 'I'll get you your breakfast and then you're going straight to bed.'

'I can't miss Susan's funeral.'

She knew that, she was going herself, but still argued. 'You look done in and you're supposed to be resting.'

He nodded as if agreeing with her. Instead, he was dealing with another problem. Cooking his breakfast would give her time to think out the weaknesses in his story unless...

'I've been thinking,' he said. 'You could drop me off at Susan's home and meet me again at St. Patrick's after the service.'

All thoughts of the bull and danger went straight out of her head. 'Me, drive? On my own?'

'Why not?'

Why not indeed? Louise had taught Vera to drive but he refused to let her out on her own in case something happened to Louise's car.

Vera floated off to the scullery, her mind full of throttles, gear-sticks and indicators.

Barlow watched her go, a grim smile pushed at the bruising on his face. No one must ever know that he held a personal grudge against Leon.

Chapter 56

The warmth of a good breakfast in his system: porridge followed by poached egg on toast, had Barlow nodding off at the table. Rather than give into his weariness he levered himself to his feet.

Vera appeared out of the scullery, dishcloth in hand. 'Where are you going?'

'To get something out of the car.'

He forced himself to walk without limping and made sure she heard the mutter. 'Worse than a nagging wife, that one.'

He fetched the Dictaphone out of the car and carried it into Krista's bedroom. He didn't put it past Gronville to come looking in the windows so she had to stay there until they drew the kitchen curtains at night. She looked comfortable and definitely better now that she had fought off the infection, but walking on those scabbed feet had to hurt.

Krista's eyes widened when he walked in.

'Either you're glad to see me or I look like hell,' he said and put the Dictaphone on the bed beside her. She took his hand and he knew she guessed better than the innocent Vera the dangers he'd faced during the night.

Plugging the Dictaphone in was something else. It meant crawling on his hands and knees while he changed plugs around, and the frame of the bed gave a good solid groan as he hauled himself back onto his feet.

His breathing came hard from the effort and Krista moved over to let him sit on the edge of the bed. Her nightdress gaped open and what he could see of her breasts was generous and firm. He dragged his eyes away.

Barlow had got into the habit of telling her things even though she spoke no English. If nothing else it clarified the worries for her in his mind. Right then, what to tell Krista was a problem. What to leave out wasn't.

'I had one heck of a night, love. No matter what I told Vera, I didn't spend it chasing a bull. Anyway, it's all over so far as you're concerned, so you can stop worrying.

‘Tomorrow morning, a man I trust implicitly will take you under his protection. In the meantime….’ He pointed to the Dictaphone. ‘I’m a policeman, and if I don’t get a statement off you, it’ll be more than my job’s worth.’

He showed her how the Dictaphone worked. ‘Press this to record, talk into this.’ His “yamyamyamyamyam” into the microphone made her laugh.

She picked it up quickly. In fact he’d a feeling that she’d used a similar machine before. All he knew was what he’d learned from Charles Denton, and that wasn’t much.

To be doubly safe that she understood what he needed her to do, he pretended to press “record” and spoke into the microphone. ‘Lithuania, and and and, England, and and and, Northern Ireland, and and and, Ballymena.’

She smiled and nodded, and took his hand and held the palm to her lips. She was wearing some of the expensive perfume that Louise had left in the bathroom. The same perfume he ached to keep forever on his pillow.

He pulled his hand free and got up abruptly. ‘Sorry. I’ve a lot on this morning.’

He left the room, feeling like a schoolboy made inarticulate by a first crush.

Chapter 57

A bath helped take the stiffness out of Barlow's muscles. He wrapped a towel around his waist and looked out his best uniform. He always kept it pristine, and his good boots only saw parades.

He dressed as quickly as he could in case Vera came in and saw the new bruising. The bruising stretched in patches from his ankles right into his hairline. Combinations first instead of the usual pants and vest, it was that sort of day outside. Uniform trousers followed by shirt and tie.

Vera gave his uniform a final brush-down. 'You'll do Susan proud.'

'Thanks.'

She wore a black skirt and jacket with a white blouse and a choker of cultured pearls. She also wore the silver laurel leaf awarded to recipients of the Queens Commendation for Brave Conduct. He was prouder of that than his own bar of medals: the War Medal, the Defence Medal and the Coronation Medal.

As promised, he let Vera drive. He'd driven straight in and parked with the nose facing the garage. Vera hung over the steering wheel, her face fixed in fearful concentration as she reversed into a narrow turn in front of the house before driving out.

Rather than go through the town he made Vera drive out the Ballymoney Road, turn left onto the Woodtown Road and across the main Cullybackey road with traffic bombing towards them from both directions. Halfway across she stalled the car and then selected the wrong gear so that the car shuddered its way to safety.

It's not that I'm terrified, Barlow told himself, but hogtied and floating down the river is beginning to look the easier option.

A turn down the Old Park Road brought them to Sourhill. From there it was a straight run to the Toome Road.

He couldn't believe the crowd of people gathered around the Day family home. Officers brought in from Antrim and Ballymoney were providing cover for the day so every policeman and policewoman from the station, plus visiting policemen from the Chief Constable down, waited outside the house. They were already forming ranks.

Captain Denton had volunteered one of his lorries to carry the wreaths. Denton himself drove it. Civilian onlookers blocked the pavements for a hundred yards in either direction.

Vera stopped to let Barlow out, stalling the traffic behind.

Immediately a policeman tapped her window. 'You can't stop here.'

Barlow stepped out of the car and put on his hat. It hurt pushing it down over the bruising, but today of all days he would have it on straight.

The policeman's eyes widened when he saw his face. 'Good Lord, Sarge.' Then he smirked. 'I heard a rumor that you'd gone head to head with a bull.'

Barlow gave the obligatory scowl back, but he was happy. Old Mick Campbell had spread the story of him jumping for his life from the irate Wee Willie, and a good story like that would lose nothing in the telling. He wondered if he could back it up by giving Daniel T an official caution for failing to keep a dangerous animal under proper control.

If the parade was falling-in, then the cortège was ready to move. An honor guard waited at the house to carry the coffin, and with them stood Sergeant Pierson.

Barlow ignored the stares and smirks of his own men and took a curved route well away from Harvey. Harvey would use the excuse of the bruising on his face to order him to drop out of the parade, but no way would Harvey let the Chief Constable or the Lord Lieutenant of the County see him chase after his Station Sergeant to give him that order.

The Honor Guard stepped back to let him pass, and he went toe-to-toe with Pierson. Pierson held a purple velvet cushion holding Susan's hat and Coronation Medal. Barlow took it off him.

Pierson tried to grab it back. 'Mr. Harvey told me to carry these.'

Barlow leaned into Pierson's face, so close he was tempted to bite off the tip of his nose. 'Susan hated you nearly as much as she hated Harvey, so fall-out.'

Before he let Pierson go he straightened his jacket buttons so that their harp design sat upright instead of at an angle, picked off fluff and ran a finger inside the collar to make it sit square.

Pierson moved off at what Barlow could only describe as a slinking march. A stare at the Honor Guard stilled any tendency to smile.

The prayers by the Church of Ireland curate finished, the Honor Guard filed into the house to lift the coffin. Barlow stayed outside feeling that right then, he couldn't cope with the charged emotions of the family. Gillespie was inside, he could see him and his crutches through the sitting room window. He trusted him to spread the RUC standard on the coffin and secure the family wreath.

Willing hands manhandled the coffin through the narrow front door and onto the Honor Guard's shoulders. Barlow followed them down the road for a short spell before the coffin was loaded into the hearse and the Honor Guard fell out. First came the hearse with Susan's coffin, then him, then McGinn's quiet, 'Left, left, left,' to keep the parade in step.

Barlow wanted to open the coffin lid and have Susan sit up with a cheery, 'Surprise.' He swallowed hard. And kept swallowing as the cortège wound its way down the Antrim Road and over the bridge. Bridge Street and its ever-increasing slope nearly drained the last of the energy out of his legs. The thought of the years stolen from Susan kept him going, so did the lines of people standing silently as they passed. The only sounds: the burble of the hearse engine, McGinn calling the step and the solid tramp of his men as they paid final honors to one of their own.

At the top of Bridge Street, they swung round into Castle Street. He breathed a prayer of thanks that his legs didn't have to cope with Church Street as well, and there was Canon Craig waiting at the church door to receive Susan.

At the church door, the Honor Party again hoisted the coffin to carry it into the church.

Barlow followed the cortège up the central isle. People stood in respect. Barlow stared straight ahead but used the side of his eye to watch out for Gronville. He spotted him about two-thirds of the way up the aisle, standing beside Sir Anthony. Gronville's face drained color when he recognized Barlow and his lips moved. He had to be saying something like, 'It can't be, he's dead,' and he must have said some of it out loud because for a moment Sir Anthony's attention wavered from the coffin.

The Honor Party laid Susan down in front of the altar. After that, their final duty done, they retreated to their seats in the side-isle. The burial itself would be a family-only affair, no accompanying parade, no volley of shots fired over the grave.

Barlow smoothed an invisible crease in the RUC standard near the bottom of the coffin. Susan had tickly toes. She couldn't bear a hand anywhere near them, and he wanted that final contact. He laid the cushion with the hat and the medal on the coffin, and placed it as close to Susan's heart as he could judge.

Chapter 58

The skies were heavy with cloud, bringing darkness early, before Barlow returned home. He had followed the cortège to the cemetery, to the very place from where Leon had fired the careless shot that killed Susan. He stayed in the background during the internment but afterwards the Day family had sought him out and insisted that he come to the funeral breakfast.

Sir Anthony had attended the internment as well. On his own, Barlow noted. No Gronville, no senior RUC officers. They were too busy filling their faces at the City Arms Hotel. The one day when Harvey wouldn't be worrying about budget overspends.

The lights in the house were on, the blinds drawn in the kitchen and the television loud enough to drown out any conversation between Vera and Krista. Toby snarled, he shoved the dog off the chair and sat down. The dog was still sore from the kicking and needed several tries before he succeeded in getting back onto the chair. Barlow didn't help him. 'That'll teach you to snarl at me.' He shifted over and made room for the dog beside him.

Vera came out of the scullery. 'Dad, you're grey with tiredness. Maybe we shouldn't go out tonight. I'm sure Sir Anthony and Lady Chard would understand.'

She looked disappointed. It was a big thing to boast about to her friends at work - her attending one of the big functions of the blue-rinse season.

'A cup of tea and a half-hour kip and I'll be fine,' he said. He stopped her before she could disappear into the scullery again. 'Be a love, bring the Dictaphone from Krista's room.'

Krista recognized her name and looked his way.

'There's a wee job I want you to do,' he said.

Vera fetched the Dictaphone, sighed wearily when he asked her to plug it in – sometimes she sounded more like him than he did – and swept back into the scullery.

Her voice carried back. 'Now if you don't mind, I've Krista's tea to prepare, such as it is.'

And it was a good thing it was only Krista's tea, he realized.

The house was all but out of food. It was surprising how much extra a third person ate, and someone could easily follow Vera to see exactly how much of everything she was putting in her bag.

He wound back the tape in the machine and listened to Krista tell what had happened to her. At least he assumed that's what it was because he couldn't understand one word. However, he did hear words like: Zeebrugge, London and Belfast. All oddly pronounced but recognizable.

He changed the tapes in the machine, put the used tape in his breast pocket and placed the machine on Krista's lap. He imitated someone typing rapidly, saying "ding" and pretending to return the carriage. 'Lithuanian, Ireland? No no no.' He kept on pretend typing as he searched his memory for the word Geordie had used. 'Ruski. Ruski?' He threw his hands out in a big query gesture and smiled.

'Ruski,' she said, and nodded. 'Ruski.'

Soon he would have to go and get out of his good uniform and put his gun away and sort out things for the night. He settled his head against the back of the chair, encouraged the dog to stretch across his legs and listened to Krista repeat her story in Russian. At least he assumed it was Russian and she told it in a sweeter, mellower tone than the one she used when speaking Lithuanian.

Her voice was ever soft, gentle and low.

He wondered where he had read that. Probably in one of Vera's schoolbooks he decided as his eyes closed. He drifted away to the cadence of her words.

Chapter 59

Sir Anthony and Lady Chard lived in what locals called the "Gold Coast" area of Ballymena. Houses were either semi-detached or detached, mostly detached, with generous front gardens and even larger back gardens. One at least with an overgrown tennis court that lay unseen and forgotten about. The Chards' house was detached, and while double-fronted like the rest seemed somehow, more modern: airy and light, when compared to the conventional neighbors.

At one minute to eight, the house held only the Chards, the hired in catering staff and two guests. At eight o'clock groups of guests hustled towards the front door. Barlow was the first to arrive, with the shoulder of a keyed up Vera bumping his for a confidence that he didn't feel. This was the first time he'd been to a black-tie event without Louise for support.

The party had cost him the price of a turquoise green silk dress out of McKillens, who knew how to charge, and Vera another half a fortune at the hairdressers. For once he didn't have to chivvy her along. She was hovering, car keys in hand long before he was ready. For that he was grateful, because this party was army style: arrive at eight sharp, leave at ten-thirty. No way would it drift on until the small hours.

A steward opened the door. Barlow gave their names and the steward said, 'Mr. Barlow and Miss Vera Barlow.'

He said it loud enough for their hosts to hear. Barlow handed him the traditional gifts brought to a private party: a bottle of wine and a box of chocolates. Louise had sourced them in Belfast soon after the invitation has arrived. It felt like giving away part of her.

A man came out of the sitting room, glass in hand. Harvey, his face flushed from an afternoon of drinking with the Chief Constable and the Lord Lieutenant.

'Ah, Barlow, you realize that you and your daughter are only here on sufferance, now your lady friend has gone.'

Vera's flushed excitement drained away. She looked ready to cry.

Lady Chard appeared at the top of the stairs. Mrs. Harvey stood behind her. Harvey had spoken loud enough for them both to hear.

'John,' Lady Chard exclaimed. 'And this must be Vera.' She came rushing down the stairs and gave her a kiss. 'My dear, I've been at your father time and time again to bring you for afternoon tea sometime.'

Harvey was drinking out of an empty glass to hide his shock. The steward stood at easy attention, hearing nothing, seeing nothing, like any good steward.

Lady Chard guided Vera upstairs. 'Come with me and I'll show you where to leave your stole. And I must apologize for the late invitation, we feel quite embarrassed about it. I wanted to invite you straight off, but Anthony said that no young lady wants to spend her Friday nights with a lot of old fogies.'

They disappeared out of sight and out of hearing. Barlow checked: Mrs. Harvey remained at the top of the stairs. Sir Anthony hadn't yet appeared. The steward still stood at easy attention, hearing nothing and seeing nothing.

Barlow grabbed Harvey by the lapels, and slammed him against a wall. A framed university diploma swung dangerously on its hook.

He ground his knuckles into Harvey's throat. 'Listen you little shit.'

Harvey clawed at his hands. 'Barlow, this will cost you your career. Assaulting your superior officer.'

Barlow gave Harvey a couple more bashes against the wall. 'Do you remember that formal complaint you made about me and young William?'

'I did no such thing.'

'Buff folder, typed sheet already signed by you?'

'Never. You're imagining things.' Harvey started to look pleased with himself. 'Search my office if you like.'

Harvey had shredded the file; he'd expected that.

Barlow smiled sweetly; it came easily. 'The thing is, Harvey, typists make a carbon copy of everything, but the carbon copy doesn't exist either. At least not in the girls' office.'

He let go of Harvey's lapels and smoothed them flat. 'You ever do anything like that again to my daughter, and a certain report that doesn't exist will be pinned to the notice board – in Headquarters.'

Harvey stumbled off. The steward still saw nothing as Barlow straightened the university diploma. Mrs. Harvey came downstairs, air-kissed him in greeting and linked arms as they walked into the sitting room. She looked like she was enjoying the night. He thought he would as well.

Chapter 60

Sir Anthony and Lady Chard always threw a good party. Their guests were the sort of people Barlow respected. Businessmen, some of whom, like Geordie, needed watching now and then. As for the ladies? They tended to be more impressed with their husbands' standing in the community than the husbands themselves.

Thanks to Louise, Barlow had come to know most of them socially. He felt easy in their company, and he took a lot of stick about the bruising on his face.

'I was chasing an old cow,' he said for the umpteenth time, making little of Wee Willie and his testosterone.

One of twin sisters, who supported each other's halting step with linked arms, fluttered her eyelashes at him. 'John, dear, I'm an old cow and I'd be easier caught.'

The other twin said, 'I wouldn't run.'

That joke travelled the room. So did Barlow's eyes, forever watching three people: Vera, to make sure she had got over Harvey's insulting greeting. She had or she appeared to have. Mrs. Harvey hardly left her side, and Harvey could hardly object to that. Not when the other ladies in the group were Clarissa Denton and her friends.

Barlow kept an eye on Gronville in the mirror over the high marble fireplace, or in the glass protecting paintings hung around the room. In the current year, fashion dictated a much thinner jacket lapel for a man's dress suit. Gronville, like many of the men, wore a last year's jacket. Somehow, in Gronville's case, it came over as an implied insult for a man of his breeding and social status being obliged to attend a bucolic evening. Harvey spent much of the time talking to Gronville. Barlow was sure his ears should be burning.

Sir Anthony had given the briefest nod, acknowledging that Barlow wanted a quiet word at some time. Eventually they managed to drift, by the way, casually together while picking over the extras at the buffet table.

'Sir Anthony,' Barlow used the "Sir" deliberately to indicate that this was business.

'Yes, Mr. Barlow.'

'Charles Denton always brings a bottle of something special to a party.'

'This evening he presented us with a rather nice brandy. Quite hard to come by, in fact.'

Barlow hesitated. This was a big ask and he certainly didn't want to answer any questions as to why. 'Perhaps after the party, a few of us could remain behind to sample that brandy? Say, you, me, Charles Denton and Major Gronville?'

Sir Anthony speared one of the last remaining cocktail sausages. 'Possibly.' He appeared to remain undecided between a rice salad and a buttered roll. 'May one ask why?'

'A half an hour of your time, an hour at most,' said Barlow, apparently not hearing the question.

'And a brandy is best experienced when shared with friends,' said Sir Anthony in a normal voice, as if agreeing with something Barlow had said.

Finished selecting food they drifted apart. Barlow ate as he went looking for Vera. Cold rice with sweetcorn and flakes of something red through it was surprisingly tasty. They should try that at home sometime.

Vera was looking for him as well. 'Dad, Clarissa is talking about a few of us going out to her place afterwards. Would it be all right? I mean, the way things are at home?'

She meant Krista.

'A party after a party?' he said as if doubtful about the whole thing, and rubbed his chin as if thinking things over. 'You're a big girl now and you could be in worse company.'

'Thanks, Dad.'

'I still haven't said yes.'

She stood on tiptoe and kissed him. 'Clarissa will leave me home tomorrow, about lunchtime.'

He could only smile as she bounced off. His little girl at ease with the nobs of the town.

He joined a group of men. They asked him, what were the chances of the local Rugby team picking up a few trophies during the season?

'Not a hope,' he said to get an argument going.

Chapter 61

At ten-thirty sharp people thanked their host and hostess for a wonderful evening and went looking for their coats and wraps. Barlow stayed on in the sitting room, apparently finishing his drink. He'd spent most of the night topping up his gin and tonic with more tonic.

There's not a chance of me catching malaria this side of Christmas, he told himself, trying to keep his mind frivolous. No way did he dare let Gronville sense that this was "business".

The last guests went out the front door. Harvey had delayed, hoping for an invitation to stay on with Charles Denton and his new friend, Gronville. The catering staff left at the same time, by the back door, and he heard Lady Chard say, 'Goodnight, dear, don't be late,' and the creak of the stairs as she went to bed.

Sir Anthony pushed the door open and came into the sitting room. He was carrying the brandy bottle and three glasses. Behind him came Charles Denton and Gronville.

'Oh, Barlow,' said Sir Anthony, as if surprised. He hesitated a moment before asking, making it diplomatically obvious that he expected an equally diplomatic refusal. 'You will join us?'

'That's very kind of you, Andy,'

Charles shuddered at that gaff. Sir Anthony invited everyone to sit down. Charles was quick to say. 'I'll fetch another glass.'

Barlow put down his drink. 'And I could do with a slash.'

He went to the downstairs bathroom, managing a stumble on the way. If Gronville thought him a drunken boor, all the better.

Charles was waiting for him in the corridor when he came back carrying his overcoat. 'What are you up to? I doubt if the wife calls him Andy.'

Barlow slipped him a small package. 'Put that in Gronville's drink.'

Charles eyed the package. 'What's in it?'

'Ground-up sleeping tablets I got at the hospital.'

'John?'

'Don't ask, Charlie, and you'll be told no lies.'

Charles slipped the package into his pocket. 'Hanged separately, or hanged together, but hang we will.'

He pushed on into the sitting room ahead of Barlow.

Barlow paused for a moment. *Hanged separately, or hanged together, but hang we will.* He'd forgotten that saying of theirs, hadn't thought about it in years. It started in primary school and carried on into their teens, and always before a bit of devilment.

He draped his overcoat over the bannisters and went into the sitting room. Gronville was sitting on the settee, not drunk but well on in that direction. Sir Anthony and Charles were using the mini-grand piano as a bar counter, with Charles insisting that Sir Anthony go and sit down while he did barman. 'Let the professional at it,' he was saying.

Sir Anthony took a seat, without even a raised eyebrow in Barlow's direction. With the drinks poured, Charles held one up to the light and expounded on the beauty of its bouquet, its provenance, the year the grapes were harvested, how it was stored...

Gronville ostentatiously yawned and closed his eyes. With Gronville's eyes closed, Charles quickly gave his drink a stir with a swizzle stick, to make sure no residue of the drug remained at the bottom of the glass, and passed them around.

The other men started with an appreciative sip. Barlow let them go first, as if unsure how to deal with a quality drink. He thought about taking a good swig, but decided not to over-egg the boorishness.

He sat in a corner seat, as if he knew he shouldn't really be there, and appreciated the heat of the silky liquid. He didn't understand a quarter of Sir Anthony and Charles' discussion on the relative merits of various brandies. Even if it cost a small fortune he intended to buy a bottle of tonight's offering. It was the sort of drink a man needed after a long week.

Gronville joined in the discussion at the start, but slowly his eyes closed and his head nodded onto his chest. The other men pretended not to notice when Gronville lifted his head again, and shook it and angled forward as if keen not to miss a word. That happened twice. The third time the head stayed down and Gronville breathed deeply through his mouth.

Barlow gave him five minutes to be sure he was in a deep sleep and another couple of minutes to get a word in edgeways. 'Sir Anthony, you've a lot of lovely pictures all over the house. You must always be buying new ones.'

'Indeed Sergeant,' said Sir Anthony, quick to take the hint. 'Sam McLarnon, of course, his watercolors.' He pointed at an oil painting of two fishermen working nets. In the background was Garron Point. 'That's a McAuley, an artist I came across recently in the glens.'

Barlow caught his eye and jerked his head towards the door.

Sir Anthony stood up. 'Charles, I know you're interested in paintings. I'd appreciate your opinion on one I have in the study.'

Barlow stood with the two men but didn't follow them as they left the room. He pulled a chamois wrapped magazine for a Glock pistol from his pocket, the pistol he had taken from the body of Jordan, and leaned over Gronville. He had to control his breathing from fear, and the bend-over hurt his ribs.

Gronville's hand was balancing his brandy schooner on the arm of the settee. Moving carefully, Barlow slipped the glass clear and swapped if for the magazine. He took particular care that his own hand didn't touch the metal.

Disturbed, Gronville's eyes flickered open. Barlow froze, stayed absolutely still rather than let him register movement. Gronville's mouth opened and closed as if trying to say something, then his eyes drooped again.

Barlow gripped the edge of the magazine and tried to pull it clear, but Gronville's hand had locked around it.

He kept a gentle pull on the magazine. Gronville's grip remained equally firm. Now his back hurt and the tendons in his legs reignited the burn of overstrain that still simmered their length.

Finally and at long last the magazine came free. That should have been it, but it wasn't enough, not with Gronville registering him standing so close. Gronville's jacket lay open and Barlow could see the bulge of his wallet in the inner pocket. Using only a finger and thumb, he slipped the wallet out. It was thin, not like his old one, which always bulged with little reminders to himself. He could ask Vera to get him a new one for Christmas. She always said he was impossible to buy for.

The wallet held a few pound notes and a Warrant Card. At least the name on it said "Major Edward Montmercy Gronville". Barlow could never be sure to whom he was really talking to when it came to Intelligence Officers.

He put the wallet back, slipped his hands into the side pockets of the jackets, and found nothing other than Gronville's invitation to the party, car keys, cigarettes and a Ronson lighter. From the tightness of the material against the thigh, he could see that one trouser pocket was empty. He tapped the other pocket and felt the give of material. *A handkerchief.*

He put everything back in a way that Gronville would know they had been disturbed.

It also gave him an explanation if the other two men insisted on knowing what he was up to.

Barlow put his own glass in Gronville's hand and left the room carrying the magazine and the drugged drink. Again, being careful not to touch the metal himself, he put the magazine in a brown paper bag and slipped it into a pocket of his overcoat. He took the glass down to the kitchen and rinsed it thoroughly under the tap, set it on the draining board and left the house without speaking to the other men.

FRIDAY NIGHT

Blank Page

Chapter 62

The night was cold to freezing and Barlow's clothes were sticky with sweat from the heat in Sir Anthony's house. In spite of the overcoat, he shivered in the car while the heater took forever to work.

With Vera away, he could always go home and change but then a neighbor might notice the car coming and going. Anyway, some nosy policeman on foot patrol would spy the car and wonder what his Station Sergeant was up to at that time of night. Best to do what he'd planned. Go straight out the Broughshane Road from Sir Anthony's house and turn up the Woodside Road into the country.

Well up the Woodside Road, he pulled into the recessed gateway at the Coursing Club and fetched a bundle of clothes out of the boot: a boiler suit and boots still damp from his near drowning. He stripped down to his underwear and threw the good clothes into the boot. His teeth chattered in the cold air and he was sorry he hadn't thought of throwing in an old pullover. As an afterthought, he pulled on his overcoat again and drove on.

Daniel T's house was the first stop. He reversed into the gateway and walked up the short drive into the farmyard. A glow of light from a back room spilled into the yard. Which room he couldn't be sure because the blinds were drawn.

Wee Willie's head appeared in his doorway. He spotted Barlow and roared. His horns clashed the metal of his restraining gate and it rang out angrily.

Barlow kept an eye on Wee Willie and stayed close to the house as he sidled into the yard. Standing sideways to the glass, he tapped the window. This was personal between Daniel T and himself and he didn't want the wife disturbed if at all possible. He kept his voice down. 'Daniel T, it's Sergeant Barlow.'

There was a squeak as if someone had jerked in a chair. After that silence.

He tried again. 'It's Sergeant Barlow. Open the door.'

The lights went out in the house. Long seconds later a key turned in the lock in the back door. The door opened. Daniel T had to be there in the darkness, looking out.

Barlow couldn't be sure because of the porch light blinding his eyes. All the same, he sensed danger and patted his pocket for the security of knowing that the Glock was there. If he'd thought to wear gloves he'd have drawn it.

'Daniel T, why did you kill Malcolm Knype?'

Silence.

His eyes began to adjust to the glare and he saw a shadow near the bottom of the stairs.

'I'm asking.'

'Who says I did?'

'Would you come out here instead of skulking back there.'

The shadow hardened into the form of Daniel T. He came to the door and, pistol in hand, craned his neck to look round Barlow. 'Did you bring anyone with you?'

It would be safer to say yes, but he needed Daniel T's trust. 'No, and I want you down at the station first thing Monday morning with the licenses for all your personal weapons.'

Daniel T stepped to the side and indicated. 'Come in.'

'No.' Barlow rubbed his chin, feeling the start of new bristles, while he pretended to think through something already clear in his mind. 'Malcolm Knype is on the run, and he'd got something everyone wants. He comes to you. You kill him and bury him in a shallow grave near Weir's farm, hoping the body will be found and Leon blamed.' He cocked his head. 'How am I doing so far?'

Silence again from Daniel T.

'As for this package or whatever it is – if the man's bringing it with him it can't be that heavy – anyway you hold onto it. Now why would you do that?'

He could see a sheen of moisture on Daniel T's cheeks but not on his forehead. He'd been crying.

'What?' he asked.

'Leon, he was here this evening. The things he did to the wife....' Daniel T's voice cracked.

A simple pickup had turned complicated. And as for Mrs. Abernathy? He couldn't blame her for her husband. He suppressed a shiver. If that had been Vera.

'So you gave him the package?'

'The wife was screaming all the time I was away getting it.'

Daniel T cried openly.

Barlow asked, 'So Leon did the sort of things to your wife that your guns do to other people?' He waited a good pause before asking. 'And then what?'

'I didn't dare call a doctor so I gave her a heavy sedative and put her to bed.'

'I mean Leon.' He knew he was being brutal but he hadn't time for Daniel T to become hysterical.

'He says he'll be back. Killing me will be part of the deal when he sells the package.'

Funny, but that steadied Daniel T. As an ex-soldier, with combat experience, Daniel T knew that he had some chance against a homicide intent Leon.

Barlow rubbed hard at his cheeks, puzzled at what to do next. The policeman in him wanted information, the personal Barlow wanted to get on with that night's work.

'This Malcolm Knype, he steals something of national importance or acquires it or whatever. He runs, not towards London but away from it. That means he intends to give it to other people: the Russians or the Chinese. He gets as far as Ballymena where he has a choice between Leon and you. Leon is all about money, a mercenary, but you he trusts, or maybe he comes here because those old fire engines make your place easier found. Which makes you a Commie spy, a traitor.'

'A double agent,' said Daniel T. 'And if the Russians find out, they'll kill me.'

Barlow wanted to hit Daniel T, and keep hitting him until his bones were dust. He couldn't keep the contempt out of his voice. 'I hope they do it slow. Those pieces of metal in the waste bin at the factory. You destroyed the weapon that killed Susan.'

Chapter 63

Daniel T didn't deny the destruction of the rifle that had killed Susan, the evidence that could have brought her murderers to justice.

Though maybe not, Barlow had to admit to himself. Big names were involved, careers at stake. Which was why they had tried to kill him and might try again. That thought brought back the shivers.

Before he went on he needed convincing that the package had gone and why was it important enough for people to die?

'What's in that package, what makes it so important?'

'Papers. Economic projections for the next twenty years.'

Barlow's voice rang with disbelief. 'The sort of garbage you see in the newspapers every day?'

'No.'

Daniel T was forever keeping an eye over Barlow's shoulder for a threat. 'Would you come in so that I can close the door?'

'No.' No way would he ever again enter that house as a friend. He'd rather choke first.

Daniel T eased himself partly behind the open door. The pistol remained prominent but not threatening. 'Forget the bomb, forget the Russians nuking us in our beds. We're waging an economic war to see who runs out of money first.'

'What's that got to do with it?'

'The Russians are selling us cheap radios. So cheap that we buy them instead of British made ones. They take sterling out of the country and the workers in our factories lose their jobs and go on the dole.'

'Okay,' said Barlow. He could see the drift of what Daniel T was saying. So what about a few radios here and there?

'Then take India. The Russians helped fund their fight for independence. Before 1947, we imported their raw cotton, turned it into material and sold it back to them at a profit. Now they sell us the finished material: more money out of the country and all the cotton mills in Yorkshire are closing.'

'Aye,' said Barlow, finally understanding the danger of the economic situation. 'If they've got our money and we've got the unemployed, they could walk in and take over any time they liked.'

Daniel T nodded. 'That report Malcolm Knype stole is the Government's plans to counter the Russians. If they get that report, then they know how we plan to stop them….'

'And we're doubly bucked,' said Barlow.

He had a think about it. 'Why don't you ring one of your contacts in the Secret Services and get him to pick it up?'

'Because they're riddled with Russian spies, and if the Russians find out I handed it back, I'm dead.'

Personally, Barlow didn't care if Daniel T ended up riddled with bullets, but there was enough bodies lying around right then without giving DS Leary anymore work.

He said, 'I'll get the report off Leon, after that you'll be safe.'

Which took him back to his first plan. 'Show me where you kept this report hidden. Convince me it's gone.'

'I kept it in the bull house,' said Daniel T.

Behind him, Barlow could hear the bad-tempered snorts of Wee Willie.

Chapter 64

The bull house!

From the snorting and the stomping of cloven hooves Barlow knew that Wee Willie still didn't like him.

He stepped clear of the doorway and jerked a thumb towards the bull house. 'Put him in the field.'

'He'll not go out this time of night.'

'Either put him out or I shoot him. That's the mood I'm in.'

Daniel T came out from behind the door, his head swiveling from left to right and back again, wary of an ambush.

No pulling on of Wellingtons this time, Barlow noted. Daniel T wore desert boots with rubber soles, and combat dress to match. Daniel T crossed the yard swiftly and pressed against the bull house wall while he spoke to Wee Willie, calming him down. Slowly the snorts eased and the stomping stopped. Eventually Daniel T was able to slide through the door and disappear into the bull shed.

Barlow stayed well back rather than risk antagonizing the bull again. He heard a subdued clang as the door into the field opened, accompanied by indignant snorts and a lot of foot stamping. It took a long time but finally Daniel T appeared and motioned at Barlow to come in.

Barlow went into the bull house, his eyes fixed on the door leading into the field. The last time, one good nudge from Wee Willie had burst it open, and that was when Wee Willie didn't know him from a bar of soap. Now there was a definite antagonism between them. He was relieved to find a length of circular steel propped against the door to give it added strength.

He looked around a room bare of anything other than a hayrack, a water feeder and Daniel T's chair. 'Okay, so where was it hidden?'

No way would he believe that Daniel T had hidden the package under the straw covering the floor.

Daniel T went to the furthest corner of the room, under the hayrack, and scraped at the straw with his foot. First Barlow saw the concrete floor, then Daniel T scraped straw dust away to reveal a metal ring. He gave the metal ring a tug and what appeared to be solid concrete swung up to reveal an opening.

Barlow stepped forward and looked in cautiously. He could see a small room with the light already on and a ladder leading down. No way would he go down there without backup. Daniel T only had to replace the hatch cover and let Wee Willie back into the house. He'd either starve to death or be gutted by Wee Willie's horns, and his body never be found.

Right then Wee Willie gave the door into the field a thump.

Just in case Daniel T had any ideas in that direction, Barlow slipped his hand into the pocket that held the Glock. 'So what's this?' he asked nodding to the opening.

'Part of the cellar of the old house.'

'What do you mean part?'

'Do you remember nineteen-twelve?'

'Before my time.'

It was hard to play the stubborn policeman with Wee Willie thumping the door. The thumps now accompanied by a bad-tempered snort.

'Nineteen-twelve, it looked like there was going to be war between us and the Catholics. My grandfather stored some of the guns imported by the UVF.'

Barlow knew of that part of Ireland's history, when the Catholics demanded independence from England and the Northern Protestants were willing to fight to maintain the Union. Both sides imported arms in expectation of a civil war.

He scowled at Daniel T. 'When Partition came, all those hidden guns were supposed to be buried forever under concrete?'

'Maybe, but after Dunkirk, when the British were arming the Home Guard with bows and arrows, the authorities were in no position to ask too many questions.'

Barlow spat at the floor instead of in Daniel T's face. 'And that's how your lot got into arms dealing?'

Daniel T nodded and said something. What he said was lost in the thunder of Wee Willie's determined charge against the steel door.

'I've better things to do than stand here,' said Barlow, and retreated to the safety of the yard.

He left Daniel T to close up the hatch and placate Wee Willie.

On his way to the car Barlow detoured into the back hallway and snatched Daniel T's stockman's coat off its hook.

Behind him, Wee Willie bellowed in rage and charged the door a second time. Even the door leading into the yard rattled.

Chapter 65

Barlow was no longer aware of being cold but he found himself trembling. Dealing with ordinary criminals, many of whom were out for devilment as much as anything else, was part of the job. But when decent men like Daniel T Abernathy became seduced by money? That he found hard to take.

He drove away from Abernathy's farm and an old friendship. Weir's farm and Leon was his next target. *But how to get there without being seen*? No way could he drive straight up to the house. *Across the fields?* Not in the dark, not with all the barbed wire that farmers now used. Which left the approach through Blacks' Estate.

He reversed the car into one of Blacks' abandoned laneways and sat for a moment wishing he could spin his life forward, *say by twelve hours*. He climbed out of the car and took off his overcoat, threw it into the boot and pulled on plastic gloves. Then he was ready to go.

He found the walk through the estate easier than he feared because Special Branch had run a trail of police tape to guide them to Malcolm Knype's body. *Typical townies.* From there he used his memory and the boundary hedge to guide himself to the opening onto Weir's land.

He could hear nearby the yap of a female fox, and something with a huge wing flicked past his face. Grass hissed as a small animal fled from under his feet. He kept his pace down and breathed quietly, and tried to be one with them.

Approaching the opening, he pressed hard into the hedge. Leary had bagged and tagged the mantrap that caught Gillespie as evidence. But who was to say that old Weir only had one? And was the replacement set on the Blacks' side of the hedge, or on Weirs.

He toed forward gently through the leaf-fall and touched a peg driven into the ground. He used his fingers to trace the chain leading from the peg to the trap itself, and found it set right in the gap.

Feeling cautiously around it, he concluded that this trap was much smaller than the original one. A gin trap, the sort of trap that men set for rats and foxes. Tempted to find a stick and spring the trap, he decided not to. The snap of metal on metal as the trap sprang shut could carry as far as the house.

He took a huge sideways step over the trap and again stayed close to the hedge for cover as he approached the dark outline of the Weirs' outbuildings.

The whole farm was in darkness. Barlow checked his watch – just after midnight, which might be normal for the Weirs – All the same, it didn't hurt to be cautious and he still had a fair bit of planning to do. Like getting into the house without anyone hearing?

He pulled on a balaclava and slipped into the farmyard between the distillery and the ramshackle hen house. Going near hens at any time was likely to get them squawking, but it was either that or risk being seen from Leon's bedroom window if he came in by the laneway.

At the gable wall of the distillery, he hesitated. Not only was the hen house door open, hens were pecking around the yard. Maybe Leon left the door open at night, wanting to entice foxes in. One way of keeping his shooting skills up.

Barlow slid around the gable wall into the yard proper, and gave thanks that the Weirs were either too mean or lazy to whitewash the stone walls and that there was no face behind any of the windows.

He reached the doorway of the distillery and stopped there to catch his breath. Why he was breathing hard he didn't know. It's not as if he was running or straining.

Barlow registered that the hens stayed bunched together around the outhouse where the Weirs had held Krista captive. Like they were hoping for food?

At the same time he sensed more than heard a metallic click.

He twisted the handle of the door and burst into the distillery even as a shot rang out. The force of the bullet striking the door ripped it from his grasp. The door ricocheted off the wall and slammed shut. The bang of the door shutting joined the sharp crack of rifle fire and echoed away into the night.

Barlow leaned against a wall and felt himself all over. He knew Leon had missed with that first shot, but his hands needed the satisfaction of finding neither holes nor blood. Now he deliberately breathed deep, trying to get enough oxygen into the system to slow his racing heart.

He only had a Glock against Leon's and his rifle. The windows in the distillery faced out into the yard, as did the only door. All the advantages were with Leon, and he wouldn't be on his own for long. Leon would have called on Running Man for help, so if he had any chance of getting out of the trap it had to be soon.

Trusting that his balaclava would camouflage his face, Barlow sidled along to one of the windows and peeked out. The hens had scattered at the sound of the shot. Was Leon still in the shed? He couldn't be sure, there was no sign of the man, and he didn't dare risk more than a quick peek.

He pulled back, hunkered down and did an undignified waddle to the second window. Surfaced just beyond it. Before he could look out, a bullet shattered the glass near his head. He ducked down again. Cold sweat poured over his body.

Leon was playing with him. Trying to guess where he might look out and sending a bullet in that direction. Eventually both would coincide.

Leon fired again, this time through the window at the door. Glass shattered and the bullet clanged through something metal.

Barlow racked a bullet into the chamber of his Glock. Shooting back would betray his position. Worse, the chances of killing Leon at that distance and in complete darkness, was nil to impossible.

His only chance was for them both to be out in the open, and if he did that, Leon would get in the first shot.

Chapter 66

Barlow knew that to stay in the distillery meant certain death but opening a window and jumping out into the yard would take several seconds. A fortune in time to a man like Leon. What he needed was something to deflect that first bullet and a ton of luck.

He tried to visualize what was in the distillery. The still was made of soft metal: copper and tin. Stuff a bullet would hardly notice on its way through.

A bullet came through a window. A second bullet ricocheted off the back wall and nearly caught him on the rebound. The muzzle-flashes lit up the distillery briefly, giving him a chance to take in shapes. Each time the flash got brighter. Leon was getting more confident, and that confidence was drawing him into the yard.

Right, go for it.

Barlow had to repeat that order to himself before he moved.

He got down on his hands and knees and crawled to the door. Once there he stood up again, his back tight against the wall, and reached around, searching for the handle. He found it, turned it and swung the door open. Gently, so that it would rest against the wall and not ricochet off it.

Immediately a bullet flew in the open doorway. About chest height from the noise it made bouncing off the back wall. Barlow guessed that Leon was playing with him, but being a professional wouldn't attempt a headshot against a moving target in poor light. Once he was down and disabled Leon would take his time and make sure of the *coup de grace*.

Barlow crawled back down the length of the distillery. Bullets flew in the windows, almost as if Leon guessed where he was going and what he was up to. Barlow reached the sacks of grain. He selected one that was unopened, hoisted it over his shoulders and started the crawl back to the door. As he neared the door, a volley of bullets smashed through the windows and in the doorway.

Barlow stood and flexed his arms and legs. He hoisted the sack of grain up until he held it tight between his chin and a curved left arm. There was a bullet in the firing chamber of the Glock. Even so, he fought down the temptation to rack in another one just to be sure.

Leon fired again. Only two shots this time, one through each of the windows. Barlow could almost feel the rifle aimed at the doorway, ready to take him down if he showed.

He felt confident that if he didn't make it Vera would be all right. The Dentons and the Gillespies would see to that. All the same he said a quick prayer that things would work out for her.

The firing started up again: far window, near window, doorway.

Going by the pauses between shots, it was a bolt-operated rifle. It needed the bolt pulled up and back to eject the used cartridge and bring up the next round, ready to fire. Not only that, Leon would be distracted wondering what shooting pattern to use next – at least that's what Barlow hoped. He was out the door before the third bullet had stopped ricocheting.

He had guessed right. He was clear of the doorway before a bullet slammed into the sack of grain. The force of the impact knocked him off balance. His back and shoulders slammed into the distillery wall, his head as well, but only enough to hurt, not to stun.

He could see Leon now, a firm shape, standing confident in the doorway of the outhouse, and he heard the *click, click* as Leon worked the next round into the firing chamber. Barlow brought up the Glock and fired. Leon folded into the yard.

Grain was trickling out of the sack. Barlow let it drop and stood for a moment making sense of things. He had bested a professional killer. Leon lay on his left side. He was moving, groaning.

Barlow approached him from behind. A lifetime of dealing awkward detainees made him realize that, in spite of his injury, Leon's movements were deliberate. Though what he was up to, Barlow couldn't guess. To be safe, he kicked Leon between the legs. Leon screamed, the first genuine sound he had ever heard the man utter.

Barlow kicked the rifle down the yard, then he leaned over Leon and rammed the Glock into his cheek. 'Move and you're dead.'

He ran his free hand over Leon's body: chest, armpits. Felt hot damp high up on Leon's right shoulder and decided there no chance of him bleeding to death that high up. No weapon, not even at the back of the neck where there might be a knife. He extended his search down Leon's legs and found a small pistol tucked into an ankle holster. The pistol had an extremely short barrel and a wide cylinder holding the bullets. At a guess an American Detective Special .38. Notoriously inaccurate but perfect for what Barlow needed.

He cocked the hammer of the Detective Special, pressed its muzzle hard against Leon's head and pulled the trigger.

Chapter 67

No matter how hard Barlow strained, his finger refused to go that extra fraction of an inch. The fraction that would trip the hammer and send a bullet into Leon's brain.

Leon started to laugh. 'Big tough sergeant, quick to throw your weight around, but when it comes to killing a man? You can't do it.'

Barlow stepped back, frustrated. It had all seemed so logical. Susan had died because Leon wasn't particular about whom he shot and he'd given his own father a horrific death. The man was out of control, but the Establishment would protect him so long as he remained useful to them.

Barlow still had the Detective Special aimed at Leon's head. 'Shoot,' he ordered himself, but still his finger wouldn't give that final twitch.

He hauled Leon to his feet and made sure he hit the damaged shoulder as he sent him staggering towards the house. 'With a bit of luck you'll bleed to death before the ambulance gets here.'

He kept the small pistol tight against Leon's spine until they were in the front door and the hall light clicked on.

Barlow pointed to the sitting room. 'In.'

For some reason Leon found that amusing. He hooked the thumb of his damaged arm into the top of his trousers and opened the door. On Barlow's instructions, he clicked on the light and retreated to the chimney wall. Sure now of not having the heavy door swung back in his face, Barlow stepped into the room.

Mrs. Weir sat in a chair beside the fire. Like the remains of the coal fire itself, she was dead.

In that moment, when his attention wavered Leon came charging at him: hand out to deflect the aim of the pistol, his knee aiming for Barlow's groin. Barlow let Leon force his gun hand up. He twisted his hips to take the knee on his thigh and drove stiffened fingers into the hole in Leon's sweater.

Leon folded onto his knees, choking on vomit held trapped by the balaclava. His left hand scrabbled to pull it clear of his mouth. Barlow stepped back and swung his boot. His kick into Leon's lower stomach was hard and accurate. Leon curled into the floor. He vomited again.

Barlow pivoted and drove a heel into the base of Leon's spine. 'Kicking someone to death is fun, isn't it Leon?'

He forced himself to step back rather than keep on kicking until Leon's body was pulp.

At least he could relax for a while and try to figure out what to do next.

He should phone the station, but what was he going to tell them? Any weakness, any grey area in the story and Harvey would delve into it until he came up with some charge. He'd be out of a job and lucky to keep his pension.

All the time he was looking from Leon to his mother.

The expression on Mrs. Weir's face mirrored the one he had seen on her husband's – sheer unadulterated fear. The reason for that fear was on the casual table beside her chair: cotton wool, a bottle of turpentine, an empty phial and a syringe that dripped fluid.

Leon had killed his mother and he had taken his time over it, setting everything out neatly, telling her exactly what he intended to do and how. At her age and the stress she'd been under, everyone would assume a heart attack.

He turned on Leon, wanting to power a boot into the back of his skull. 'Why did you kill your mother?'

Leon gave a long sigh as he finally got control of his pain. 'I got a phone call to say you might be heading in this direction. It disturbed her as well. I'd warned her time and again that I can't have people coming about the place, so I thought finish it all now.'

Barlow spat in Leon's face. All the woman had ever wanted was enough money to put meat on this monster's plate.

Leon wiped the spit away. 'Barlow, I'll never see jail, but you will. The men I work for will make sure of that, and when they do….' He sniggered, a sick, perverted sound that put Barlow's teeth on edge. 'Who's going to take care of your daughter? Save her from the bogeyman?'

Barlow made sure his thumb went deep as he grabbed Leon by the injured shoulder and hauled at him until he was leaning over his mother. Then Barlow rested the Detective Special between Mrs. Weir's hands, and put her still pliable forefinger inside the trigger guard. Pushed his and her hands forward until the muzzle of the pistol rested between Leon's eyes.

'Never, ever threaten a man's daughter.'

This time the trigger went the whole way back.

Chapter 68

Only a trickle of blood showed from a small bullet hole in Leon's forehead. The real damage was invisible.

Something in Barlow died the same way. Was so dead he didn't bother trying to revive it by justifying what he'd done.

Leon's body had flipped back and lay in a tangle of limbs on the floor. Barlow left the Detective Special in Mrs. Weir's hands and walked out of the room. He wanted the night done, he wanted the next ten years done. By then he might have learned to live with himself. And he wanted rid of the Glock with Gronville's palm print on the magazine.

He took it out of his pocket intending to leave it on the hall table, but that seemed too obvious. The gun had to be "lost", dropped somewhere in the dark and left behind because time was getting on and, supposedly, Gronville had to set up his alibi.

That was as much planning as his shocked thoughts could come up with. He turned off the light in the hallway and walked out of the house and down the yard.

He was throwing himself onto the ground before he could even work out what he'd heard: the crackle of a foot on half-frozen dirt. A gun flashed from the opening into the laneway. The bullet passed overhead, would have cut through him if he hadn't ducked.

A second shot. The gunman had overcompensated. The bullet sparked off the old cobblestones and whanged off into the night. Barlow fired two quick shots into the gun-flashes.

Stretched out in the open yard he felt vulnerable. The gunman, Running Man probably, could be taking his time to be sure of a head shot. Could be creeping around the Weir house to come at him from a different angle. Could be waiting for him to move, to pinpoint his position.

At least he now knew where Running Man was or had been, and the gap between the distillery and the chicken house was only a quick crawl away. Barlow crabbed along the ground towards the gap between the buildings, never taking his eye or the aim of the pistol away from the opening into the laneway.

His hands burned with chill from the cold ground, every stretch an agony for tired muscles. Finally he was in the gap between the two buildings, aware that Running Man could be waiting for him, ready to fire at point-blank range as he struggled to his feet.

Barlow waited, gun at the ready. He heard nothing and saw nothing other than a vague outline of chickens beginning to peck around the yard. So Running Man wasn't coming that way.

He checked the way he had to go and saw only the dark translucence of a grass field and the solid black of the boundary hedge. The longer he waited the bigger the danger. He scrambled to his feet and took to his heels, trusting that a dark shadow in a black night would make an impossible target. The long stalks of grass and the sodden ground dragged down his speed as he angled towards the hedge and the darkness of its cover.

Halfway down the field he stopped and looked back. Nothing or no one had followed him, neither footsteps nor a spread of bullets, and no dark shadow moved among the buildings.

Barlow remembered what Leon had said about the first killing being the most difficult and after that….

He flung the pistol into the hedge, hating himself for shooting at a second man without even thinking about it.

Chapter 69

Barlow remembered the gin-trap when his foot was nearly on it. He twisted clear and after that walked blindly until he stumbled across the police tape left by Special Branch.

He knew he should be focusing, looking out for ambushes, especially as he neared his car, and didn't care. Or rather, couldn't bring himself to do anything about it.

At the car, he pulled off the plastic gloves and the boiler suit and bundled them into the front footwell. Dressed again in his "black tie" outfit he crashed into the driver's seat.

His body ached to turn left, for home and the oblivion of sleep. He turned right. With two suspicious deaths, DS Leary would search the countryside for clues, the sort of thing a man in a hurry would dump at his heel. Things like boiler suits with bloodstains and gunpowder residue.

He went deeper into the hills, until he came across the winking safety-lights at a roadworks. He left the bundled-up boiler suit there. One of the workmen was bound to spot it and claim it for his own. He stopped on a bridge and threw the rubber gloves into the water.

After that he could go home. Into the drive. Into the house. His shaking hand had trouble putting the key in the lock. He headed for the bathroom, needing to purge himself of dirt and residues that would hang any man.

In the bathroom, he stripped off, stepped into the bath and turned on the shower. He washed himself thoroughly and stood under the battering flow of water until the hot tank ran cold. Like an old man, he planned every hand and foot movement before stepping out of the bath.

He found Krista at her bedroom door, waiting for him. She wore one of Vera's newer nightdresses and had a rug thrown around her shoulders. He was carrying his dress suit in one hand, the other using the towel to dry his hair. He didn't care that he was indecent.

He said, 'It's over, you're safe. Tomorrow, I'll take you to people you can trust.'

He went into the bedroom, threw the good suit on a chair and climbed into bed. Without his wishing it, his body lay partly on its side, one leg bent forward as if taking a step.

When that happened, he knew sleep wouldn't come.

Chapter 70

The bedroom door opened and light from the hallway spilled in. Krista's shadow elongated along the floor and up the wall. Barlow pretended to be asleep.

Instead of leaving, he heard her limping steps across the carpet and he smelt her perfume as she stood over the bed. Time passed, she stood on. Finally, her fingers touched the tendons and muscles running along the top of his shoulders.

'Hard, bad,' she said.

He should tell her to go away, but the fingers were cool, and their coolness somehow worked its way into his overheated brain. First, her hands kneaded out the tensions in his shoulders and then her thumbs dug along the tendons running up his neck while her fingers worked the back of his skull and around his ears.

He gave up pretending to sleep and moaned at the sensuous relief she was bringing him. He lay on content as her fingers reached further and further down his back. Her hands encouraged him to lie flat on his face, the sting of the cold air as the bedclothes fell away was a blessing.

Her hands slowly travelled the length of his body, finding and soothing away pains he didn't know he had. Then up again, harder this time, the fingers coursing the lines of muscles, seeking out damage. She straddled him as she worked his back and shoulders, demanding flexibility and relief from strain. Now she really hurt him with her fingers scouring deep into his flesh and he let go groans of pain, knowing that they were also part of the cure.

'Turn,' she said.

He couldn't, not with her there, not that close.

She arched over him. 'Turn.'

With her weight off him and with her hand pulling his shoulder around, he had no option, no strength to resist. He kept his eyes closed as she worked again at his neck and shoulders, and arms and down his sides.

His eyes snapped open when her hands drifted lower. Even in the poor light he could see that she was naked, the nightdress thrown off at some point. Sweat stood on her body from effort, the sheen of the sweat setting up shadows where her flesh sank between the still too bony ribs.

She moved up, hanging over him, ready to take him in, and he wanted her.

'No,' he said.

'Woman gone,' she said.

He wasn't telling it to do anything but his hand reached out. The hand touched Louise's pillow then came back to rest on his heart. 'Still here.'

Blank Page

SATURDAY

Blank Page

Chapter 71

The rattle of a door-handle and the click of a door closing brought Barlow out of a deep sleep. He lay on not knowing what had wakened him, and not caring. He was warm and snug and curled into Louise's pillow, the way he used to snuggle into her body.

His ears strained and caught another sound that his brain refused to process, the closing of an outer door. The churn of a cold engine failing to catch first time, snapped his eyes open. The second churn brought his head up. It had to be Louise's car. He felt under the pillow, Krista had taken the keys.

He fought his way from under entangling sheets and blankets and ran into the corridor. Krista's door lay open. He didn't bother checking to see if she was there.

The teeth aching grind of gears drove him on. He'd left the car nosed in across the front of the house, she'd have to reverse first. It gave him a chance.

He ran out the inner, glass-paneled door, then the solid front door, leaving both swinging behind him. The driver had finally managed to find the reverse gear and reverse the car around the side of the house. He was right, it was Krista. Even in the poor street lighting he could make out the shape of her head. She only had to find first gear and she'd be gone, and then all sorts of hell would be let loose.

Krista found the first gear and slammed her foot down on the accelerator. The car kangarooed forward as the engine choked on too much fuel. Out of breath from annoyance, his feet hurting from grit on the tarmac path, Barlow swung open the passenger door and jumped in beside her. 'Where do you think you're going?'

She looked at him, wide-eyed, even as she drove the car down the drive and out the gate. 'You, no clothes.'

He already had a hand over his groin, but could do nothing about his gut. He'd developed one recently. Vera thought it hilarious. That gut was nearly as embarrassing as his nakedness.

Not that he intended to show it. 'You run, and you're dead when British Intelligence catches up with you,'

He leaned across and clicked on the car's headlights, and felt like he was sitting in the middle of a spotlight. Anyone seeing them passing would know that he was naked, and big, tough Station Sergeant Barlow would be the laughing stock of the countryside.

He could imagine Gillespie. 'What's the dress code for today, Sergeant, *au naturel*?'

She was driving hard down the Ballymoney Road into town.

'There's a speed limit,' he reminded her. 'You don't want to be pulled over by some bored policeman with nothing better to do at this time of the morning.'

She was watching him as much as the road, a defensive elbow at the ready if he tried to grab the wheel. He didn't want to force her to stop, and he didn't want to drag her down to the station and have her go out of his protection.

He pretended a casualness that he didn't feel. 'Edward's a great man, the things he learns from newspapers you wouldn't believe. Like after the war, Russia invaded the Baltic States including Lithuania.'

Her head whipped around and she stared at him through the near darkness. He risked a hand off his groin and pointed at the fast approaching Pentagon roundabout. She turned back to her driving.

He said, 'The KBG knew that it takes more than terror tactics to control a people. So, being clever men, they embed a lot of Russians in those little countries to act as overseers.'

'Ruski.' She imitated a spit.

He waited to see which street she'd select off the roundabout. She went straight across and up Mill Street. A bad choice, in his opinion, but he wasn't going to tell her that.

'That time in the hospital, when you were frightened for your life, when you killed Jordan. You cursed in Russian.'

'No English,' she said.

He ignored her. He needed to tell someone something, he'd been silent too long. 'I got you to make your statement of the rapes and torture, by the spoken word. First in Lithuanian and then in Russian. Now as you know, I don't speak a word of either language, but I listened carefully to both tapes. Your Lithuanian was slow and careful, but your Russian started off hesitant as if you were unsure of the words but were flowing fast and angry near the end.' He ignored the threatening elbow and wagged a finger in her face. ‘In my book that makes Russian your first language, and that makes you a Russian national. And that makes you a Russian spy.’

She looked at him, frowning in puzzlement. ‘You say?’

‘As a Russian spy, you were sent down some sort of escape trail for two reasons: firstly to find Malcolm Knype and recover whatever he was bringing to your lot. Secondly, and more importantly, to find out who in your organization is a double agent working for the British.’

He wished she spent more time watching where they were going. Now they were almost on top of the crossroads at the other end of Mill Street.

‘I say you’re a professional spy. I say you were already embedded somewhere in Britain. I say that recovering the report is important but identifying the traitor is vital.’

He made it a question. The sort of question where he didn’t really want an answer. ‘What could a grubby little clerk like Malcolm Knype get his hands on? Details of our Blue Streak rocket programme? The new nuclear submarine base in Holy Loch?’

‘You say?’

He pushed on doggedly. ‘Somewhere along your escape route Malcolm Knype goes missing, yet your lot know from other spies in the Civil Service that the report hasn’t been found.’

They were at the crossroads. He pointed downhill and she turned that way. The route she needed to escape took her downhill and over the bridge. Maybe she knew that already. Maybe she had learned to trust him.

‘No spy,’ she said as the car dipped down the hill and his gut seemed to stretch onto his thighs. That made him determined. There would be no more fries for a while.

He ignored her obvious lie. ‘You got passed down the escape route as far as Leon Weir’s farm, and there things went wrong, He assumed you had some idea where the missing report had got to, and rather fancied grabbing it for himself and selling it on to the highest bidder.’

Now he seriously started to guide her through the lower end of the town, talking all the while. ‘Leon, raped you?’

‘Two. Leon, Tommy.’ She spat the words.

He could feel the tension of upset in her. He patted her thigh to comfort her, but the feel of her flesh, even under her dress, brought back vivid memories of her naked body straddling his. He hurriedly pulled back the hand. 'So when that didn't work and Tommy was killed for other reasons, Leon decided to force things.'

'Leon.' She drew a hand across her throat.

He nearly said "You're too late", but bit it back in time. What had happened the previous night was between him and God. People might guess but they would never know the details from his lips.

They were running along the river by now. He stopped talking and watched for the turn coming up, a gap in the wall. It appeared in the lights of the car, a greyness against the dark of the lava-stone wall.

He pointed. 'In there.'

She swung the car through the gap, without slowing. She could have been launching straight into the river for all she knew. The car dipped into the darkness. Barlow forgot his nakedness and grabbed the dashboard to stop his head from hitting the windscreen.

Chapter 72

The car's headlights swept the far bank and the buttresses of the bridge, then it nosed sharply down until the beams glistened off the river. A turn in the track focused them on a wooden hut set under an archway. Sitting on a bench outside the hut was Edward, who was waiting for the dawn.

Krista stopped the car in the narrow gap between the hut and the edge of the river. Barlow drew breath. He didn't know who had taught her to drive or where, but Gillespie would never allow her near one of his beloved squad cars.

He pointed beyond the bridge to where the riverbank widened out. 'Turn the car there while I have a word with Edward.'

She could reverse up and leave him stranded. There was a tension in her that made him place a hand on hers. 'You've trusted me this far.'

He got out of the car and closed the door, and waited. She drove on under the bridge and started a sweeping turn. Relieved, he turned to Edward who was looking at him with great interest,

'Sergeant Major, you appear to be at a sartorial disadvantage?'

Nakedness in the army, in front of fellow soldiers, was a normal thing but coming naked from the presence of a young lady was something different. Barlow refused to give in to embarrassment. 'Major, I would appreciate your help this morning.'

He used "Major" deliberately, letting Edward know that this was business. He was also getting a strong smell of drink. Edward had supped well the previous night in the Bridge Bar, so no way could Barlow risk him driving Louise's car.

He told Edward what had happened to him during the week, being completely truthful as to what he had done and why. During the war, Edward had demanded honesty off his men and, in turn, lied like a trooper to protect them from the wrath of the higher-ups. He had traded shamelessly on his George Cross to get many a guilty man off.

Krista had turned the car. She parked beside them and rolled her window down, trying to listen in. Barlow wished she'd turn off the lights because, in spite of everything, their joint nakedness of the last night was still in his head.

Edward nodded when Barlow had finished his explanations. 'And you want me to....?'

'Do you know the current GOC for Northern Ireland?'

Edward nodded. 'You mean Lieutenant General Sir Douglas Packard. Regretfully we enjoyed only a brief acquaintance. His wartime service was mainly abroad, Italy to be precise.' Edward cocked an eyebrow. 'You are reaching high, Sergeant Major?'

Barlow nodded, relieved that Edward at least knew whom to ask for. 'It's simple. Krista could disappear into the hands of our Intelligence people and never be seen again. But the more people know she exists, they more they are likely to ensure her safety, if only to protect their own necks.'

Edward stood up. He searched an inner pocket of his greatcoat and produced a printed card. 'Business cards supplied during my all-to-brief period of employment in Denton's establishment. "Major, the Honorable Edward Adair, GC, MC",' he read out. 'That will at least get me as far as the Adjutant.'

'Perfect,' said Barlow.

Full Generals wilted under Edward's charm offensive. A mere Adjutant hadn't a chance.

Edward insisted on a formal introduction to the "charming young lady" before getting into the car. At long last Barlow had time to go to the boot. He retrieved his overcoat and buttoned it up, right to the neck. It gave him instant protection from the chill morning, though a cold draft still ran up his legs.

He got into the car beside Krista.

'No English,' she was saying in reply to Edward's blandishments, and looked fixedly ahead as if wishing she had taken off on her own when she had the chance.

Barlow stared at her as he said, 'Major, no matter what she says, Krista speaks some English and understands it even better.' He put a hand on hers to show that he wasn't angry at her deception. The hand was warm under his chill one and he gripped it harder than he had intended. 'If they were trying to uncover a traitor in Moscow, they wouldn't waste their time sending someone like me who didn't speak a word of Russian.'

Krista frowned as if not understanding what he'd said.

Chapter 73

Barlow told Krista, 'On you go, we have to pick up your boyfriend, Geordie.'

She followed his "lefts and rights" back into town, out the Antrim Road and into Victory Park where Geordie lived.

Barlow waited in the car while Edward went to collect Geordie. Knowing Connie, Geordie's wife, and her sense of humor, he'd have to fight her off from viewing the family jewels.

Geordie came out wiping his mouth clear of breakfast. He wore only a white shirt against the wind that had left Barlow trembling with cold. The shirt was fresh on. Connie made him put on a clean shirt every time he left the house. In Connie's eyes, Geordie was the Raffles of Ballymena. Something Barlow couldn't understand because the woman wasn't stupid.

Barlow wound down his window.

Geordie stuck his head in. 'Sergeant Major, this had better be good, I've a scheme or two working today.'

'Then it's a good thing you're telling the Sergeant Major and not that bastarding Station Sergeant you're always complaining about.' He thumbed backwards. 'Get in.'

The car lurched to the left and rear as Geordie got in. Then it steadied when he leaned forward to plant a kiss on Krista's cheek. 'Darlin' you look a treat.'

Even in the near darkness Barlow could see Krista give the first smile of the morning.

'On,' he said, and pulled the edge of his overcoat up to cover a bare knee. 'Home, please. Mine. Then we'll organize your deliverance.'

All the same, he worried about Krista taking the head-staggers and heading out into the country. He only relaxed when she turned the car back into town.

That route he chose took them through the center of the town, which was already starting to come to life. The alternative was up Waveney Avenue and down the Galgorm Road past the police station. Definitely not the route to take, not the way his luck had been running recently.

To distract his mind from what troubles he faced during the coming day, and from the sardonic look on Geordie's face, he gave them their final orders.

'I know it's shorter and it avoids a lot of traffic, but do not go by Dundrod. Stay on the main road: Antrim then Belfast, right through the city center, and from there to Lisburn.'

'Sergeant Major, do you anticipate the possibility of problems arising?'

The bodies waiting discovery at Weirs' farm swam into Barlow's mental vision. 'Possible but unlikely.'

Geordie rubbed his hands in delight. 'This will earn me a couple of free pardons from the Station Sergeant.'

'A pint if you're lucky.'

'Accompanied by a chaser?' enquired Edward.

'Naturally.'

At long last, and to Barlow's relief, Krista swung the car into the driveway of his house and stopped.

The front door hung open the way he had left it but, thankfully, Toby stood guard in the doorway. Toby saw Barlow get out of the car, and snarled.

Geordie was taking over the driving. Instead of getting straight back into the car, Krista came over and gave Barlow a hug that lingered.

'You'll be all right now, darling, but let me know when you're safe.'

She kissed him, her tongue teasing his lips, before letting go.

She said, 'John Barlow, if they sent you to Moscow, with or without Russian, you'd succeed. You're that sort of man.'

Her accent was cut-glass English, the way he imagined the Queen spoke.

'Goodbye,' he said, and watched as she got back into the car and drove out of his life.

'Another time, another place,' he told himself, and shocked Toby by giving him a pat.

Chapter 74

Barlow cycled into work. Before leaving he had taken the time to change the sheets on his bed.

'Time I grew up,' he said aloud, but he felt a change in himself. Especially when he strapped on his pistol. It now felt part of him instead of something he wore because *Regulations* demanded it. He also made sure he left home before the postman passed. Things would be bad enough that day without knowing that there was still no letter from South Africa.

The police station was quiet, unbelievably normal. He let Sergeant Pierson handle the Morning Parade and hung around the Enquiry Office. One of the WPCs, Clare, brought him a cup of tea. Her eyes filled with tears when she saw his hurt that it wasn't Susan.

'Sarge, we'll get the men who did it.'

'Aye.'

He drank the tea while he leafed idly through the Incident Book, and found the normality of ongoing petty crime, soothing: the uneducated and unskilled, nicked. The nobs seen safely home. He also supplemented Pierson's uniform inspection by criticizing the appearance of every man who passed him.

'You're still on the sick, so I'm ignoring you,' said McGinn, and wandered on with Rex.

All the time, Barlow's ears stayed cocked for the panicked emergency call.

After an eternity of waiting, one of WPCs came rushing up. Barlow was the senior sergeant, Pierson the Duty Sergeant.

She looked somewhere between the two of them. 'Sarge, it's bad, Cromkill.'

Barlow nearly betrayed himself by saying, 'You mean Weirs' farm.'

The WPC continued, 'A lorry's overturned.'

Pierson imitated Harvey by vibrating indignation. 'That is no way to make a report.'

The WPC caught her breath. 'A lorry overturned on the Antrim Road, at Cromkill. The driver's dead, trapped under a load of steel.

‘How does they know he’s dead?’ asked Pierson.

‘He’s dead.’ She said it with a flat intonation, obviously not wanting to repeat the caller’s description of a body turned to mush.

‘Well send an ambulance anyway,’ said Pierson. He rushed off to practice his sucking-up by telling Harvey and Inspector Foxwood of the death.

Somehow, the men on duty in the station had sensed a tragedy. The vague hum of voices became whispers and the old floorboards creaked as men came to their doors to find out what was going on.

The front door banged open. Gillespie stood there, balancing of a pair of crutches.

‘Come in before you let the heat out,’ said Barlow.

Gillespie stumped into the room. Barlow closed the door himself rather than have Gillespie fall and really break something.

‘So what are you doing here?’ he asked, uncomfortable under Gillespie’s searching gaze.

‘The same as you, Sarge.’

Gillespie, like many a good policeman, was there because he sensed trouble brewing. This time Barlow knew it for a fact.

Frank Wilson came in the door. Like Gillespie, he was in uniform.

Barlow scowled. ‘You’re on compassionate leave, so clear off.’

Gillespie said, ‘I needed Frank in uniform to break me out of that darned hospital.’

Barlow ignored the “Frank”. He didn’t know what the world was coming to when people insisted on using first names.

‘Well tell him to break you in again, and then clear off.’

Gillespie said, ‘Huh!’ and stomped down the corridor, following the sound of voices from the Radio Room.

Wilson smiled apologetically as he sidled past Barlow and went after Gillespie. Barlow gave a long-suffering sigh to show that he was still annoyed, and followed them. Really he couldn’t have asked to have two better men handy on what was going to be a long, trying day.

The small Radio Room was crowded with those who were entitled to be there. DS Leary’s gut took up half the space. Onlookers crowded the doorway. Barlow bulled his way into the room to hear

Harvey give orders, making sure it was Inspector Foxwood rather than himself who went to the scene of the accident.

The red bulb on the wall flashed and a buzzer sounded as a second emergency call came through.

Chapter 75

The WPC at the switchboard answered the emergency call. 'Police, Ballymena.'

A man's voice sobbed, 'They're dead. They're all dead, and there's blood everywhere.' A whoosh came down the line as he vomited.

Barlow thought of Leary and his men having to wade through vomit. The more contamination the better. However, it turned out that the caller, the postman on his rounds, wasn't phoning from Weir's hallway but from a neighboring farm. Totally inconsiderate, in Barlow's opinion.

He made a face at Gillespie and jerked his thumb. Gillespie was to disappear before Harvey registered his presence and ordered him home. For once Gillespie obeyed without argument. He thumped off.

Barlow listened in while Harvey gave his orders. Harvey intended to take personal charge at to Weirs' farm. People were dead, violent deaths according to the postman. Everyman must check their individual weapons and, Barlow, break out a couple of rifles, just in case the killer is still around and armed.

That was something about the man that Barlow couldn't understand even as he admired it. When his officers' lives might be at risk, the pedantic paper-pushing Harvey became a different man, inspired even. Harvey's uniform sported the ribbon of the Police Medal, won for gallantry during the wartime bombing of Belfast. Barlow had come to the reluctant conclusion that it was hard earned.

Foxwood set off for Cromkill. The men detailed to go with him were equally reluctant. Like Foxwood, they wanted to be where the action was.

Harvey delegated men to come with him in his car. If the postman had been able to hurry from Weirs' farm without someone threatening him, then the killer must be long gone. Even so he, Harvey, would assess the situation before allowing the medics or the detectives onto the property. Barlow was to follow with more men in a second squad car.

Harvey's eyes lingered on Wilson. Wilson was tense, the strain of the past week showed clearly on his face.

'Wilson will be all right with me, Sir,' said Barlow.

Because of the kidnapping and torture of Krista, the boy knew that somehow Leon Weir and Weirs' farm were involved in the killing of Susan. Being there, getting involved in the enquiry, might give him closure.

Barlow unlocked the door into the armory and signed out two Lee Enfield rifles and ten rounds of ammunition for each weapon. He also made a personal check that every officer's gun was loaded and in good working condition.

The men didn't know it, but the only thing likely to take umbrage at them tramping around Weirs' farm were the chickens. And I don't know it either, he reminded himself.

He let Wilson drive. 'Don't rush, son. Mr. Harvey will need time to check out the farm before he lets us in.'

'Ah, Sarge.'

Barlow relented and authorized the bell and the strobe light, but ordered Wilson to keep the speed down. He didn't want to go anywhere near Weirs' farm. He wanted to be first in, so that his presence in an authorized capacity would camouflage his presence there the previous night. Three bodies, the postman had said, so he'd killed Running Man as well.

He felt guilty for that death. For killing a man who was only carrying out orders, even if those orders were illegal and more than tinged with a personal bias.

Gronville had a lot to answer for and Barlow intended to make him do just that.

Chapter 76

The fields were white with frost as the sun's rays struggled through a mist. From a distance Weirs' farm looked picture-postcard perfect. Barlow was anxious to get his footsteps everywhere. There was no knowing what potential evidence still stuck to the soles of his boots though he had given them a good clean.

Harvey ordered him to set up a police line around the farmstead. No one to come near the farmyard or the buildings until the detectives had a good look around first.

Barlow tramped from one end of the police line to the other, watching Leary make a preliminary assessment of the yard. At times Leary stood in thought. Other times he positioned himself at the distillery, or the outhouse, or the chicken house or near the entrance to the yard, and used his fingers to point, as if he was firing a gun.

News filtered out that the detectives had found Leon and Mrs. Weir dead in the house, and that a stranger, a man, lay dead in the yard.

They already knew about the man in the yard. They could see him lying against a wall. He had bled out, the ground around him stained rust-red with dried blood. Barlow felt ridiculous for even thinking it, but he wanted to go over to Running Man and apologize for killing him. That it wasn't personal. He sucked at an imaginary antacid tablet to keep vomit down.

Gillespie stood beside him. He'd cadged a lift with McGinn, sitting in the back of the van with the dog. Gillespie was mostly silent, but he asked, 'Are you okay, Sarge?'

'Aye.'

All the time he had to appear normal. Act normal.

He found himself checking his hands for blood and determinedly put them behind his back.

Finally and at long last, the Police Doctor appeared. Barlow felt authorized to escort him through the police line to declare the victims dead. With the frost lifting, the yard was now sticky underfoot, which took care of the contamination on his boots.

'You're quiet today, Barlow,' said the Police Doctor.

‘It’s Saturday, Doc, and the weekend. My brain’s still in bed.’

They stopped at Running Man. Leary waited there for them. At their first meetings: at the hospital and in the People’s Park Barlow had thought Running Man to be in his mid-forties. With his face relaxed in death he looked much younger, mid-thirties. Just the right age to have a young family. He put that thought out of his head.

The doctor skirted as much of the blood as he could to touch the carotid artery. ‘Dead,’ he said. ‘Ruptured aorta.’ His gloved hand pulled the zip-up jacket clear to have a better look. ‘Tear in clothes, possibly consistent with a bullet.’ He rolled the body partly onto its face. ‘No exit wound, so the possible bullet is probably still in the body.’

Barlow forced himself to say, ‘I like a man who gives a definite opinion.’

He kept telling himself that Running Man was meat, that it was pure business. He could only remember Running Man turning in the People’s Park to shoot him, then thinking better of it.

He felt an emptiness around his heart expand until his body threatened to fold in on itself. The thump of crutches on cobbles steadied him. Gillespie had blandished his way through the police cordon.

That man gets off with things that the Chief Constable wouldn’t dare do, thought Barlow in another attempt to distract his thoughts

‘You’ll slip and kill yourself on those cobbles,’ he told Gillespie.

‘And make your day? No fear.’

The Police Doctor stepped back from Running Man and wiped the edge of his shoes on the frosty ground to scrape off some blood. The mist had lifted, the sun getting stronger, the frost starting to melt.

Barlow was glad of the excuse to escort the Police Doctor as far as the house, to get away from Running Man. Much as he ached to contaminate the house, he didn’t go in. Later on, Leary might start to wonder why he had entered a crime scene unnecessarily, setting up possible contamination before Forensics had done their job.

Barlow leaned against the wall at the doorway and searched his pockets for a packet of cigarettes. He’d bought them for Krista to keep her going until the security services got round to getting her some, but, with one thing and another that morning, she'd left without them. He didn't normally like Woodbines, but right then he was glad of its heavy drag in his lungs.

Gillespie used the wall on the other side of the doorway to take the weight off his crutches. Mercifully, he stayed quiet.

Harvey, Leary and the Doctor came out of the house. A doctor, even a Police Doctor, was an important man and Harvey personally escorted him back to his car, to hear the interim report and to sign off the paperwork.

Leary detailed a Detective Constable to guard the house against unauthorized people gaining entrance. Then he said, 'Barlow, I'd like a word.'

Chapter 77

Leary wanting a word worried Barlow. His heart thumped. 'Do you now?'

Leary led the way down the yard and stopped halfway between the outhouse where the Weirs had held Krista prisoner and the distillery. He was already breathing hard from the strain of what was going to be a long day.

'Preliminary thoughts,' he said and pointed to each location as he detailed them. 'The outhouse and the ground around it is littered with used .303 cartridges and the Lee Enfield we found nearby has spots of blood on it. The door and the windows of the distillery took multiple hits.'

He kept pointing. 'Two cartridges outside the distillery, two more at the gap between the buildings and another two with the body near the laneway. Query nine millimeter in each case.'

Gillespie had come with them. He used a crutch to point. 'What's with the bag of grain?'

Attracted by spilled grain from the bullet hole, the hens had worked the hole into a large tear to get at the grain inside.

Leary shrugged by way of reply. It came too quickly for Barlow's peace of mind. What was Leary holding back? What clue had he left behind for the wee fat man to find?

'And nobody heard anything? None of the neighbors?' he asked to be saying something.

Leary shook his head in disgust. 'I sent a man to ask around. The neighbors hardly admitted to knowing the Weirs. Until, that is, my man confirmed that Leon was dead, assured them that he personally had seen the body. Apparently, right from when he was a nipper, if anyone made a complaint about Leon, things happened to their livestock or equipment.'

Somehow, that news made Leon's death easier to live with.

'I should have known that,' said Barlow, annoyed with himself. He should have, all those years back, and done something about it at the time.

'Okay,' said Leary. 'I've a scenario I want to run past you.'

Again he pointed as he spoke. 'The dead man is a stranger.'

Barlow knew it would cause comment if he didn't tell at this point. 'He's the man at the hospital when Susan was killed. The one I chased through the town.'

Leary was already nodding in agreement. 'I thought so. He matches the description of that man you called "Running Man".' Then he shook his head in frustration. 'At least the "Jordan" character in the hospital had an ID, even if it was false. With Running Man, there's no ID on the body and nothing in his pockets other than a car key.'

'So where's the car?' interrupted Barlow. Other than police cars, the only car he'd seen was Leon's car parked up the side of the house. 'It has to be somewhere handy.'

'Some of your flatfoots could go look for it,' said Leary.

Barlow caught Gillespie's eye and nodded. Gillespie swung off on his crutches to give the order. Men jumped into cars and roared off down the laneway.

Leary waited for Gillespie to come back before continuing. Gillespie returned muttering about warped cylinder-heads and broken springs in his beloved cars.

'Right,' Leary said. 'The man comes into the yard in the dead of night. Somehow Leon knows he is coming and sets up an ambush in the outhouse there.' Again he pointed. 'Leon shoots and misses and the man takes shelter in the distillery. Leon keeps shooting.

'The man knows that if he stays it is only a matter of time before he's hit so he makes a break for it, firing as he goes. He gets lucky with the second shot and tags Leon in the shoulder, knocking the Lee Enfield out of his hands. But Leon has a pistol. Running Man heads for the laneway and escape, Leon runs to the gap in the buildings. They again exchange shots. Running Man misses but Leon hits him at least once, fatally wounding him.'

Barlow didn't dare agree to Leary's version of what had happened the previous night. It left too many loose ends. Worse than that, he sensed a subtle distinction between "the man taking shelter in the distillery" and "Running Man."

There were too many gaps in Leary's version of the events for Barlow not to query them, so he asked, 'Why did Leon run across the yard instead of taking cover in the outhouse?'

He pointed from the outhouse to the chicken house and from the distillery to the laneway where Running Man lay. The lines crossed where they stood, so he knew Leary had that problem worked out as well. 'They should have run into each other right here.'

'There's an even bigger problem,' said Leary. 'Count them: two and two and two. Six nine-millimeter shots fired, but only two came from Running Man's pistol.'

'How many rounds did Leon fire?' asked Barlow.

'Aye, there's the rub,' said Leary. Sometimes he read more than the Daily Mirror. 'Leon didn't have a nine-millimeter, at least not one that we can find. He had a snub-nosed pistol in an ankle holster and a bandolier of reloads for the Lee Enfield, but no shoulder holster. So what does that tell you?'

'There's a missing pistol,' said Gillespie in the voice of a man who knows he won't have to look for it.

'And a third gunman,' said Barlow. That's what Leary was angling at so he couldn't hold back on the suggestion. He was sorry now that he hadn't stayed outside the police lines, and avoided what amounted to little more than a polite interrogation.

'Especially after what happened in the house,' said Leary.

'What happened there?' Gillespie asked, before Barlow could even think that he should ask that question. He was supposed to know nothing.

It had been a long week, with little sleep and a lot of hard knocks. Leary could easily trip him up.

'The house,' said Leary, waving his hand in its general direction. 'Leon had killed a man or been involved in the killing and he owned un-licensed weapons.' The casual chat became a glare at Gillespie. 'You and Wilson searched the house the day Tommy was killed. Why didn't you spot the weapons then?'

Barlow remembered Leon's smirk, challenging him to find anything when he did his own look-around. 'They were well hidden.' He made it sound like speculation.

Gillespie said, 'We even checked the roof space.'

He sounded annoyed at himself for missing something important. If he had found the guns, three people might still be alive.

Leary said, 'Maybe Mrs. Weir saw who killed Running Man and tried to ring the police, and for some reason Leon decided to kill her as well. But Mrs. Weir fought back and shot him with the little snub-nose just as he finished injecting her.'

'Is that what you think happened?' asked Barlow, trying to quell a feeling of relief.

'It's too neat,' said Leary.

Chapter 78

Harvey arrived back from seeing the doctor off, his breath steaming like fire. 'Where did those men go in the cars and why? Who authorized it?'

Barlow pointed at Running Man. 'We think he came in a car and parked it somewhere nearby.' He wished someone would cover the body, make it anonymous under a sheet of blue plastic.

'Oh, yes, right. Good thinking, Leary.'

'Thank you, Sir,' said Leary.

'And Barlow, what have you done about the missing pistol?'

'We were wondering where we should concentrate the search. Would you have any suggestions yourself, Sir?'

'Um … um ...'

Gillespie coughed politely to get everyone's attention. 'We're assuming that Leon Weir and Running Man were expecting a third man and had set up an ambush.' He pointed to the two spots in turn. 'Leon in the outhouse to cover the yard and Running Man, the laneway. Even so the third man reaches the yard before being spotted.' Gillespie nodded towards the gap between the buildings. 'So he came across the field.' He rubbed his injured leg. 'Through that frigging gap in the hedge.'

Even at the best of times, Gillespie wasn't beautiful, but right then Barlow could have hugged him. Police boots tramping over the field would cover any tracks that he himself had left the previous night, especially if he only instructed the men to search for a pistol.

With four officers away searching for Running Man's car there were only two men available to search a four acre field.

'We need more men to do a proper search,' said Harvey, glaring at Barlow as if he was at fault.

'And WPCs with tea and sandwiches.'

He knew the girls would want to be there, and any excuse would do.

'Good thinking. Good thinking.'

Leary grimaced but didn't dare object when Harvey strode off to the Weirs' house to phone the station. Barlow went over to the police tape and told two men to search the field for the missing pistol. One of them was Wilson. The second man detailed for the job was McGinn with Rex.

McGinn looked at the field as if he'd never seen it before. 'Tell the wife to start Christmas dinner without me.'

'Be systematic,' Barlow said. 'Start at the boundary hedge and work out.'

Leary glared at Barlow as if every contaminated crime scene was his fault. 'If you find anything, don't touch it. Call for a detective.'

Barlow watched them go off, confident that they would find the pistol where he'd thrown it. He heard car engines and turned, expecting to see the patrol cars back. Instead, he saw Sir Anthony's limousine and an unmarked police car edging gently over the rough surface.

Obviously, before he left the station, Harvey had phoned Sir Anthony to give him an update. Barlow supposed that Sir Anthony had a right to know. All the same, visitors should be discouraged from visiting active crime scenes.

He pasted a smile on his face and went over to open the door for Sir Anthony. This was an official visit so he honored him with a cracking salute. 'Good morning, Sir Anthony.'

'Good morning, Sergeant.'

Gronville followed Sir Anthony out of the car.

Sir Anthony looked like he had spent the previous evening resting at home and gone to bed early. Gronville wore mufti, the army's word for civilian clothing: sports coat and flannels, check shirt and a mustard colored tie. He looked definitely rough around the edges.

Barlow rubbed at the stubble on his chin. Having Gronville there might work out handy.

A Special Branch Superintendent and his men piled out of the second car. Barlow nodded to them and went back inside the police tape.

Only the Superintendent followed him in. Barlow appreciated this gesture of goodwill even though "D Notices" with their message of "Hands off and go away you common lot" seemed to ricochet off the walls.

Leary said, 'I'm glad you came early, Sir. It saves me the trouble of doing my job.'

The Superintendent, a tall man with greying wavy hair brushed straight back, said, 'We've all got our orders, Detective Sergeant.'

The "Detective Sergeant" he said without any pointed reminder of their difference in rank.

The Superintendent pulled out a packet of Benson and Hedges and shared them around. Using long drags on his cigarette for cover, he negotiated politely with Leary. Leary was shorthanded that day. A motoring accident, if Superintendent had heard right, so if his men could help in any way?

Equally polite, Leary accepted the fact that Special Branch intended to be involved in the investigation.

That settled, the Superintendent raised an enquiring eyebrow at Barlow. 'Aren't you supposed to be on the sick?'

'There's no show without Punch, Sir.'

Right then Rex barked and McGinn shouted. They had found the pistol.

Chapter 79

Boosted by the authority vested in him by no less than a Special Branch Superintendent, DS Leary took immediate charge of the new crime scene. A pistol caught up in the roots of a thorn hedge? Not even a trek across wet grass in town shoes dampened Leary's enthusiasm.

Barlow remained in the farmyard and convinced the detective guarding access to the house to spread a plastic sheet over Running Man. Gronville watched it happen from the other side of the tapes. Barlow felt waves of hate coming in his direction.

Leary returned from the new crime scene, with the pistol held prominently in a clear plastic bag. 'Nine-millimeter,' he said, almost as if someone had disputed the caliber of weapons used.

It was only cold metal, shaped by an assembly line of machines. Barlow remembered the weight of it in his hand, and his feelings of hate and fear as he pulled the trigger. He could barely raise a smile of congratulations.

Harvey came to examine the gun, bringing Sir Anthony and Gronville along with him. Leary was annoyed at civilians invading his crime scene. As far as Barlow was concerned, Harvey was welcome to bring the Brigade of Guards. Even Wilson, McGinn and Rex were now inside the tapes. Normally he'd have sent them packing, but not today.

'Fingerprints,' said Harvey, somewhere between a question and an order.

'I plan to do that at the station, Sir,' said Leary.

'Perhaps in the circumstances…?' said the Superintendent.

Harvey waved Leary towards the house. 'The killings took place in the living room. We can use the kitchen.'

At least Barlow now knew officially where the deaths of the Weirs had taken place. Leary hadn't said. He knew he'd have to be careful around that wee fat man. It would take very little to make him suspicious. If he wasn't already.

Though why, Barlow couldn't figure.

Harvey led the way into the house, down the hallway and into the kitchen. Barlow jerked his head for McGinn and Wilson to follow. Especially Wilson. A rage was building in the boy, and Barlow needed to keep that in check.

To his relief, someone had closed the door into the living room. As the most junior officers present – himself, Gillespie, Wilson and McGinn – they stayed at the kitchen door and behind Harvey, where he couldn't see them and order them out.

It was chill standing in the doorway with the door into the farmyard left open behind them. The fire in the cast-iron stove had burnt out. Un-brushed grey ash lay around it in a flat arc. The kitchen smelled of damp clothes.

Without being aware of it, Wilson's hand was on his pistol. 'They were men who killed Susan, wasn't it Sarge?'

Barlow forced the hand clear of the pistol and re-clipped the holster flap. 'We don't know anything yet.'

Leary's murder bag sat on the worktop at the sink. He spread fresh plastic sheeting over the kitchen table before easing the pistol out of its bag. It wasn't often that he had an audience and he used the presence of the two civilians – Sir Anthony and Gronville – as an excuse to show off by explaining the procedure. Sir Anthony looked on, apparently fascinated. Gronville's eyes hardly left Barlow.

'Gentlemen, you observe that I am wearing gloves. The gloves prevent me from destroying any prints already on the pistol.' Leary laid the gun on the plastic sheeting and produced a packet of powder. He used a makeup brush to spread the powder over the pistol. 'Not too much. Everyone's skin has oils to keep it soft and pliable. The idea is that the powder will react with those oils, and when the surplus powder is removed the whorls of the perpetrator's fingerprints will be clearly seen.'

Next, he used a photographer's lens brush, with a little bulb for squirting air, to blow off the excess powder. He examined the pistol in minute detail. 'In this case the perpetrator wore gloves.' He let Sir Anthony have a closer look. 'Sir Anthony, you can see the marks of fingers on the metal, but no ridges so the pistol was last handled by someone who knew to take precautions.'

'Then the pistol is of no use to you in your enquiry?' said Sir Anthony.

Harvey pushed in to display his knowledge. 'A test firing will enable us to compare the bullets from this gun with ones found in the body of the man in the yard. And of course we may be able to trace the registered owner by the serial number stamped on the pistol.'

'There is no serial number, someone used acid to obliterate the numbers,' said Leary.

Harvey flushed at missing something as obvious as that, and glared at Leary for embarrassing him.

Realizing his error, Leary quickly covered. 'However all is not lost. Sometimes people get tired, become careless and make mistakes.'

He ejected the magazine from the pistol and dusted it with powder. A palm print showed clearly on the metal.

'Well done, Detective Sergeant,' said Sir Anthony.

Wilson clenched his fists and shouted, 'Got him.'

Harvey nodded to Leary, one professional to another. 'Well done, Sergeant. As usual a first class job.'

Gronville's face shaped its first smile of the day. 'Got you,' his eyes telegraphed to Barlow.

'That's what you think,' Barlow telegraphed back.

Chapter 80

In spite of finding a palm print on a murder weapon, Leary still looked annoyed.

Barlow couldn't blame him. Thanks to Harvey, the unnecessary presence of uninvolved people had compromised the crime scene. Even the dog had slipped into the house to stand beside McGinn.

'What do you do now?' Sir Anthony asked Leary as busied himself taking a Polaroid photograph of the palm print.

'Well Sir, for evidential purposes in Court, we normally photograph the prints with an old-style camera. In the circumstances, I thought we should use the Polaroid to give us an instant print. I will then compare the print with those on the three bodies, just in case there is a match there.'

Harvey gave a tut of impatience. 'Unlikely in the circumstances.'

Leary ignored him. 'Then we compare it with prints held in Central Records, starting with those of likely suspects, of course.'

'Barlow,' said Gronville.

Every head turned in his direction. Barlow's three subordinates hardly seemed to move but he found himself held in the protective triangle of their bodies.

'Gronville, perhaps you'd care to explain yourself?' said Sir Anthony.

'He's been interfering in this case right from the start.' Gronville shook a finger at Barlow. 'I recognized you that night at the hospital. It was you who killed Jordan and helped that woman to escape.' He spat the words out. 'Krista Riekstinš, if that was her real name, is a Commie spy, which makes you a Sleeper, a Red under the Bed.'

Barlow wanted to grab Gronville and pound him to pulp, but Gillespie had a crutch jammed between his legs, ready to trip him up if he tried to burst through the crowd.

Barlow ripped open his jacket and his shirt, and held his vest up. There was a general gasp when the others saw the bruising and blood scabs on his body. 'You paid Leon to kick the shite out of me before they threw me into the river.' Self-conscious of his potbelly, he jammed his vest down again.

Much as he hated doing it, he had to ruin a man's reputation. 'And you made Daniel T Abernathy destroy the murder weapon.'

'Never!'

Somewhere in his head, Barlow registered his own loss of control. All the same, it was a great feeling, venting every held-back anger and frustration: speaking for himself, what he thought and what he felt, not concerned for anyone else or their opinions.

'And you drove the getaway car the day Susan was killed,' he yelled.

He felt Wilson break the triangle as he made to lunge for Gronville. Barlow used his forearm to force the boy back.

'It was you,' Gronville said, the words snarling out of him. 'You and that criminal friend of yours, Geordie Dunlop, who spirited Riekstinš away. Allowed her to evade British justice.'

Harvey had a go at asserting his authority. 'Barlow, I warned you before about associating with a known criminal.'

'If you mean, did Geordie and I prevent Gronville and his friends from murdering a defenseless woman. Yes we did and we'd do it again.'

Sir Anthony said, 'Sergeant, I am of the opinion that you misread the situation.'

Somehow the Superintendent had managed to get between Barlow and Gronville. The Superintendent stood, arms folded. 'Do I take it, Gronville, that not only did you supply Jordan with a chemical designed to kill Krista Riekstinš, but you were also involved in the murder of a Police Officer: WPC Day?'

'Who do you think you are, accusing me?'

'We'll talk later,' said the Superintendent. He stepped aside again.

Sir Anthony turned to Leary. 'About this palm print?'

'Barlow's, who else?' snapped Gronville. 'You think I didn't know you went through my pockets last night? You think I didn't know you were up to no good?' His finger stabbed out each word of accusation. 'You came straight out after the party and killed everyone here.'

'No way,' said Barlow, and his denial rang true. He hadn't come straight out and he hadn't killed Mrs. Weir.

The knuckle of Sir Anthony's first finger touched his lips as he gave a polite cough. 'Gentlemen, we appear to be at cross-purposes. Perhaps we could speedily resolve this impasse if Sergeant Barlow here agreed to Detective Sergeant Leary comparing his palm prints to the one on the magazine?'

Barlow pretended reluctance. 'Why only me? Why not everyone else concerned with this case?' He nodded as if coming to a decision to act reasonably. 'I'm willing to let DS Leary compare my palm print with the one on the magazine if Mr. Harvey and the Superintendent agree to do the same.' He made it a challenge. 'And Major Gronville.'

The Superintendent shrugged. 'Why not.'

'I never heard of anything so ridiculous in all my life,' spluttered Harvey.

'There's also the partial trace of a fingertip,' said Leary.

Chapter 81

Barlow gritted his teeth and refused to even consider being sick with worry. How had he managed to touch the magazine with a bare finger and not notice? He should have checked the gloves for a tear.

All the same, he had agreed to the comparison of prints, and people were already giving way, allowing him to approach the table where Leary stood. Leary already had the fingerprint kit: the inkpad, the bottle of ink and the cards for recording the prints, out and ready.

Barlow stepped up to the table. "A partial" Leary had said. Hopefully not enough to make a definite comparison.

He held out his right hand. It remained surprisingly steady as Leary gripped it and rolled it on the inkpad and then on the Record Card. He repeated the process with the left hand. After that, Leary leaned over the table, his body metronoming from side to side as he compared the prints.

Barlow could only hope that it was Gronville's fingerprint. He didn't think so.

Leary was taking forever to make the comparison. Somewhere outside hens clucked. Even further away, at the edge of his hearing, a tractor spluttered into life.

'Can I help, Detective Sergeant?' asked the Superintendent.

Everyone jumped at the shattering of the expectant silence in the room.

Leary straightened up. 'I'm just being absolutely sure, Sir.' He placed Barlow's Record Card in a brown envelope and put it the murder bag. 'Okay, who's next?'

'You're not serious, Sergeant?' said Harvey.

'That was the agreement,' said the relieved Barlow. It had to be Gronville's fingerprint then. How that had happened was beyond him. He'd been so careful working with the sleeping man.

'It has to be Barlow's. Check it again,' said Gronville.

It was difficult not to look triumphant, knowing that he had his man. Barlow cocked a finger to draw Gronville forward. 'Your turn, Major.'

'Certainly not.' Gronville stuck his hands in his pockets. 'I refuse to go through with this charade.'

He might act arrogant and speak arrogantly, but there was a shift in his eyes, an uncertain flick.

'We all agreed,' said the Superintendent.

'No.'

'A gentleman's agreement,' said Barlow.

'I never agreed to anything.'

Barlow only realized that McGinn had left during the fingerprinting, when he came back carrying a fingerprint Record Card in his hand.

'I remembered,' said McGinn. 'It just came to me, we already have Major Gronville's fingerprints. That day, I got the cards all muddled and I managed to give him the wrong one to tear up.'

Harvey flushed with annoyance. 'You're on Report.'

The Superintendent asked, 'You mean you gave a suspect his fingerprint card?'

'Orders, Sir, orders,' said McGinn, somehow managing to look downtrodden and ineffective. 'I didn't dare say I'd got it wrong so I kept it in the van, meaning to destroy it.'

He's worse than Gillespie in his own sweet way, thought Barlow.

The Superintendent turned on Harvey. 'Is this normal procedure in your station?'

Harvey went into a splutter of explanations.

Leary whipped the Record Card out of McGinn's hand. 'Let's see.'

He bent over the table again. This time his backside bobbed to and fro like a family pet spotting a favorite treat.

Gronville backed away from the table, looking worried. 'What happened last night, Barlow? What did you do besides search my pockets?'

'I never touched you.'

'Maybe you'd care to double-check, Sir,' said Leary, and the Superintendent bent over the table beside him.

'It's a match,' said Leary.

'No doubt, Sergeant. It's as clear as day.'

The Superintendent straightened up. 'Gronville…'

Sweat stood on Gronville's face. 'It wasn't me.... I never touched that gun....'

It was nowhere nearly as bad as being hogtied and thrown in a river. All the same, Barlow enjoyed his moment of revenge. No matter what happened now, no matter how many "D Notices" the Establishment created to bury their guilt, Gronville's career was over. He'd embarrassed the Establishment, left them open to censure.

The Superintendent produced a set of handcuffs. 'Major Gronville, I am arresting you on suspicion of the murder of....'

A pistol appeared in Gronville's hand, pointed straight at Barlow.

Chapter 82

Gronville shook with anger and insulted pride, but the point of the pistol never wavered from Barlow's chest.

'No way are you arresting me, Barlow. No way. You framed me.' Sweat stood on Gronville's face but generations of privilege held him ramrod straight.

His pistol was another automatic. Gronville could put half a clip into Barlow before anyone had time to draw their gun and shoot. Barlow shuddered at the thought of bullets flying in that crowded room.

He made himself act cool and casual. He even rubbed his chin as if thinking things through. Everyone else stood still, anxious not to do the wrong thing. Except for Wilson. He had the flap of his holster undone. Barlow stared at Gillespie until he caught his eye, then he gave the smallest of nods in Wilson's direction. Immediately Gillespie's hand went out and pinned Wilson's gun hand against his side.

'This is personal between me and Gronville,' said Barlow. 'No one else is to interfere.' Leary and the Superintendent were behind him. 'Perhaps, gentlemen, if you care to move out of the line of fire.' He heard the shuffle of feet on the tiled floor. 'Quietly please.'

'None of you will ever put a hand on me,' said Gronville. The "you" had a tone of disdain that went back generations. His ancestors had addressed serfs with more respect. 'Barlow framed me, how I don't know. I'm going back to London and I'll sort it out from there.'

'It doesn't work that way,' Barlow said.

No matter what happened, Gronville wasn't walking free. He was going to feel cold metal on his wrists and shudder as a cell door shut him in.

Barlow knew that the palm print on the magazine wasn't conclusive evidence of guilt. Gronville could come up with a good reason why he'd touched a subordinate's weapon, and when.

The shirttail hanging over his holster and his jacket lying open spoiled the image Barlow wanted to create as he ever so slowly unclipped his holster flap and drew his weapon.

Still moving slowly he brought his pistol up until it pointed between Gronville's eyes. 'I've had a week of your arrogance. I've had a week of dealing with bullyboys you sent to kill me. I've had a week where I've lost one of the sweetest girls ever and had to fight to keep another woman alive.'

He noted that Gronville's breath came in shaky spurts, the way his own had come after his near drowning in the cold river.

Gronville said, 'I'll compromise. I'll agree to house arrest at Palace Barracks in Belfast while I sort this ridiculous charge out.'

'It doesn't work that way.' Barlow thumbed back the hammer. Now he only had to squeeze the trigger and the pistol would discharge. 'I'm going to count back from ten to zero, and if you haven't surrendered that pistol by then, I'm pulling the trigger.'

The rest of the men might think it bluff but he knew the truth. He would pull that trigger. He hated Gronville for giving him that ability to kill people.

'Ten.'

'Barlow, you're being ridiculous,' said Harvey, but he didn't move to interfere.

'Nine.'

'Perhaps Palace Barracks is a reasonable compromise?' said Sir Anthony.

'Eight.'

Rex growled.

'Seven.'

Gronville lowered the pistol a fraction. Now it threatened Barlow's paunch. 'I can prove it wasn't me. The police saw me. I went straight to bed.'

'Six.'

Gronville went back a step.

'Five.'

Then another.

'Four.'

Barlow sweated internally. He would shoot on zero, and he didn't want to.

'Three.'

Gronville was in the doorway now, the threat of the pistol sweeping to and fro forcing people to make way for him.

‘Two.’

At this angle, the bullet would go through Gronville’s head and impact the lava-stone wall at the front door.

‘One.’

‘Shoot me if you want, Barlow, but you’re not arresting me.’

He turned and ran.

Barlow dropped his pistol to the end of its lanyard and burst down the gap created by Gronville’s retreat. Wilson’s hand and pistol were up, his aim steadying on Gronville’s spine.

Barlow forced the hand higher. ‘Who are you and what are you doing?’

‘He killed Susan.’

He kept Wilson’s hand raised while he grabbed a handful of lapel and slammed the boy against the wall.

‘Who are you?’

Wilson’s eyes were still unfocused by hate, his tears running onto Barlow’s hand. ‘I loved her. She was everything to me.’

This time the slam was so hard that things rattled. ‘What are you doing?’

‘I’m going to….’ Wilson’s eyes started to focus.

‘Who are you and what are you doing?’

Wilson drew breath. ‘I am Police Constable Frank Wilson, Number 34257. I am in the process of apprehending a person wanted for questioning in connection with a series of violent crimes, including murder.’

Barlow looked down the farmyard. The policemen left at the police line stopped in mid-chew or mid-drink as Gronville veered away from them. It didn’t seem to occur to them to do more than stand and wonder.

Gronville ran into the gap between the distillery and the chicken house and disappeared.

Barlow let go of Wilson and stepped back. ‘Officer, apprehend and restrain your man.’

Chapter 83

Wilson flew out the door and down the yard, running so fast that his heels never touched ground. The brainless lot at the police line stood on. Some of them started drinking and chewing again.

Gillespie thumped crutches as he followed Barlow to the door. 'You sent the boy, Barlow, because you're getting fat and slow.'

Everything hurt so much he doubted if he could call up more than a fast walk. 'It's called "delegation."'

Barlow knew that Gronville might shoot Wilson if he got too close. He bellowed, 'You dozy lot over there, go give Wilson a hand.'

Cups went flying, half-chewed sandwiches spat out. Men jammed their caps tight on their heads and took off. Their shouted comments and questions to each other about who they were chasing and why made them sound like a pack of bloodhounds on the trail. Two WPCs went with them.

Barlow walked across to the police line. Only Clare remained there, with a cup of tea and a sandwich held out enticingly.

'You got here pretty quick,' he said.

'Sarge, we were expecting your call for the mid-morning cuppa.'

'Atta girl.'

He couldn't face food until he knew Wilson was safe and hadn't done anything stupid, so he walked back to where he could watch the pursuit. The extended line of policemen blocked his view of Gronville and Wilson, but they had to be nearing the gap in the hedge.

Then the line wavered and a cheer went up. Barlow punched the air in delight. Wilson had got his man.

Then there was something wrong about the line, something about the way the men were running forward. They reached the gap in the hedge and stood there in a rough semicircle. He could see one of the senior constables order the WPCs back to the farmyard.

Barlow started to run.

He passed the WPCs. They were sobbing. 'Sarge, it's awful.'

There hadn't been gunfire. If only he could catch a glimpse of

Wilson and know he was okay.

He remembered the gin trap in the gap in the hedge. 'Serve Gronville right.'

All the same, the men were just standing around when they should be helping to secure the man.

Finally he reached the semicircle of men, who made way for him. He could only stand and force breath into lungs that had to be punctured, because they took all the air he sucked in and wanted more. He could see Wilson kneeling over Gronville, speaking to him, a hand gentle on his back. Wilson was all right, but he was making no move to cuff Gronville, who writhed in pain. Barlow tried to think of a bollocking that mixed in praise and sympathy.

Then he realized that the gin trap in the hedge had been a decoy. Last night, Leon had known that he would be expecting it, but not a second trap. It was set in a straight line between the gap in the hedge and the farmyard. In the dark, he must have missed it by inches.

Still running, Gronville had stepped on the second trap. His speed had pitched him forward.

Barlow reached for his handcuffs. Only when Wilson looked up at him, white faced, even to the lips, did he finally understand.

Caught by the gin trap in the field, Gronville had tumbled forward and landed on the gin trap in the hedge. The trap had snapped shut, catching his head. Barlow hoped it was his imagination, but had the pressure of the spring in the trap compressed the head, making it narrower?

Wilson asked, 'Sarge, what do we do. He's still conscious.'

The eight bones forming Gronville's skull crackled like dry sticks as they finally separated.

Chapter 84

Much later Barlow was able to pull a bench out of the ruined distillery, shake off the broken glass and make himself comfortable against the wall. He appreciated what little warmth the sun had brought to the day.

Finally he had time for that mug of tea, though he still had no interest in food.

One of the WPCs carried it to him. 'You look done in, Sarge.'

Rather than go to the effort of opening his eyes against the glare of the sun he fumbled around until he had the mug safely in his hand. 'I'm not done in. I'm bucked.'

Gillespie shared the other end of the bench, his injured leg resting on an upturned bucket. Wilson they kept between them. The boy was bearing up well, he had a line of inner strength that always surprised Barlow. Even so, he'd been through a lot recently and he had the sensitivity needed for his hobby: that of a painter. His current notebook was full of pencil sketches of Susan. Where she wasn't smiling or obviously happy Wilson had caught her mimicking the "Papa Bear" face she accused Barlow of making when he was in a bad mood.

The tea was warm, yet cool enough to swallow in big gulps. Eyes still closed, he held the mug up for a refill. It came swiftly. That was one of the pleasures of being the Station Sergeant, a prompt service.

The undertaker had taken the body of Running Man to the hospital for a post-mortem. The bodies of Leon and his mother would soon follow. He didn't want to even think about Gronville.

In the meantime, Barlow had organized men to sweep down the yard, to hose the blood into the drains, and hump the bag of grain into the field to draw away the hens. Without Leon around to protect them the foxes would soon have them for dinner, but at least they would be die with full stomachs. It also meant that the bullet Leon had fired into the sack, when trying to kill him, would disappear into the mud and never be seen.

He didn't need to open his eyes to sense Leary look in his

direction. Something the man did every time he came into the yard. Look, hesitate, but not approach.

A shadow came between Barlow and the sun. 'Sergeant, may I have a word?'

It was Sir Anthony, and on his own. He had finally slipped clear of Harvey.

'Certainly, Sir Anthony.'

The effort of getting to his feet didn't matter. He probably should be walking around anyway to keep the men effective and his own joints from stiffening up. It was just… He didn't know how to explain it to himself, let alone others, but something in him had changed. It wasn't the utter weariness he felt, or the strain from the constant danger of the last few days. It was, somehow, the pointlessness of what he was doing: the lives and reputations he'd helped ruin, the ruthlessness of people grasping for wealth or power. He'd been doing it too long and all those hurts for other people, the innocent, had built up until they were choking him.

They walked into the middle of the yard.

'Are you all right, John?'

'I'm fine, Anthony.'

'Well you don't look it. There's nothing you can do here. Why don't you go home and rest?'

'Soon, soon.'

Sir Anthony gave Barlow's elbow a friendly squeeze. 'I've a flask of something special in the car if you care for a pick-me-up.'

Barlow shook his head at that and they talked on, Sir Anthony seeking as much information as possible for the report he would have to submit to "the appropriate authorities." Barlow repeated what Leary had told him, but refused to speculate as to why Gronville would want to kill Leon. As for Running Man? He had no idea what he was doing there unless he'd come with Gronville. Forensic tests on the bullets would tell them who had shot whom.

He was grateful when Wilson came down from the police line and told him that he was needed. He made his apologies to Sir Anthony and walked across to where Geordie waited to speak to him.

Geordie indicated Wilson. 'The young buck here said I was a great person but they still wouldn't let me down the yard.'

'*Persona non grata*,' muttered Wilson.

'Aye, that,' said Geordie.

He handed over the keys to Louise's car. 'Those army toffs, the higher the rank the more decent the man. He stood us a bit of lunch in his own house.'

'Is that all you've got to tell me?'

Geordie shrugged. 'Other than the fact that the Russian bird and General Packard got on like a house on fire. It turns out they have mutual friends in London.'

From the color on Geordie's cheeks and the daft talk, the lunch had been partly liquid. Army men tended to pour with a heavy hand. He could only hope that Louise's car was still in one piece.

Anyway, it was one of those days when nothing came easy, but if there had been a problem Geordie would tell him. He'd get a fuller report the next time he saw Edward, who was almost certainly in the pub. The general had started him drinking early in the day; he'd be legless and in need of a lift home at closing time.

Tomorrow then, he'd fill Louise's car with petrol and check the oil, the water and the tires, lock it in her garage and slip the keys through the letterbox. Call an end to that part of his life.

Meantime, he knew exactly what to do. 'Wilson, put Geordie in a police car, the front passenger seat for a change, and run him home.'

Half an hour of Geordie's nonsense would do the boy good and if he got out of the Dunlop household with less than two slices of cake in his stomach, then Barlow didn't know Connie.

Geordie walked off with Wilson, and then slipped back for a quiet word. 'I was thinking, those army houses have a lot of valuable kit in them.'

'Piss off.'

Chapter 85

Barlow went back to his seat in the sun. In spite of sitting with his eyes closed and his feet propped up on a second bucket, he remained aware of the various power plays going on in the yard.

Harvey insisted on supervising Leary and the other detectives, giving unnecessary orders to demonstrate a hands-on approach, to his superiors. The Superintendent in turn, quietly and with a lot of tact, used a shared cigarette break to sideline Leary and his men. Leary grumped a bit, but he didn't really mind Special Branch taking over the investigation and, with it, a month of paperwork.

Barlow could sense the Superintendent's impatience to get down to the real reason for his presence. The discovery and recovery of the missing package. While he waited for Leary to finish his forensic investigation of the house, the Superintendent had his men search the outbuildings and fork through bedding. Harvey volunteered men to help move bales of hay and straw. In Barlow's opinion, they were wasting their time, but anything was better than them hanging around earning easy overtime.

He ordered two of the WPCs to lend a hand by raking through the loose straw, and made sure WPC Clare Conway was one of them. Conway had a habit of being busy with non-work when a real problem needed tackled.

'You could always give them a hand as well,' he told Gillespie.

'I could,' agreed Gillespie, who had only left the bench to swallow a plate of stew magicked up by the WPCs. Barlow's plate sat on the ground beside him, barely touched.

Sir Anthony moved between the groups of men, but somehow stayed apart from them all. Quite often, mostly in fact, his focus seemed to be on Barlow.

That didn't surprise Barlow. Sir Anthony still had to account to his superiors for the missing Krista. He had to know from Gronville that Barlow and Geordie had spirited her out of the hospital and, the same night, Geordie had hidden her somewhere faraway. Now Geordie had appeared driving Louise's car. Sir Anthony suspected that this had something to do with Krista.

Barlow wondered if he should put Sir Anthony out of his misery by telling him where Krista now was, but he didn't feel up to dealing with the barrage of questions that would inevitably follow.

At long last, an ambulance drove into the yard, turned and backed up, and stopped close to the front door of the house. Barlow stood in a respect he didn't feel as Mrs. Weir and Leon were stretchered into the back of the ambulance and driven away. He noted that not one of the police officers present saluted as the ambulance passed. Some even turned their backs. Nobody had told them, but they knew who had killed Susan.

With the departure of the bodies, the tempo of work intensified. The Superintendent hurried Leary and his men out of the house. The only thing he allowed Leary to take with him was his "murder bag." Everything Special Branch deemed relevant they packed in boxes and put the boxes in the Superintendent's car.

Leary waddled across the yard to Barlow, where he used his ample hips to find room for himself on the bench.

'Special Branch,' he said and spat.

'What did you expect?'

'Nothing better.' He spat again. 'They can't wait to get searching the house for this famous package. The shambles they made shoving things into boxes. I've seen bricks handled with more care.'

At that, Leary subsided into silence. He seemed tense and on edge, as if psyching himself up to share something, but couldn't bring himself to do it.

Taking pity on Leary, Barlow signed to the WPCs. Mugs of tea and a plate of biscuits swiftly appeared. Leary supped tea and ate most of the biscuits while officers came and went, seeking instructions or giving reports. At long last, someone had found Running Man's car. Not parked on the road like any honest man, but in a field a mile away. A hire car they guessed with nothing in it of importance except a hotel key. They gave the key to Barlow who passed it straight on to Leary.

The tea drunk and the biscuits finished, Leary pulled a handkerchief out of his pocket and blew his nose before he stood and stretched. 'Ah well, back to the fray.'

He walked away

Barlow noticed that in pulling the handkerchief out of his pocket, Leary had dropped a small evidence bag containing a spent bullet and a few grains of seed. He scooped it up, noting that the evidence bag lacked an assigned number. He crunched the bag in his hand while he considered slipping it into his pocket, but didn't dare. He couldn't risk being seen doing anything unusual – like concealing potential evidence.

Which didn't stop him from being his own awkward self.

He lobbed the bag to Gillespie. 'Leary dropped that. Run after the man and give it to him.'

He put his head back against the wall and pretended to doze. Gillespie hadn't jumped up and hobbled after Leary, but he didn't know that because he was asleep.

After a long pause Gillespie said, 'Did you know, Sarge? They hang fools but lock up raving lunatics.'

He pretended not to hear.

Chapter 86

'Let the fun begin,' said Gillespie as the Superintendent marched his men into the house. Sir Anthony followed in a supervisory role.

'You're right there,' said Barlow as men from Special Branch carried the settee out into the yard and used utility knives to slice and dice the covers down to its wooden frame.

A soft chair appeared and received the same destructive treatment. McGinn slipped forward when the men went back into the house for the first of the mattresses. He snaffled a cushion cover, shoved its foam lining back in and carried it over to where Barlow and Gillespie sat.

'I didn't know you'd piles?' said Gillespie.

'It's for Towser,' said Barlow, catching on quick.

Rex trampled around on the cushion a few times to flatten the stuffing, before settling down. McGinn eased his bones onto the bench and tipped the cap over his eyes. 'These long hours are bad for a man.'

From the house came shouts and bangs, and the occasional sound of glass breaking.

Over McGinn's snores, Gillespie said, 'I was thinking, when my leg's better we should head for Killybegs for a bit of deep-sea fishing.'

'Sounds a good idea.'

'Yeah, you can shout and scream your frustrations at the wind and the sea. I'll be too busy hauling in fish to hear a word.'

That, Barlow knew, was the only reference Gillespie would ever make to what he suspected had gone on at Weir's farm. He didn't think he needed to talk things through, but a couple of days on a boat would blow away a lot of cobwebs.

The farmhouse wasn't that big. With daylight fading, Barlow could judge the Special Branch's progress by watching lights flick on in the various rooms. It only took the Superintendent and his men an hour to rip and tear the place apart. In the end, they came out, leaving all the lights on, their feet dragging from weariness and disappointment.

Barlow went across to meet them and heard the Superintendent tell Harvey to put a strong guard on the farm overnight. Tomorrow morning, first thing, Special Branch would be back with the right machinery. They planned to take the buildings down to bedrock if necessary but come hell or high-water they'd find that package.

'If it's here,' said Harvey.

'Knype's body was here so the package must be here as well,' said Sir Anthony.

After a long day even his mood was irritable.

Barlow did a quick calculation in his head. All this overtime: today, tonight, Tomorrow and probably into Monday, would leave him with hardly an officer alert enough to man the Enquiry Office during the coming week.

He coughed to gain the Superintendent's attention. 'I'm not promising anything, Sir, but would you give me half an hour?'

'Don't be ridiculous,' said Harvey. 'If the experts can't find it, what makes you think you can? And in half an hour.'

Gillespie's elbow nudged Barlow's back, and he got the message. 'Shut up before you talk yourself into trouble.'

But if that package was as important as everyone said it was, then he had to take that risk.

'Half an hour?' queried the Superintendent and looked at his watch as if checking the time. Really he was thinking things through, because when he looked again at Barlow his gaze was penetrating. 'That bruising and the scrapes on your body makes me think you know more about this case than you're saying.'

Harvey did one of his annoyed vibrations. 'Barlow, what have you been up to?'

Gillespie muttered, 'Told you.'

Barlow's stare back at the Superintendent was just as hard. 'What bruising, Sir? What scrapes?'

The Superintendent opened his mouth as if intending to say something, then closed it. He tried again, speaking slowly, allowing the thoughts to form in his mind. 'This case is all about the package. Once it's found, none of this ever happened.'

For the first time in his life, Barlow liked the idea of "D Notices". If he found the package, case closed and Harvey could go choke on his indignation.

Wilson was back, standing with the other men. Barlow waved him over and was pleased to see that the boy looked less strained. Something he couldn't really understand, because ten minutes with Geordie had him wondering if he should get his blood pressure checked.

'Right, Wilson, I need you in on this.' He didn't "need" Wilson but he deserved to be there. 'And, Superintendent, if you please, a couple of your men.'

Special Branch had made the mess and, in Barlow's opinion, that made it their job to clear it up again.

He led the way into the house. The whole gang of men followed him. He'd known they would and didn't mind, up to a point. When it suited him, he'd tell them to back off.

The hallway was sort of all right, more untidy than wrecked. The sitting room looked bigger without the settee and armchair. The carpet and underlay sat heaped under the window. The display cabinet had been pulled out, the glass of its door broken. A bar of First World War medals lay on the floor. They had belonged to Leon's grandfather. Barlow picked them up and placed them on the mantelpiece.

'Not here,' he said, and led the way to the kitchen.

Rather than waste time going in he stood in the doorway, making his assessment. The kitchen had a solid floor. Even so someone had smashed the tiles to make sure there wasn't a hidden hidey-hole. Every cupboard had pulled off the walls, half of the Delph smashed.

'Onwards,' he said, and led the way upstairs.

He spent time in Mrs. Weir's bedroom. Like the rooms downstairs that look-in was mainly for show. Leon was a control freak. If they found anything it would be in his bedroom. However, Barlow stopped in the doorway rather than go into the room itself.

Clothes and bedclothes and Leon's knickknacks lay heaped on the floor. The posters torn off the wall and thrown on top of ripped-up floorboards. Barlow sensed not so much a search as an orgy of frustrated revenge.

He pointed to the two junior Special Branch Officers, not caring that both were technically his superiors. 'Boys you made the mess, now sort it. Floorboards replaced, anything portable dumped in Mrs. Weir's bedroom. And open the window, this place needs fresh air.'

The Superintendent stood looking thoughtful. 'Barlow I hope you know what you're doing.'

He took that as a threat.

Chapter 87

Barlow led the way back downstairs, giving the two Special Branch Officers room to work. He felt like one of those moments in wartime when he walked from safety towards an unstable bomb. He'd dedicated his life to serving the Crown, and taken an oath to that effect, even if that meant spending the rest of his life in jail.

Harvey pushed himself forward into Barlow's consciousness. 'Barlow you are totally out of order.'

Someone made a sound, a grunt of agreement. Gillespie of course.

He ignored them both and handed Wilson his car keys. 'There's an old coat in the boot of the car. Put it in the biggest evidence bag Leary has and bring it here.'

Wilson nodded eagerly and ran off.

Barlow shouted after him. 'And wear gloves.'

Not that Wilson wouldn't, but he didn't want the boy to know that he trusted him implicitly.

Wilson raised a hand in acknowledgement and rushed on.

After that Barlow waited, hemmed in by the Superintendent on one side and Sir Anthony on the other. All they needed was the handcuffs and his arrest on suspicion of lots of things would be complete.

He realized that lack of food and sleep were making him lightheaded.

The sound of things thrown and the odd curse echoing from the house changed to the bang of hammers driving nails back into place. Eventually one of the Special Branch Officers appeared at Leon's bedroom window and gave his superior the thumbs-up.

Barlow led the way back into the house and up the stairs. The two Special Branch Officers stood like dogs waiting for a pat and praise. They had taken Barlow at his word and dumped everything portable in Mrs. Weir's bedroom. Only the cast-iron bed with its bare springs remained.

'I need that window closed,' Barlow told the two Special Branch Officers. They glared back at him. Rather get into an argument about who outranked whom he explained, 'Please, there is a reason why it has to be one of you two. I don't want anyone else in this room until I have finished.'

The junior of the two shrugged and obeyed.

Meantime Barlow went into Mrs. Weir's bedroom and fought his way over heaped furnishings to the window. He opened it and looked out.

Both McGinn and Rex were still at the bench. Awake and interested in the goings-on across the yard, but keeping well away from any involvement. Barlow cocked a finger, ordering them over and up the stairs.

He stumbled his way back through the heaped debris onto the crowded landing. Gillespie, Leary and Wilson stood halfway up the stairs, with Wilson holding the plastic bag. McGinn was at the bottom wondering how he was going to get himself and the dog up.

Barlow sighed. He could hardly tell a Superintendent and Special Branch Officers and a "Sir" to bugger off, but he was tempted. 'Gentlemen, if you would let my men through, please.'

People made room for McGinn, Leary and Wilson to come up. Gillespie took it upon himself to assume that he was required as well, and thumped and stumped up after them. Somehow, the weight of a crutch landed on Harvey's toes. Harvey was most indignant.

Barlow took the bag off Wilson and handed it to McGinn. 'If you say Towser's got a head cold, you're both on report.'

McGinn opened the bag. 'A stockman's coat.' He wrinkled his nose at the whiff coming out of it and peered around Leon's bedroom as if looking for something. 'There's no cows here, they're too big to hide.'

'Get on with it.'

He didn't want to cross his fingers in public so he crossed his toes. Daniel T had held onto the missing package for months. In that time he had handled it more than once. Probably lots of times while he wondered what to do with it. Leon might hide the package from view, but Barlow doubted if he'd ever thought of police dogs and scent trails.

McGinn placed the bag on the floor and opened it wide. Rex stuck his nose in and immediately sneezed from the bovine hydrogen sulphide trapped in the material. McGinn borrowed Wilson's gloves and turned the stockman's coat until Rex could sniff the armpits.

'Find,' said McGinn and Rex walked into the room, still sneezing. He walked about, and sniffed and sneezed. Hesitated at the fireplace and walked on. Did another circuit then stopped at the fireplace. Not facing the front grate, but the side nearest the window.

He barked and wagged his tail.

'Right,' said the Superintendent, pushing himself forward. 'Everyone out.'

'No,' said Barlow. He checked his watch. 'You still owe me ten minutes.'

Chapter 88

The Superintendent frowned at Barlow's claim that ten minutes of the half-hour still remained. Finally, he nodded his agreement to the ten minutes. The nod also acknowledged that if Barlow didn't find the package he'd arrest him for withholding information and suspicion of murder, but that he'd do it with regret.

Barlow let McGinn take time patting Rex and rewarding him for the find. Pleased with the way things were going he bent down and patted Rex on his way out. Rex growled. It made Barlow wonder if Rex and Toby compared notes.

With the room clear and with people hanging expectantly in the doorway, he concentrated on the fireplace. He knew that something lay hidden in there, something that Daniel T had touched.

Leon had decorated his bedroom in the recent past or, more likely, he liked to keep it that way. The only marks on the wallpaper was where the posters had been pinned to the wall. Only one pin remained in place, the top left-hand pin on the fireplace wall. A piece of torn poster hung from it.

Willing to make a fool of himself, Barlow stepped forward and pressed hard on the pinhead. He heard a click. A click as sharp as a stick breaking.

'Wow!' said Wilson.

There was a movement of people into the room. McGinn raised his voice in protest as he found himself shoved to the back of the crowd. 'Mind the dog's feet.'

Barlow blocked the on-comers' path and pulled Wilson forward. 'Your honor, son.'

A door to the side of the fireplace had swung open, the bulge of its hinges concealed in the stretch of wallpaper curving from the wall proper onto the fireplace. The opening end of the door finished neatly where two strips of wallpaper met.

Wilson stepped forward, already slipping on gloves before Barlow could say the word. He pulled the hidden door wide open. Everyone crowded in behind Barlow and him.

The hidden cupboard was narrow: high enough to hold rifles

upright and lined with Cedar wood planking to protect them from damp. Someone, Leon presumably, had screwed two sets of clips to the back of the hidden cupboard. One set held a rifle and its telescopic sight. The other set was unused. Even looking at the unused clips gave Barlow the shivers. He touched the bruise above his heart.

Boxes of ammunition and cleaning materials lay on the bottom shelf.

No package.

Barlow breathed out slowly. 'Oh boy.'

And yet the dog had smelled something of Daniel T.

He ignored the mutters of disappointment coming from the men grouped around him and dumped the ammunition and the cleaning materials onto the floor. Grasped the rifle and pulled it from its clips, and felt the panel of wood move against the pull.

He gripped the clips themselves and hauled. The whole back of the cupboard came away to reveal a second recess, boxed in by aged firebricks. Within the recess sat a package slightly larger than a family encyclopedia. The package was wrapped in soot-stained wax cloth, held secure by cord pulled tight enough to crinkle its edges. Red sealing wax impressed with important looking seals doubly secured the knots in the string.

Barlow pushed Wilson forward. 'Your honor, son.'

Wilson lifted the package out of the cupboard and stood, unsure what to do next.

Sir Anthony stepped forward, his hands out. 'I'll take that, Constable.'

Barlow snatched it away from him. 'Over my dead body.'

Chapter 89

With Barlow's almost gratuitous insult of Sir Anthony, the atmosphere in the room went from celebratory relief to an awkward silence. A silence broken only by the click of Rex's toenails as McGinn took him downstairs and away from thoughtless feet.

'Barlow!' snapped Harvey.

Barlow prevented Harvey from saying anything further by ramming the package into his hands. 'You hold that, and if you even think of giving it to Sir Anthony you won't have to worry about an ulcer. I'll break your neck.'

He drew breath and stared at the senior officers gathered around him. 'Gentlemen, look at it this way.' Just to be certain the package stayed safe he stepped between Sir Anthony and Harvey. 'Malcolm Knype gets his grubby little mitts on this package and takes off for Moscow. I'm assuming this happened in London because Krista Riekstinš lived in London and was probably his controller.

'If I was heading from London to Moscow, I'd take a plane to, say, Germany or catch the boat-train to France. Yet Knype heads North, maybe Wales, maybe Scotland and from there to Northern Ireland.'

He had caught their attention, everyman was listening hard.

Barlow licked dry lips. Now he had to give facts that only he knew, and couldn't divulge without someone passing on the information to Moscow. At the same time, the men in Moscow weren't stupid, they'd work it out for themselves in the end.

'Knype goes straight to Daniel T Abernathy, one of a number of trusted men who helped him on his way. However, Daniel T is a double agent and loyal to the Crown. How or why he killed Knype, I don't know, but he buried the body in Blacks' Estate and held on to the package.

'Thanks to Burgess and Maclean and the hunt for the "Third Man", the country knows that the Russian have their spies in every Government Department. Daniel T couldn't return the package to the Government without Moscow finding out. And Moscow, as you know, deals harshly with traitors.'

He looked to see Wilson, now relegated to the back of the room. His face already showed hurt and disbelief that Susan had died protecting a Russian spy.

For the sake of the boy, Barlow decided to minimize the events concerning Krista. 'Moscow wants that package and Krista is ordered to go and investigate. Nobody is particularly concerned about Knype. Priority number one is to recover the package. Secondly, she was to find out how and why Knype disappeared.'

Now that he thought about it, Krista was probably a trained killer.

That gave him the shivers as he continued. 'Krista follows Knype's trail as far as Ballymena and knowing Leon Weir or about him, she decides that he is the most likely suspect. Unfortunately for her, she mentions the missing package to Leon. Leon wants it for himself to sell to the highest bidder, so he tortures Krista to find out what she knows.

'Krista gets lucky and escapes. This time she heads for the highest hill in the area. From there she can see Daniel T's farm. I'm guessing her contact told her to look for old fire-engines in a field. Unfortunately for her, Daniel T had finished work for the day and she doesn't know who else is in the house, so she hides and waits for him to appear.'

He threw in a compliment for McGinn. 'We arrive, and our highly-trained police dog spots her.' He then used his hands to express a shrug. 'The rest you know.'

He stopped there. He could tell from their faces that they didn't yet know what had happened to Krista, but as far as he was concerned they could guess as much as they liked about her and all the deaths. He wasn't for telling.

Harvey folded his arms and stood resolute. 'And that's it? That's your reason for insulting a man as important as Sir Anthony?'

It was and it wasn't. Everything else was guesswork that could cost him more that his job.

Sir Anthony gave Barlow a sympathetic smile. 'I understand that you have been under great stress recently. For the sake of our friendship, I am willing to overlook your irrational outburst.'

'I'm afraid I can't,' said Harvey. 'Barlow you are suspended from duty with immediate effect. Charges will be brought against you, and this time they will stick.'

'I'm not finished yet.'

It felt good, snapping back where he normally had to pretend respect.

It was pure speculation, but suddenly he felt confident that he was right. 'Look at it this way. Malcolm Knype heads for Ballymena, when, logically, he should have headed for the continent. Because of that, the package ends up first in the hands of Daniel T and then Leon. Obviously they weren't the main man.

'Then there is the question of why people wanted Krista dead. Only Daniel T made contact with the main man and nobody dared trust Leon. But Krista knows, or perhaps suspects enough to be dangerous.'

'Who told you all this?' asked the Superintendent.

Barlow could feel Gillespie's eyes burning into him, warning him to be careful. 'Daniel T, days ago.'

'Withholding information,' said Harvey, like he was writing up a charge sheet.

'And have you blab it around the countryside?'

He stared at Sir Anthony. 'There's a lovely graduation scroll in your hallway, from Trinity College, Cambridge. Burgess and Maclean were Cambridge men and, according to the newspapers, there are a lot more traitors in the Cambridge Spy Ring that we don't know about. A hell of a lot.'

He wanted to spit. How people, educated people who should have known better, could betray their country, was beyond him.

'Really! Barlow,' said Harvey.

Sir Anthony said, 'Harvey, draw up the charges. I will happily endorse them.'

Harvey reached out the package to Sir Anthony. The Superintendent intercepted the pass and handed it one of his men. 'It's filthy, Sir Anthony, and it would ruin that lovely suit of yours. Whereas us…' He rubbed at the dirt on his hands. 'There's nothing like searching a house to ruin a good suit.'

Harvey reached for his handcuffs.

Chapter 90

Even as Harvey reached for the handcuffs, Gillespie somehow stumbled and his crutch rapped off Harvey's knuckles. Harvey yelled in pain and hugged the hand to his chest.

'Sorry, Sir, someone bumped into me,' said Gillespie.

'That's twice you've hurt me, Gillespie. Don't let it happen again.'

The distraction bought Barlow the seconds he needed.

He gave Sir Anthony an unfriendly smile. 'Then there is the question about what you knew about Major Gronville and Jordan and Running Man.'

'Who?'

'You know who they are. After I left last night you, rang Running Man to the Avenue Hotel in Belfast and ordered him to get here a.s.a.p.'

'Nonsense! I went straight to my bed once you and Charles Denton had left. My wife will confirm that.'

'Funny, but the Night Porter says he put a call through to Running Man's room and he left immediately afterwards in a great hurry. Could hardly wait for the Porter to unlock the gate to get his car out.'

That was complete speculation. Nobody had gone yet to speak to the Night Porter, but Sir Anthony wasn't to know that, and his eyes flickered when he'd mentioned the Avenue Hotel. That put another tick against Barlow's certainty of the man's involvement.

However, Sir Anthony had been too long in Government to show a crack in his resolution. 'I was aware that the late Major Gronville had men to do what he referred to as "the leg work", but who they were or how to contact them I left to Gronville. If anyone made any calls last night, it was him.'

That sort of arrogance, of leaving the dirty work to deemed lesser men, had always annoyed Barlow. Made him want to stretch out his hands and wring necks.

'Sir Anthony, according to last night's reports in our Incident Book, a mobile patrol discovered Major Gronville standing at the coin box just up the road from your house, on the junction of the Broughshane Road and Warden Street. Gronville offered my officers a pound note in exchange for a handful of pennies. Apparently, he wanted to make an urgent phone call.

'My officers, judging that Gronville was incapable of driving, searched him looking for identification. On finding both his Military ID and a room key for the Castle Arms Hotel, they put him back in his car and took him there. One of the officers had to assist the Porter in escorting Gronville to his room and seeing him safely into bed.'

Barlow decided that the bluff would be more believable if he made it sound like a throwaway piece of information. Like the phone call to The Avenue Hotel, it still needed checked out.

'The Porter confirms that at no time during the night did Gronville ask to be put through to an outside number.' Still using the light tone, he gave Sir Anthony the look he'd given many an idiot caught red-handed. 'Which means, Sir Anthony, that it was you who made the call to Running Man. Which also means that you are more deeply involved in this affair than you care to admit.'

Sir Anthony stood stiff with indignation. 'May I remind you, Sergeant, that you are dealing with a Knight of the Realm and a Privy Councillor, a man who can make and break Chief Constables. Yet you expect me to stand here and listen to your insults. Enough and no more.'

He stepped sideways and away from Barlow, and snatched the package out of the unresisting arms of the Special Branch Officer. Barlow reached to stop him, but Sir Anthony's elbow slammed against his cracked ribs. The aim was accurate and carried the force of someone well trained in unarmed combat.

Barlow found himself on the floor, struggling against a blackout that bubbled in from the edges of his vision. The pain in his chest all but stopped him breathing. He put a hand over the ribs and drove the pain to new heights when the ribs moved under his touch.

He shook his head, and rubbed at his eyes with the back of his hand, and tried to force air past the compressing barrier of broken ribs. What little he could see was of trouser legs surrounding him, but he could hear clearly. Hear Sir Anthony's determined step on the stairs and the tiptoe step of Harvey as he rushed after him, abject with apologies.

Cold metal touched his wrists, then arms hauled him to his feet. His vision cleared. He found himself standing between the two Special Branch Officers with the Superintendent relieving him of his pistol.

'Barlow, I'm arresting you on several counts of murder, and don't confuse me with that fool Harvey. I'll make it stick.'

Chapter 91

Barlow found himself bundled out of Leon's bedroom. Wilson headed down the stairs in front of them, looking back anxiously at Barlow. The Superintendent ordered Gillespie and his crutches into Mrs. Weir's room until they had passed.

Special Branch Officers pushing and pulling him down the stairs, hurt. Barlow's mouth dried with fear at what his arrest would do to his daughter.

'Vera,' he yelled to Gillespie.

'Don't worry about her,' Gillespie called back.

The Superintendent told Gillespie. 'You will not communicate with the prisoner.'

They reached the doorway. Low cloud covered the sky, bringing dark night. Only weak electric bulbs in the outhouses and the sidelights of waiting cars illuminated the yard. A car's interior light came on as Sir Anthony's chauffeur opened the door for him. Beside the tall outline of Sir Anthony was a Special Branch Officer carrying the package, and Harvey still apologizing for Barlow's actions.

McGinn and Rex were within hearing so Barlow said, as if to the Special Branch Officers. 'You need to arrest Sir Anthony.' Then he dug his heels in, making them all stagger back into the hallway, shouting as he did so. 'Get him, Towser.'

The Special Branch Officers were too busy taking their revenge by pushing him around to hear McGinn's low, 'Rex, seize.'

Thanks to the Special Branch Officers, all the pain was back but this time Barlow's vision stayed clear. He saw the low shadow of Rex streak across the yard. And another dark shadow, waiting anxiously for orders.

'Wilson. The package.'

A fist grinding into his chest missed the damaged ribs but still hurt. He found himself on his knees.

The Superintendent stood over him. 'Barlow you're not doing yourself any favors.'

From the far side of the yard came a cry of pain and yells of alarm. Barlow could only hope the cry of pain came from Sir Anthony. Faced with a choice of four men in a close grouping: Sir Anthony, the Special Branch Officer holding the package, Harvey and the chauffeur, Rex could have attacked the wrong man.

Barlow staggered to his feet. 'And you, Sir, were you not trained to first assemble the facts, then allow in some speculation before deciding on a course of action?'

'What do you mean?'

'You're reacting here, not thinking.'

The Superintendent sent one of his men to investigate who had been hurt. 'To see what additional charges we can bring,' he told Barlow, but Barlow sensed the man was using it as an excuse to delay while he did some thinking.

From across the yard came more yells and Rex's continuous snarl.

The Superintendent bunched his fists as if tempted to hit Barlow himself. 'Did you ever hear the expression "give up"?'

'No.'

The Superintendent told the remaining Special Branch Officer to let go of Barlow but to stand between him and the front door. Then he un-bunched his fists and sat against the hall table, with his arms folded. 'Convince me.'

Now he had a chance to state his suspicions, it didn't hurt to be polite. 'Sir, bear with me.'

A man needed his hands free to do much of the talking for him. However, there was nothing he could do about that. Handcuffs were uncomfortable on and these ones were too tight. He'd warn his men against that at the next parade, and then realized that there wouldn't be another parade.

'If you remember, Sir, I said that Leon and Daniel T weren't the main men?'

'I'll accept that.'

'Now think of it logically. If the main man lived in the south of Northern Ireland or in the Irish Republic, then Knype would have headed south from the ports at Larne or Belfast, or from Nutts Corner airport. But he heads north, and not only north but to Ballymena, as does Krista, so it's someone around here.'

'That's pure speculation.'

‘Everything is in this case.’ He stopped himself from leaning forward, from appearing too anxious to convince. ‘Firstly, there was all this talk about Burges and Maclean and the “Third Man”. Somebody warned them that they were about to be arrested. Then we hear about the Cambridge Spy Ring and the ongoing hunt for other traitors.’

‘You mentioned that before.’

‘I did, at which point Sir Anthony made great play of being a Knight of the Realm and a Privy Councillor, whatever that is.’

He knew what a Privy Councillor was, but it didn’t hurt to appear ignorant. People loved telling things that they knew, to other people who didn’t. It also distracted them from the problem in hand.

It worked. The Superintendent looked pleased as he said, ‘A Privy Councillor takes a personal oath of loyalty to the monarch. As a Privy Councillor, they are entrusted with ultra-important secrets that they must never even hint of.’

The Superintendent’s voice died away as he realized how important it was that he got things right. If Sir Anthony, as Barlow said, really was a traitor… He gave a mock shudder to dispel that ridiculous thought, put a hand near his neck and gave a jerking motion. ‘Barlow, there could be more than your career on the line after today’s events.’

The noise from across the yard had grown in volume. Barlow could hear Harvey shouting and Rex barking, the barks savage and threatening.

The Superintendent grabbed his arm. ‘I have to sort that out before someone else ends up dead.’

He and the Special Branch Officer hustled Barlow out of the house. Once in the yard Barlow pulled them along, anxious to get across and sort things, and he had to be sure that the package was safe from Sir Anthony.

He knew that, no matter what happened, he’d spend several years in jail. If need be, he’d kill Sir Anthony and plead insanity.

Chapter 92

Barlow was under arrest and facing a possible hanging. Even so, the professional shambles unfolding across the yard put his teeth on edge. He could see Sir Anthony, sitting half in-half out of his car, hunched over in pain but with a hand still out for the package.

Wilson had the package clasped to his chest and Harvey was trying to reach him to take it off him. Rex stood wrapped around Wilson's legs going frantic with the urge to attack Harvey.

It was tempting to order Rex to 'seize' Harvey, and enjoy the consequences. He was for jail anyway.

The Superintendent slowed Barlow's rush across the yard. 'You've got ten seconds. Convince me.'

Ten seconds? He could talk for a week and still no one would believe him. Even so it was worth a try. Even if it only to put everyone off guard until he was close enough to grab someone's pistol and shoot Sir Anthony.

'A Knight of the Realm, Sir, now that's important. Only big businessmen are awarded a knighthood, them and Civil Servants who have got to the very top.' He paused hoping the Superintendent would make the connection, before he actually said it. 'Now a man as important as Sir Anthony apparently is, what's he doing in Northern Ireland?'

'He liaises between here and Whitehall.'

That came out too quickly, almost as an excuse. Barlow could see that the Superintendent was listening hard.

Barlow said, 'A Knight of the Realm, a man who reached the upper echelons of government, concerned only with Northern Ireland?' He made locker room gossip sound dismissive. 'It might be an exaggeration, Sir, but rumor has it that one little man in a Whitehall garret, manages all the Northern Ireland affairs for the British Government, right down to the plans for our police stations. Look at the one we got in Dungannon. It should have gone to the North West Frontier. So that little man, in that little garret is responsible for both.'

The Superintendent nodded again, briefly this time, almost as if things that puzzled him were clicking into a bigger picture.

‘Think Cambridge, Sir. Think The Third Man and the search for other traitors, and Knype and Krista heading in this direction.

‘Think this. If you have suspicions but no proof, you sideline people. Sir Anthony’s appointment to Northern Ireland removed him from day-to-day intelligence gathering and from the tittle-tattle of friends over a drink.’

They reached the edge of the warring group. Harvey was still trying to get the package but couldn’t get near Wilson because of the dog. Wilson was pretending to be terrified of Rex. He kept saying, ‘Help. Help.’

Unfortunately, as Barlow knew too well, Wilson couldn’t tell a convincing lie, even for the sake of a joke, so his “Help. Help” sounded like the bad acting it was.

Every other Officer present stayed well back, unwilling to get involved. Barlow could hear the murmur of voices when someone spotted the handcuffs on his wrists and passed the word on.

It was weak, he knew, but it had to be his clincher. ‘Who cares about Northern Ireland anyway?’

Harvey drew his pistol. ‘Wilson step aside. I am going to shoot that dog.’

‘I can’t.’

Now that’s real fear, thought Barlow and tried to run forward and thump Harvey. He didn’t even get one-step before the Special Branch Officer hauled him back.

‘You’ll shoot the boy,’ he roared at Harvey.

Barlow hadn’t heard McGinn follow them up the yard or Gillespie swinging hard on his crutches to keep up. But suddenly McGinn was there, bursting past them and throwing himself between Harvey and Rex.

‘You’ll not shoot my dog,’ said McGinn, his hand already on the butt of his pistol.

‘How dare you!’

‘He’s telling you it’s a job for himself,’ said Barlow and said it loud enough for Harvey to hear him over the noise of the dog barking.

How he was going to sort this mess, and him in handcuffs, he had no idea.

Gillespie caught up with him, breathing hard from the rush up the yard. He nodded to the handcuffs. 'Sarge, the only silver I thought you ever saw was a knife and fork.'

'Shut up.'

His words echoed around the yard because McGinn had silenced the dog. Even so, Rex still stood tight against Wilson, teeth bared in Harvey's direction.

Harvey looked at the men and WPCs standing around. 'One of you, recover that package from Wilson.'

The officers looked Barlow's way. He gave his head a firm shake and they all stepped back into the darkness beyond the lights of the yard and of the cars.

The Superintendent said, 'I wish I could control my men like that.'

'They're all magic. Mention work and they disappear.'

The Superintendent snorted a laugh then he shouted. 'Harvey, put that gun away.'

It was nice watching Harvey full of righteous indignation re-holster his gun. Especially when he didn't dare glare back at a superior.

Barlow sensed that the Superintendent had come to a decision when he let go of his arm. 'I don't know how you did it, Barlow, but somehow you've been well ahead of us this week.'

'Wasn't I sitting at home with nothing better to do than add two and two, and occasionally make four.'

'A lot of fours,' said the Special Branch Officer.

On the Superintendent's nod, he too released Barlow. A second nod and he produced a key and removed the handcuffs.

'Right Barlow.' The Superintendent sounded both relieved and apprehensive. 'Assuming you're still ahead of us, what do you suggest?'

Barlow knew he was still in big trouble but at long last he had control of the package and what happened to it. It would also sweeten Harvey against taking revenge against the rest of the men for his humiliations of the day.

'You and DI Harvey escort Wilson to Headquarters where he will hand the package to the Chief Constable in person.'

'Why Wilson. Why not just the two of us?'

The Superintendent sounded like a man robbed of the congratulations and advancement given only to the clear victor.

'Sir, this case really started with Wilson and Susan, and he'll finish it with her. You mightn't see her, but Susan will be there.'

The Superintendent pulled a packet of cigarettes from his pocket and lit up. 'And Sir Anthony?'

'Your men take him to hospital and have his cuts seen to. Then escort him home and stay around in case he needs to go somewhere overnight.'

'Like he has a relapse?' The Superintendent sounded dry with disbelief.

'Like a relapse,' agreed Barlow.

By morning the Establishment would have assumed responsibility for Sir Anthony and whisk him away to some comfortable little retreat for interrogation and a debriefing.

'And Barlow.'

'There's nothing else, Sir.'

'No, I mean I'll spend the next few days putting my own two and twos together for a report. Personally, I'd hate to do it, but if Forensics find any trace of you in the items we've taken, I'll have to arrest you.'

In all the excitement he had forgotten about the fingerprint.

Chapter 93

A long, drawn-out Saturday had at last started to wind down. A few more things to sort, mostly seeing his officers off the premises, and then Barlow could go home. What to tell Vera was beyond him at that point. She was entitled to know that he was likely to face charges of murder and, at the same time, he couldn't just tell her the truth. That would make her an accessory after the fact and liable to prosecution if the police ever found out.

Suddenly it was no longer "us", it was "me" and "them." The last time he'd felt that lonely he was standing over his mother's coffin.

Gillespie had taken it upon himself to order the police lines taken down, things packed away and for the attending officers to head back to the station to sign out for the day.

The first of Barlow' problems was the car holding Wilson, Harvey and the Superintendent. The Superintendent had elected to drive. Harvey, instead of sitting up front, where he could suck up to the Superintendent, sat in the back with Wilson.

Barlow knew that Harvey intended to bamboozle the boy into letting him handover the file.

He walked across and swung open the back door. 'Wilson.'

'Yes, Sarge.'

'I can't tell you how vital that package is to the future of this country. If it gets into the wrong hands it will destroy our economy for generations to come. The country would be bankrupt.'

The whites of Wilson's eyes glowed wider in the near dark of the car. 'It's really that important.'

'Yes, son, it is. Therefore, I am giving you one last order. That package does not leave your hands until you pass it over to the Chief Constable in person.'

Wilson's head nodded eagerly. 'Yes, Sarge, you can depend on me.'

'So if anyone, anyone tries to take it off you, for any reason, you are to shoot them.'

'Anyone, Sarge?'

Barlow smiled at the fury boiling on Harvey's face. 'Anyone, and make sure they're dead.'

Wilson had a habit of obeying orders to the letter. Sometimes it could be annoying. Right then it seemed the best trait in the world.

Barlow swung the door shut and waved the car off. He turned to find DS Leary standing, wanting a word. Maybe it was the biting cold of a wind that had got up, but Leary looked shrunken with worry.

'Barlow I might need you to cover for me.'

'What's wrong?'

'That time in the house when Gronville pulled the gun on you.'

'Yes?'

'I was behind you, at the table, and I'd left my gun in the car. I thought if I could reload the weapon we'd found… Well the thing is, I was working with my hands behind my back and I think… I know I did. I touched that fingerprint on the magazine. I'm sure it's destroyed.'

That created a break in the chain of evidence. Not only would Harvey go mad, it also gave him something for a good defense counsel to use.

He tried to sound concerned. 'There's still the Polaroid.'

The Superintendent was sharp. He'd order Forensics to double-check that Polaroid against his prints, and get a match. It had to be his fingerprint, though how he'd managed to do that was beyond him.

'The thing is…' said Leary.

Right then a car pulled up beside them, and Sir Anthony said, 'Barlow. Now!'

Really he wanted to ignore the man, to spit in his face, gouge out his eyes, but there he was in the car with the window rolled down. The junior Special Branch Officers in the car with Sir Anthony didn't dare to order the chauffeur to drive on.

So he had to speak to the man, but on his own terms. Leary was drawing back, turning away.

Barlow gripped his sleeve to delay him. 'Leary, Special Branch didn't do it, so I presume your men are bagging and tagging that rifle we found and the ammunition?'

Leary tried to pull away, seemingly anxious not to be seen

talking to an alleged criminal. 'They are.'

'Then tell them to take the First World War medals as well, before someone nicks them. It'll help Weirs' extended family remember that not long ago they were decent, God fearing people.'

Sir Anthony spoke louder, making sure other people heard him. 'You're so clever, Barlow, always thinking of others, or so you would have us believe.'

Barlow stayed a step away from the car to stop himself from really going for Sir Anthony. 'If you've anything to say to me, say it. Otherwise clear off.'

'You're a social climber, trying to be what you're not, a gentleman. I'm delighted Louise Carberry saw though you in time.'

Barlow was surprised, he'd never put Sir Anthony down as a poor looser. He had enjoyed his times with Louise's friends and they seemed to like him. Only last night, he could hardly believe that it was only a few hours back, they had laughed and joked together.

He jerked a thumb at the chauffeur. 'Move on, you're blocking the traffic.'

The car started to move forward, slowly enough for him to hear Sir Anthony's lowered voice. 'Barlow, you don't know it yet, but you're a dead man. If they don't hang you, the men from The Regiment, the SAS, will kill you.'

'You think so?' Barlow walked alongside the slow-moving car. 'I'm reckoning that if the friends of Jordan and Running Man come looking for me, it will be to discover how an unfit policeman could beat the best our country has to offer.'

There had been little of that day for him to enjoy, but winding up Sir Anthony brought a glow to his heart.

'Whereas you had those same men involved in illegal acts, the torture and killing innocent people. You also ordered them to kill me out of some personal spite.'

'I told you before, Gronville…'

'Gronville told the men what to do, but you told Gronville.'

The car reached a good stretch of laneway and speeded up. Sir Anthony wound up the window, refusing to hear any more accusations.

Barlow shouted after the car. 'It's you who should worry. Don't walk near cliff edges or deep water. And beware of friends.'

He waved a few more cars off as well, which left just his and the detectives' car. Gillespie was hanging around, waiting for a lift home and the chance for them to plan what to do about Vera when things turned nasty.

Leary was back again, looking more hangdog than ever. Barlow wouldn't have minded if his only worry was a missing fingerprint.

'Yes, Leary?'

'Barlow, it's not only the fingerprint.'

'Think latterly, lie. Blame Special Branch.'

'Well it is their fault really, the way they chucked things around when they were packing up.'

'So what's missing or broken?'

'The Polaroid ... Barlow?'

Somehow between Leary saying "The Polaroid" and "Barlow" seconds had passed that he wasn't aware of. Leary couldn't remember what he'd done with the Polaroid. It had to be in that envelope with his fingerprints. Now if he could find some excuse to call at the Special Branch offices, he might… he might…

'You must remember where you put it,' he said.

'Yes in the envelope with your fingerprints. But when I went back and looked, someone had taken the Polaroid out of the envelope and before I could find it those idiots from Special Branch told me to clear off and threw everything into boxes.'

Barlow liked that. The movements of the Polaroid not properly recorded and the original print on the gun destroyed, preventing a direct comparison. A half-decent defense lawyer would have the Polaroid thrown out of court as being non-admissible evidence.

He nodded, as if coming to a decision. 'As I said, blame Special Branch and don't waver. It was them who lost it, nothing to do with you.'

'And you'll back me?'

'To the hilt.'

Right then he was tempted to hug the fat little man.

Leary shook Barlow's hand, pressing something into it as he did so. 'No one else will ever say it, Barlow, but thank you for giving Susan closure.'

He walked away, wiping at his eyes.

Barlow walked across and got into his car. It took Gillespie longer to wriggle in his injured leg and the crutches. That gave Barlow time to check what Leary had given him. The Polaroid of his fingerprint. He buried it deep in a pocket for destroying later.

'Fancy a pint before I run you home?' he asked Gillespie.

'The wife will kill me.'

'So what's changed?'

Blank Page

LATE DECEMBER

Blank Page

Chapter 94

It was one of those days that could go either way. Which way Barlow wouldn't know until the chill mist lifted off the tops of the trees in the convent grounds beyond his back wall.

The post came early. The unheard flutter of an envelope, followed by the snap of the letterbox flap pursuing the postman's fingers. The letter was probably another Christmas card for the sleeping Vera.

He fetched it anyway, wondering where to put it. The house was already coming down with cards from her many admirers. Buried among them was a pleasing number of cards from the new friends he had made through Louise. He had replied with a card and a little personal note, as his mother had taught him to do, though he intended to keep away from the friends themselves until well after the New Year.

He just couldn't bring himself to nod seriously and agree that it was a tragedy and a loss to the whole community, and wonder how such a simple accident could have resulted in the death of Sir Anthony.

The letter was for him personally. One of those light blue, pre-stamped envelopes available at Post Offices, where you wrote your message on one side of the page, folded the page in two, licked the pre-gummed strips down three sides, wrote the name and address of the recipient under the stamp, and posted. Job done.

This letter was from America, he could tell that from the eagle stamp. However, the sender had used a marker to black out the paper around the pre-printed stamp so that the cancelling stamp by the Post Office wouldn't betray which city the letter had come from. Neither was there a return address on the back.

He opened the letter, carefully pealing back the gummed edges. There was no "Dear John" or "Dear Mister Barlow". The message was a cartoon.

The drawing showed a big bully of a woman towering over a minuscule little man. The little man was in his pajamas and had a very obvious bulge at his groin. A word bubble stretched from the woman's mouth. It said "You want what? Sex is when you make my tea."

He felt a lift in his heart. It was from Krista letting him know that she was safe and well and living in America. As he'd hoped, she had agreed to a debriefing by the Western intelligence community, rather than face years in jail.

He studied the cartoon over a second cup of tea, then he stirred up the embers in the grate until a flame flickered. He put Krista's letter on the flame and watch it burn. When it had turned to ash, he could still see the outline of his name and address, so he poked at it until only illegible dust remained.

Barlow took Vera up a cup of tea to get her awake for work. After that, he let Toby out before pulling on his jacket and checking himself in the mirror. Brylcreem could only darken the streak of grey that had appeared in his hair. Naturally Vera liked it. 'It's rather becoming, Dad, it gives you an air of gravitas.'

He checked the weather outside and decided to walk to the station. The stomach paunch was persistent.

Other than that, it was one of those rare days when no one or nothing could annoy him – except Edward, or Geordie, or Sergeant Pierson, or Harvey, or Vera making eyes at that young solicitor working for Solicitor Moncrief. And, anyway what was she doing out so late last night…?

Acknowledgements

My wife, Patricia, of course, and our two children, Lucie and Daniel, all of whom are ever encouraging. Kevin Hart for his weekly slices of homemade apple pie and advice.

Professor Ciaran Carson and the guys at the Creative Writing Group, the Seamus Heaney Centre, Queens University, Belfast for their chapter by chapter critiques of my work and Liz Wasson who, having edited the book, read it again for pleasure.

Ashley Bingham of Dogtag Creative for the eye-catching cover and Consultant Stella Hughes for her medical input, which I always appreciate but sometimes ignore.

My wider family and friends for their encouragement and support and Sammy Gillespie for the use/misuse of his name. Dara Vallely and Anne Hart for 'edging' my writing in different directions. Hugh Woodcock my Ballymena spokesperson and various retired police officers who have tried to keep me right on facts, procedures and tall tales.

Fabio & Luisa, Luigi & Nadia who keep an eye on me when I'm in Italy writing.

Printed in Great Britain
by Amazon

43917419R00165